OPERATION ʤ

A Science Fiction Novel

P.F. DONATO

Second Edition

PAGE PUBLISHING, INC.
Conneaut Lake, PA

First originally published by Page Publishing 2018

ISBN 978-1-64350-580-0 (pbk)
ISBN 978-1-64350-582-4 (hc)
ISBN 978-1-64350-581-7 (digital)

Printed in the United States of America

To Teddy & Teah for always being by my side.

To My Children:
You are never too old for adventures,
You are never too old for fun,
You are never too old for magic,
You are never too old, my son.

To John:
You may have been supportive, but I know you'll
never read it. Perhaps you'll watch the movie.

To Mary - Michelle - Cecilia:
Thank you for always believing in me.

Not even an outcast can escape her destiny.

–P.F. Donato

CHAPTER 1

NATALIE CREPT UPSTAIRS from a darkened basement to a kitchen, its cupboards full and its sink overflowing with dishes, perfectly preserved as if abandoned overnight. She peeked out the window. Houses lined the streets, and cars were parked in the driveways. The only thing missing were the people. *Where did everyone go?*

The sun fell past the horizon, and an ominous blackened haze loomed in the sky. She sprinted across town until the street ended and a chain-link fence with barbed wire began. Nothing but woods covered the outer shell of this ghost town. She followed the fence to a main gate, chains binding its two doors. She grabbed the gate and heard a click, then a gunshot. The dirt spat just short of the fence. She backed away and saw a sign that read "Welcome to Wells Springs, Wyoming." She couldn't understand what was going on. Clearly, she wasn't leaving, at least not yet.

Natalie heard footsteps behind her. She glimpsed two dark figures with rifles over their shoulders across the street, heading straight for her. Panicked, she ran. She needed a place to hide, not knowing who they were, what they wanted, or what else might linger in the darkness. Where could she go? She didn't even know where she was.

The storm clouds seemed to follow Natalie as she scurried down the center of the small, nondescript town. She ran down the sidewalks lined with antique lampposts. The streets were filled with rows of run-down historic buildings that had been turned into small restaurants, boutiques, galleries, and antique stores. She tried the doors, all locked. It felt as though no one had been there in years.

Natalie walked along the row of cars in front of the shops and peeked in each car's window until she found one that was unlocked.

She looked in both directions, bent down, and lifted the handle ever so gently, trying not to make a sound. The lever released with a click, and the door squeaked open. She ducked inside and locked the doors. The key was still in the ignition.

Not knowing if it was safe to leave, she sat in the driver's seat and pulled the hood of her sweatshirt up over her head. When she tucked her hands into the pockets, she found a cell phone. She mashed the buttons, hoping to call someone, anyone, for help. *No service, damn it.*

As she put the phone back into her pocket, she felt something else and pulled out a license that read "Natalie Thompson." She stared at the picture. *Is this me?* She looked in the rearview mirror at her hazel eyes, fair complexion, and reddish-orange hair, then back at the picture. Quite the opposite, the license revealed a woman with dark hair, brown eyes, and olive skin. *It doesn't look like me.* She stared at the unfamiliar face using her identity. Her name was Natalie Thompson, but whose picture was it?

She held the license in her hand and rested her head against the driver's door window. She shot a glance upward and saw the moon glimmer through the hazy sky. The moon's light mingled with the darkened mist, accenting colors of yellow, green, blue, and red. The wind began to pick up, and a few water droplets speckled the windshield.

Through bleary eyes, Natalie gazed at the raindrops that rolled down the windshield as she tried to remember how she'd gotten there and who wanted her stranded in this godforsaken town. She thought back to the locked gate. Maybe there was a curfew and the gate was closed at night, but why would someone try to shoot at her? Whatever was going on out there, it would undoubtedly be safer to wait in the car until morning. At least she had the car key if something went wrong.

Suddenly, the deafening roar of thunder rattled the car windows, snapping her out of her daze. She hadn't even noticed the lights on the lampposts were lit. Had hours passed? She couldn't remember how long she'd been there.

She thought about her life and her parents. She might have slept through her alarm clock and could never get up without her mom waking her, but she was the highest ranked grad student at her school. Her parents would have figured out by now that she hadn't come home, and they were going to be mad that she'd skipped her classes. Still, they must be worried. She could see the distress on their faces when they woke to find her missing.

The night fell still, reminding her how tired she was. Her hands became cold and clammy as she slipped into a light sleep, but woke with a startle. *Stay awake, Natalie.* She wondered if she could make it until morning.

Lightning crackled as it flashed, striking the lamppost in front of the car. It startled her and she jumped, dropping the license on the seat beside her. The streetlights flickered, then went out, and Natalie could see nothing. A few crackling sounds lingered in the distance. *It's only a storm,* she had to remind herself, trying to put her fear behind her.

Another crackle filled the air, and sheets of rain swept over the town. The steady patter of raindrops struck the windshield hard as the storm picked up steam and turned into a downpour. She squinted out the window for any sign of movement. There was only darkness and torrents of rain. The lightning flashed once again, briefly illuminating the storefronts and the dark, deserted street.

The sound of the raindrops became a soothing, rhythmic song, and the road seemed to disappear into a river before her weary eyes. It wasn't long before her eyelids grew heavy and drew closed.

All of a sudden, the thump of a fist on the car window startled Natalie, waking her. She forced her eyes open and squinted out the windshield, nearly blinded by the sunlight. *It's morning already?* Dazed and confused, she rubbed her eyes.

The gray clouds that had followed her the night before seemed to have passed. Only a few water droplets remained, dripping down the windshield, proof that the storm had ever happened.

Natalie whisked her long bangs out of her eyes and wiped the fogged-up glass with the side of her fist. When the glass cleared, she could see the profile of a man, but the sunlight was so bright she had to turn away.

Narrow-eyed, she strained to see an old man with gray thinning hair, wearing a navy-blue corduroy blazer and baggy tan trousers standing outside the car. The old man's wrinkles showed many years of wear. He had to be well into his seventies.

The man glared at her through oversized glasses with unblinking eyes. He stared at her so intensely; she could almost feel his breath on her neck. She resisted the temptation to crawl into the back seat and hide.

"Miss, are you okay?" the old man asked.

She ignored him as she fought her disorientation. She put her hand to her forehead. Her head felt fuzzy and somewhat hungover, as if she had partied the night before.

How did I get here? she wondered as she tried to recall what had happened and where she was. She forced her eyes to stay open, but her exhaustion got the best of her. In a state of shock and fatigue, her eyes fell shut again. The sunlight bathed her skin through the glass. She felt as though she were wrapped in a warm blanket. Memories of home danced around the edge of her consciousness.

The man knocked on the window again. "Miss, can you hear me?" he asked, growing concern in his voice.

The voice hazily entered her mind as Natalie's eyes flew open and thoughts swirled around in her head. She didn't want to think about what had happened, and she certainly didn't want to deal with it yet, but she knew it was time.

She squinted and tried to focus; her gut twisted up in knots. A bolt of fear struck her when she remembered why she had run and how she ended up in the car. Could this man be the person who had tried to shoot her through the fence? She didn't want to find out.

Natalie feared what might lie ahead. Her hand moved to the key in the ignition. She was ready to start the car, but she didn't know where to go. She couldn't leave through the gate, and there was no way of knowing if there was another way out. She placed her head on the steering wheel and let go of the key. She knew she couldn't run. They would eventually find her.

Another rap on the glass brought her attention back to the old man. "I own the shop right over there." The old man smiled and pointed with his age-spotted hand to a small ramshackle shop across the street. "If you want, you can come with me, and I'll make you some coffee."

Natalie, more confused than ever, wondered if it was all a dream. *Did I wake up in that basement? Am I locked in this town? Did someone try to shoot me?* She let out a heavy sigh as she analyzed the situation. "Well, if he owns a shop here, he must be all right," she mumbled to herself. The old man seemed harmless, and she didn't see a weapon. Besides, if he was after her, he would have done something by now.

Alone and exhausted from her night in the car, she thought it would be all right if she went with him. Maybe he could shed some light on what had happened and why she was there, and where *there* was. He must know something.

Natalie pushed the hood of her sweatshirt off her head and hesitantly said, "Yes, a cup of coffee would be nice. Thank you." She plucked the license off the seat and placed it in her jeans pocket when she noticed a handbag on the passenger side floor. Something was sticking out of it. She leaned over and opened it. Set inside was a small monitor attached to a handle. *Strange, what could it be? Why would something so odd be left behind?* Intrigued at her find, she wanted to know more about it. She peered back at the old man as he waited for her. Unsure what it was, she left it in there to inspect it in more detail later, away from prying eyes.

She flung the strap of the handbag over her shoulder, opened the door, and stepped into a puddle left behind by the storm. Cold water soaked through the edge of her sneaker, chilling her foot. She stomped her foot to shake off the excess water and followed the old man across the street and down the sidewalk.

His stride was slow, but steady. He hunched over a bit, but easily traversed puddles left behind in the broken cement. He pulled on his suspenders a few times to haul his trousers up over his belly so the bottoms wouldn't get soaked; every time he did this, he exposed his brown socks and old, worn-out leather loafers.

Natalie tried to follow his route while staying a few steps behind him. "Is it still early?" she asked.

"For what?"

"For this town. Shouldn't these stores be open by now?"

The old man didn't answer, leaving Natalie wondering. She began to watch his every move, not fully convinced she should be following this stranger, but knew she had no other option. He passed a few stores and stopped in front of one with peeling paint, revealing years of colors layered over one another. Natalie watched as he dug deep into his pocket and pulled out a set of keys. As he fingered through them, Natalie fought the urge to leave. She wanted to trust this old man; he'd been kind enough to help her in her time of need.

She took her eyes off him for a moment and searched the streets for anyone else. She would feel safer knowing there was someone who noticed her, but the town was deserted, not a soul in sight. The streets should be busy, even at this early hour.

"Here it is." The old man separated one key from the bunch. His aged hand trembled, scraping it around the keyhole, while the rest of the keys jingled on the metal ring until, at last, he managed to insert the key into the lock.

The key turned with a click. He glanced back at Natalie and smiled. His smile made her feel strange, as if he were telling her he held many secrets behind this storefront. She tried her best to fake a smile, keeping her distance.

The old man grabbed the doorknob and turned it, but the door wouldn't budge. With a nudge of his shoulder, the door flew open, ringing the old shopkeeper's store bell attached to the doorframe. "There we go." He adjusted his thinning hair back over his bald spot and shuffled inside. "I'll get right on that coffee." He headed to the other side of the store.

Natalie read the sign over the door. "Abigail's Antiques." *Sounds like an interesting store.* Drawn by curiosity, she stepped across the threshold and into the old-fashioned, quaint-looking antique shop.

"Feel free to take a look around while you're waiting." The old man strolled up to an old, worn, wooden counter covered with a layer of dust. He grabbed the coffeepot from under the counter and placed it beside the antique cash register that read "No Sale" in faded letters. He plugged the pot in and turned it on, causing the lights in the shop to dull then flicker for a moment.

As the lights blinked on and off, Natalie noticed that half of them didn't work. Flakes of paint spotted the floor, and broken tiles crunched under her feet. A pungent, musty smell, almost sweet to the taste, hung in the air and seemed to coat the inside of her mouth and nose. She resisted the urge to sneeze, feeling as though she should be extra quiet.

"The coffee will be done in just a minute," the old man said, breaking the silence.

CHAPTER 2

NATALIE PACED AROUND the tiny unorganized store jam-packed with vintage memorabilia. Her thoughts kept returning to last night. *What happened to me? How did I end up here?* She rounded the corner of the room and asked, "Is there a way out of this town?"

"What do you mean?"

"Well, I tried to leave last night, but there was a gate that closed off the main street. Is there another way out?"

"Oh, that. We've been having a lot of trouble with coyotes around here, so the mayor decided to put up the fencing. It should be open by now."

"Oh, so that explains why I heard a gunshot at the gate."

"Yes, the townspeople go out in the middle of the night to scare the coyotes away. But there's no need to hurry off so quickly. Why don't you stay awhile and enjoy our town?"

"Thank you for the offer, but I need to get home. My parents must be worried about me."

"At least finish your coffee."

Natalie turned to the old man, who smiled at her. She smiled back. "Yes, of course. Thank you for your hospitality."

As she pushed her way through the narrow aisle, her eye caught on some oddly dressed mannequins in tattered, out-of-date clothing that didn't fit in with the display. They stood clumped together, tucked away in the far back corner, in front of a closet doorway that had been roped off. The door had been left open but was latched to the wall. She examined two long slide bolts anchored across the top and the bottom. It seemed odd for a closet.

Natalie walked toward the mannequins, unable to take her eyes off them. There was something about them that disturbed her. Inching closer, she placed her hands onto the rope, and leaned in. She stared into their glazed, hungry eyes; they almost seemed to be staring back at her.

"The coffee's done," the old man called from across the store.

"Oh, you startled me!" When Natalie spun around to see him pouring coffee into a cup, she caught movement out of the corner of her eye. She turned back around and studied the mannequins, but they were in the same pose they'd been in before. Everything else was still. *Odd.*

Natalie returned to the old man, confused, wondering if she should ask about the mannequins. Next to the old man, a tan-coated German Shepherd with spatters of black around his nose and eyes and a black patch across his back sat. She bent over and patted the dog. "What's your companion's name?"

"Buster." His tone was suddenly icy.

"Is he your watchdog when you're away?"

"Something like that," the man answered brusquely.

"He seems too loving to be a watchdog." Buster's long tail wagged, sweeping the floor. His ears pointed upright as he licked Natalie's face.

The old man poured coffee into another cup and placed it on the counter next to her. "Here's your coffee."

"Thank you for your generosity. I won't be long. I have to head out soon." She wasn't sure how to mention what had happened to her last night. Maybe he would think she was crazy if she told him.

She stood and took a sip of her coffee as she scanned the area one last time. "Your store is amazing."

"Thank you," he replied.

"I couldn't help but notice the name of your store. It's lovely. Is Abigail your wife?"

"My late wife," the man said, his voice devoid of emotion.

"I'm sorry for your loss."

"It's okay. That happened many years ago," he said flatly. "Now my life is dedicated to tending the store."

"That's wonderful, you keep the store running in the memory of your late wife." Natalie began to feel guilty about her initial misgivings of this stranger. When her uneasiness subsided, she realized this man, who had been so kind to her, didn't even know her name. "We haven't been properly introduced. My name's Natalie. What's yours?"

"Walter."

After a few sips during an awkward silence, she placed her cup down and headed back to the mannequins. She wanted a second look before she left. They had seemed so real, so lifelike. Buster followed as she reached out to touch the mannequins near the edge of the doorway.

"Don't touch that." Walter's stern voice made her jump.

"Oh, I'm sorry." Natalie's eyes were still fixed on the mannequins. "I don't want to sound crazy, but it seemed like they were moving on their own earlier."

"Yes, sometimes it looks like that," Walter said.

Natalie leaned over the rope to examine them further. When she inspected the mannequins, the mouth on one of them seemed to twitch. "I must be tired." Natalie rubbed her eyes. "That was the second time I thought I saw one move. I know I didn't get much sleep last night in the car."

"I wouldn't get that close if I were you," Walter said. "That rope is there for a reason."

Without warning, the store's front door opened, ringing the shopkeeper's bell. It surprised Natalie, and she almost fell over the rope. She turned to see a tall, thin man and a short, plump woman enter the store.

Buster's back legs bent as he leaned forward, poised to attack. He began to bark.

"What's the matter, Buster?" Natalie heard shuffling behind her. She glanced over her shoulder and looked back at the closet. "Where did they go?" Her gaze held steady. "How did they move on their own?" No matter how hard she tried, she couldn't pull away—she was waiting for an answer that never came. It took every part of her being to refrain from making a scene as she blurted out, "What are they, robotic mannequins or something?"

"Robots?" The man who had entered the store headed over to Natalie. "Do you have a show going on?"

"Okay, dear, you have fun at the show. I'm going to browse a bit." The woman waddled to the other side of the store, barely able to fit through the crowded pathways.

Confused, Natalie tried to peek into the closet from behind the rope, but she couldn't see what it hid. It appeared to be nothing more than a closet, but how were they able to move on their own?

"When does the next show start?" the man asked Natalie. His voice rose with excitement.

"I-I don't know. You'll have to ask the shop owner over there." Natalie pointed to Walter.

"There is no show," Walter hollered from across the room.

"What? You mean I missed it by two seconds? Oh, man," the man said.

"Oh, honey, don't pester him." The woman dug deep into a pile of children's toys and held up an old porcelain doll. "Look here, honey, this would go nice in my collection, don't you think?"

"Uh-huh." The man stared at the closet.

"Now stop that. I know you're not even looking at me. We've been in this town for a whole five minutes and you're already at it. You know this trip was for antiquing, not for robots."

"Since I missed the show, can I take a gander at them anyway?" the man asked, ignoring his wife. "I'd love to see your robots. They sound fascinating."

"Sure, go ahead," Walter said, his voice cold and lifeless.

Natalie didn't understand what was happening. Why was this man allowed behind the rope but she wasn't?

"You'll be entering at your own risk." Walter took his eyes off the man and turned the page of his newspaper.

"What kind of risk is there in staring at some robots in a storage closet?" The man chuckled. "At least I didn't come in here just to look at some old crap with my wife."

"Fred, cut that out," the woman shouted. "Just because I've been stuck with you for thirty years doesn't mean other people have to put up with your nonsense as well. Now leave that man alone and come here."

Fred ignored his wife and walked over to the roped area.

Natalie approached the woman. "Ma'am, how did you get to this town? Wasn't there a closed gate?"

"No, it was open," the woman said. "I thought it was odd to gate a town, but I heard this place was great for antiquing."

Natalie headed back toward the closet as Fred ducked under the rope.

"Wow, it's dark in there. Is there a light I can turn on?" Fred leaned into the closet and disappeared as though he'd been sucked in. Natalie's imagination ran wild. The closet door quivered, followed by a thud. A small grunt echoed for an instant. Buster yelped and stood guard next to Natalie.

Natalie's eyes met Walter's, where he stood at the counter, drinking his coffee. "I warned him." He dropped his gaze back to his newspaper.

Natalie backed up, trying not to cause a scene. *He's all right. It's only a closet. He just dropped something in there, that's all,* she told herself, but she didn't really believe it.

"Fred? Where'd you go?" The woman threw the doll back onto the pile and headed for the closet. "If you're in there with those robots, you better come out this instant and spend some time with me. I'm not on vacation alone, you know." She passed an old grandfather clock in the corner. The clock ticked hard and loud as if it had a heartbeat while her footsteps pounded across the rickety floor in sync with its movement. She navigated around the piles of assorted crafts and vintage clothing, all thrown around in disarray. She brushed up against a few items, knocking them to the floor. She stormed past Natalie, ducked underneath the rope, and approached the closet.

"Remember, you're entering at your own risk," Walter said to the woman.

Natalie watched the woman pause and glance over her shoulder at Walter, her face tight. She stepped closer. Natalie could read the worry in her eyes as she whispered, "Fred? Are you in there, Fred?" The woman squinted. "It's so dark in there. I can't see a thing."

Just as she was about to stick her head into the closet, a mannequin popped out, its arms fully extended. Startled, the woman let out a small scream and jumped back. Buster gave a bark, and Natalie jumped as well, almost knocking down a pile of awkwardly stacked boxes behind her.

Natalie's eyes widened and her mouth dropped open. She looked at Walter, but he ignored them both, busily reading his paper. Her lips moved, and she tried to speak, but nothing came out. She felt paralyzed with fear and couldn't do anything but watch the woman, but it would be all right. Natalie could almost guarantee it wouldn't happen again.

The woman stepped up to the mannequin. "Sorry, sir, your mannequin fell out of your closet. I'll put it back for you." She took another step to peer around it. "It's dark in here. Do you have a light switch on the wall?" A second later, she was pulled in as well.

Hearing a faint cry from within, Natalie ran to Walter. "Something happened to those people," she said, trying to keep panic at bay. "Aren't you going to help them? They might be hurt."

Walter sipped his coffee and turned the page of his newspaper.

"Why aren't you going in there to help them?" Natalie shouted.

"I warned them, and they didn't listen. What's done is done. We all must die sooner or later."

"If you knew there was such danger, you should have better security to close off the closet. A rope barrier isn't going to help anyone," Natalie yelled.

"Don't worry, death will only follow if the dead becomes one with the life placed before it," Walter said calmly.

"What are you saying?" Natalie stepped away from him.

"They only want our human life, so anyone could survive in there as long as they don't come into contact with those beings."

Natalie realized she should have gone with her gut and stayed in the car. This man couldn't be trusted. "I was right! I knew you were hiding something in this store."

Appalled at Walter's apathy, Natalie pulled out her cell phone—still no service. "What's going on?" She placed her phone back into her pocket then focused on the darkened closet and the couple in need of help. "I can't believe you! How could you be so cold? If you aren't going to help them, I will."

Natalie threw her handbag down on the counter and ran back to the rope. She grabbed it with one hand and ducked underneath. She glanced back at Buster. He made no move to follow her, but he whined and paced the floor in front of the barrier.

CHAPTER 3

NATALIE MARCHED UP to the closet with a bravery she didn't actually feel and stopped to stare into the shadowy doorway. *Will I get swallowed up too?* she wondered, but she felt it was a risk she needed to take. There was no one else to help that couple. Even though she was afraid, she felt an enticement to go in, an invitation, it seemed.

She tiptoed toward the opening, inching closer. A chill filled the air as the smell of rotting flesh wrinkled Natalie's nose. She held in a cough as she struggled for a breath of fresh air. There was only total darkness before her, as if no light could escape. Natalie stared at the closet, unsure what she'd find inside.

As she approached, her body tingled and the hairs on her arms stood up. A pressure surrounded her and seemed to pull on her body. The closer she got, the stronger it became.

She paused and stared at the opening. "How can I get close enough without getting pulled in?" she muttered. Natalie gazed at the door latched to the wall then the frame. She bent down and gripped the side of the doorframe tightly.

When she peered in again, she could see into the closet. A dual spherical, ring-shaped mass consumed it. A rippled effect filled the inner ring as the outer frame pulsated. She tried desperately to hang on as she searched hard through the thick darkness, but when she leaned in, it began to pull her with more strength.

Her head slipped into the doorway, and the darkness cleared at the entrance. Natalie stared in amazement as her eyes fixed on an odd group of trees—three trees, all dead.

"What is this place? Is this some sort of magical door?" she yelled to Walter. "This definitely isn't a storage closet."

"Beautiful, isn't it? It's an interdimensional doorway—a portal. It's not every day you can see such magnificence, a world being created right before your eyes," Walter said from across the room. "This once-unseen extension of our world, possibly formed from dark matter and merely a shadow of ours, just tucked away between life and death, is now reality as you stand before it."

A creation from our world? Natalie's eyes twitched as she gazed upon the three trees, activating a part of her brain that she couldn't control. She felt a sense of attachment to the place, a connection of some sort that she couldn't comprehend. It was as if she'd been there before.

"The portal doorway possesses an enormous amount of energy to allow rapid travel between two dimensions. Strange enough is that the matter around the portal doesn't change. Our world isn't affected in any way, and the portal doesn't break apart and explode," Walter explained.

Natalie didn't understand what the old man was babbling about or what she was looking at, but she didn't have time to figure it out. She needed to find the couple, and fast, so she could leave this horrid place.

Natalie ignored Walter and tried to search beyond the trees for the couple. All she could see was a dense darkness, but off in the distance, a faded light shifted behind the trees, creating silhouettes. The light exposed a woman lying on a dirt path. She appeared to be unconscious. *That's the woman from the store.*

The light brightened, and a forest emerged in the still air. Creepy and silent, this place seemed to hide some ghastly secret. Natalie hoped to keep a level head and get through this.

"Miss, can you hear me?" Natalie called out in a loud whisper, trying not to make too much sound. The woman lay motionless under the shadows that crossed her body. "Miss, can you get up?" The woman didn't move.

A man's moan came from behind the trees, followed by the noise of something being dragged across the ground. "Fred, is that you?" Natalie called. "Are you hurt? Follow my voice, and I'll get you and your wife to safety."

A stronger, more intense smell of putrefied flesh came over Natalie as dark figures appeared from behind the blackened trees and cast their own haunting shadows over the unsuspecting woman. Natalie watched their stiff, jerky movements.

She kept her eyes on the unconscious woman as she lay helpless, unaware of the impending danger. The stiff shadow figures hovered over the woman, then threw themselves down and fastened to her. A brief, loud scream came from the woman and echoed for a moment, but was abruptly cut off. It might have been too dark for Natalie to see what was happening, but she could hear the sounds of cracking, crunching, and squelching all too clearly.

The shadowed figures rose and emerged out of the darkness.

Are those the mannequins? Natalie's eyes widened, noting some familiar facial features, but before she could examine them fully, she realized one remained behind. As they stood, they no longer obscured the dimmed light. It shone down on the woman and exposed what they had done to her.

The woman lay motionless with a creature crouched beside her; this one wasn't finished with her yet. Its mouth twitched and drooled as it chewed through her skin. While it feasted, the mannequin's once-hardened body, loosened.

Its arms began to bend at the elbows and its hands closed onto hunks of the woman's flesh. It pulled and tore into her as it cracked her bones, forcing her limbs and ribs apart. Its thin lips moved with every bite as it exposed razor-sharp teeth. Corpse-white flesh formed on its gangling body and ripened as it expanded.

It made Natalie's stomach churn, but she couldn't take her eyes off it. "They're coming alive," she screamed. The mannequin continued to rip into the woman, bloodied hands shoveling meat into its hungry mouth. The more it consumed, the more life it absorbed, and the more humanlike it became.

Heedful of their change, Natalie panicked as she watched the dead evolve before her eyes. She fought hard against her panic as the mannequin features disappeared. The once-lifeless statues that had stood behind the rope were now full-bodied creatures, vicious with life.

Sickly and frightful, the menacing, vile creatures' heads hung tilted to the side; their straggly, fine hair moved and exposed their decomposed ears. They lifted their heads and smelled the air. Their eyes set in sunken sockets locked onto Natalie. Natalie's eyes met theirs, and she was paralyzed with fear. Their black eyes stared back at her, crazed and rabid with hunger.

The last creature dropped the remaining flesh and bones and stood with the others. Seeing another life-form made their teeth chatter. Clumsily, their bodies lurched forward. They veered right and left, stumbling toward Natalie.

They moved in closer, threatening her. All she could do was watch in horror as the mannequins came forward, slavering for her flesh.

Becoming accustomed to their newly formed bodies, the mannequins hobbled and lumbered along slowly. Some limped and dragged their legs while others dangled their swaying arms.

Natalie struggled to remember how to move. She forced herself to break free from the sight. Frightened beyond reason, she tried to pull herself back into the store, but she wasn't strong enough to fight the pull of the unknown world before her.

Natalie watched them get closer. She pushed off with her one free hand and let out a loud grunt. She pulled on the doorframe with the other, but she couldn't budge. Their pale arms heaved and advanced straight for her. "Someone help me!" Natalie pleaded for her life, knowing it was about to end.

All of a sudden she felt a tug on her clothing. The force made her lose her grip, and she found herself falling backward into the rope surrounding the closet. She landed on the floor, knocking over the stacked boxes. As her eyes focused on the ceiling, Buster hovered over her and licked her face, wagging his tail.

"I told you to stay behind the rope," Walter shouted. "Now look what you've done. Not only will they be angry that I saved you, I'm late in closing the doorway." Walter unlatched the door from the wall. "Now hurry and help me close this door!"

Natalie jumped up and ran to Walter. She pushed on the door just as a bloodied, decomposed hand emerged through the crack in the doorway, clawing at her. Natalie screamed as the dry, brittle hand grabbed her. It clutched her arm and tried to pull her in. Walter held the door with his shoulder and grumbled while he yanked her free, but the hand continued to claw at Natalie.

Walter and Natalie slammed the door several times, trying to force the hand back in. Walter gave one final heave with his shoulder, the door sliced the fingers off the creature, and then slammed shut. The severed fingers flopped around on the floor next to Natalie's foot. Walter grasped the top latch and secured it, relieving Natalie. She let go of the door and backed away as Walter attached the bottom latch.

"I must say, that was a close one. I never had the homondie reach out like that before."

Natalie listened to scratching sounds that turned into pounding, and she feared the creatures would burst through. Petrified, she backed away from the door, but she couldn't tear her eyes away. As she stared, she thought about what Walter had said. "Homondie?" she mumbled, her voice soft and dazed.

Walter stomped on the fingers until they stopped moving. "At least the homondie are still in there and not out here." He stood with his back to the door and took a deep, relieved breath. He pulled a handkerchief from his pocket with a trembling hand and wiped sweat off his brow.

Natalie heard more scratching at the door and saw the knob twist, then as quick as it began, the scratching stopped and fell silent. A cold chill ran down Natalie's spine. *Why did they stop?*

Walter grabbed the doorknob one final time and jiggled it. "They won't be getting out of there right now, but I don't know how long that'll last."

When she was able to tear her eyes from the door, Natalie noticed bloodstains on her sweatshirt. She pulled it off and threw it onto the floor on top of the crushed fingers. As she straightened out her T-shirt, she asked, "What are homondie, and why are they in your storage closet?"

Walter turned to Natalie. "They're from a place we call Homondiem, now awakened, and they're trying to find a way into our world."

Natalie was confused. She crossed her arms and asked, "What is Homondiem?"

"It's an alternate world, parallel to ours."

"Why did they eat that poor woman?" Natalie's stomach twitched and she felt sick, remembering what she had witnessed.

"Before the portal opened, they were no threat. Once they interacted with live humans, they found out what it was like to be alive, something they didn't have, but now they crave it. The only way for them to become alive is to extract life from us. So because of the change in the configuration of cells, a new breed of species has been created. For now, these homondie can't survive outside their world, past the rope, but if they do find a way to escape, we're doomed."

Natalie stood slack-jawed. "If you knew all about the homondie and their world, why did you let those poor people go in there?" She narrowed her eyes at Walter. "You obviously didn't care what happened to them."

"I mustn't interfere, but you could have." Walter left her by the closet and returned to the counter. He took off his frayed corduroy blazer and placed it on the back of the rickety wooden counter stool. He pulled up on his suspenders and sat. The stool creaked as he twisted back around to face Natalie who had followed him.

"What are you saying?" she asked.

"You could have saved that woman, but you let her go in after her husband," Walter said. "You had a chance to tell her not to go into that closet, but I saw you let her step right up. You knew what would happen to her, the same thing that happened to her husband, and you didn't say a word. You're no better than I am, so don't kid yourself."

Her eyes widened at his words. "I didn't understand what was happening and I froze. I was scared." Her face softened. "I tried to speak, but nothing came out." Natalie held in her tears. It made her skin crawl to admit it, but he was telling the truth. She had a feeling that something bad had happened to Fred. She should have said something. Even so, Walter could have stopped them from the very beginning.

Walter picked up the coffeepot with a quivering hand and poured himself more coffee. He took a sip. The steam fogged the lenses of his glasses and briefly masked his eyes.

Natalie glared at Walter, gathering her strength. "You can't put this all on me! You knew about the homondie world, yet you did nothing to stop them!" She backed away. "You knew what would happen to the man before he went in, and you said nothing."

"If someone wants to go into the homondie world, I'm not going to stop them," Walter hollered.

"You stopped me, didn't you?"

"I had to!" Walter slammed his fist on the counter. His glasses flew off his face. He picked them up, wiped off the layer of mist, then put them back on.

"How many people did you send in there with those creatures?"

Walter fell silent, eyes fixed on his newspaper.

"I don't understand." Natalie grabbed her handbag off the counter, slung the strap over her shoulder, and hurried to the door.

Walter ran after her and grabbed her arm as Natalie reached for the door handle. "They're gone now, so you needn't be concerned with what happens in there."

With one hand on the handle and the other trapped in Walter's grasp, Natalie replied, "It *is* my concern." She wrenched her arm from Walter's grip and looked him dead in the eye. She pushed him back and ran out the door.

CHAPTER 4

NATALIE RAN OUT of the antique store and down the street. As she looked back over her shoulder to make sure no one was following her, she turned a corner and bumped into something.

She almost screamed but paused when she saw the wide-shouldered, thick-chested man she'd collided with. He wore a black T-shirt and tan fatigue pants. His black hair was trimmed high and tight, and he held a coil of rope over his shoulder. A little girl with braided black hair and beads on the ends was fastened to his leg. She wore a pink dress and white shoes.

"I'm so happy to see you. Please help me. I don't know what to do," Natalie cried.

"Listen, lady, we all have our problems here. I have my daughter I need to protect." The man walked past Natalie.

"Please take me with you." Natalie followed the man. "I can help protect your daughter."

"I don't know who to believe in this town," the man said, not stopping. "I just need to find a way out of here."

"I'll help you. I'm trapped here too."

The man stopped and pulled out a kitchen knife from the front of his pants. He held the tip of the blade toward Natalie's face.

Natalie stepped back and put her hands up. "I'm sorry, please. I'm unarmed. I just saw a homondie eat a woman's flesh, and I'm scared."

The man lowered his knife and placed it back into his waistband. "So I take it you met Walter."

"How did you know?" Natalie asked.

"He's one of the scientists here."

"A scientist? He told me he owned the store."

"He's the one using us as bait for the homondie."

"What?" Natalie gasped. "All of us?" She peered down at the little girl.

"No one's safe here." The man stared at Natalie, brow furrowed and squinting. "I haven't seen you around. What branch of the government did you enlist in?"

"Enlist?"

"Yes, we're all from different parts of the military and were reassigned to this town. We were told to pack up and bring our families, but they didn't tell us what we were supposed to do once we got here. But we found out pretty quickly once the homondie were exposed."

"There are more people in this town?"

"Yes, what's left of us. Everyone here are homondie meat. A lot have already gotten sucked into that nomadic world, and I don't know if anyone can survive in there."

"Well, I'm not from a government facility," Natalie said. "At least I don't think so. I woke up in the basement of a house down the street, and I don't know how I got here. The only things I can remember are who my parents are and that I'm a college student. The rest of my life is a blur."

The man and his daughter walked away from Natalie. "Come on. We need to keep moving. Don't know where or when a portal will open. If we're not prepared, those homondie will eat every last one of us."

Natalie caught up to them. "While I was in the store, a couple came in and said the gate was open. We should head over and check it out."

"They open the gate so unsuspecting people come in to make sure they have enough food for the homondie. I'm sure it was closed right after they entered. Besides, the exterior is heavily guarded, and if you try to leave, you'll be shot. No." The man paused. "We have to find another way out."

"My name's Natalie," she said, looking down at the young girl.

"Briggs," the man said, "and this is my daughter, Emily. Her mother stepped too close to a portal as it opened and got sucked in. We don't know if she's alive or dead."

"I'm so sorry."

"A few of us tried to grab her and pull her out, but with the suction the portal creates, we couldn't get close enough. By the time we found a rope to throw in, the portal had closed. If only I could figure out how they control the portals, I could get my wife out and maybe find a way to escape this hellhole."

"Maybe Walter can tell us?"

"Yes, it's time I get him to talk." Briggs picked Emily up and sprinted down the street with Natalie following close behind.

Natalie, Briggs, and Emily entered the store. Walter stepped out from behind the counter. "I told you earlier, Briggs, I don't know anything. I was given one mission, and this is it. They didn't divulge anything else to me. You know how secretive the government is."

"I don't believe you." Briggs placed Emily on the floor beside Natalie and stepped up to Walter. He grabbed Walter's shirt and raised him off the floor.

"Please, it's not my fault you're all here. I'm just following orders," Walter whimpered.

Emily looked up at Natalie with her big brown eyes; she reached out a hand.

"It's okay," Natalie spoke softly to the young girl as she took her hand.

Natalie shot Walter a glare and collected her thoughts. She couldn't understand how this man could allow this to continue. "If you're involved in this mess, you have to help us. You can't be that cold-hearted to allow this poor child to die."

"Of course, I don't want her harmed," Walter said. "I never thought they would involve children."

Briggs lowered Walter. His feet touched the floor, and he straightened out his clothes.

"I have to be honest with you. It's Jameson that has full control over this operation. You're all here because of him, not me," Walter said.

"Who's Jameson?" Briggs asked.

"He's the lead scientist."

"Where can we find him?"

"Now that's a little tricky."

"Why? You two work together, right?"

"I know he's here somewhere on this compound in an underground bunker, but I'm not exactly sure where it is. I do know that he has cameras around town to keep an eye on things, and could be watching us right now."

Natalie glanced around, looking for cameras. She didn't find one. Still afraid of Walter, but also curious, she edged back toward him and whispered, "Do you know how I ended up in this town?"

"I don't know. I'm not a recruiter. All I know is Jameson told me you would be here, but he didn't say how." Walter gazed down at his newspaper on the counter.

Natalie didn't believe him. She looked out the window. "Who were the two men carrying rifles who chased me in this direction last night? They obviously have something to do with all this, or I wouldn't have ended up here with you."

"I don't know what men you're talking about. The only ones who have access to this town are Jameson and me. The recruited don't have any guns. No one else is privy to this operation, and they aren't allowed to come past the gates."

"Why would he want me here?" Natalie asked.

"He thought you needed to see Homondiem to understand what's going on."

"The only thing I understand is that I'm being held prisoner and I want out." Natalie backed away and stood next to Briggs.

"Why would the government intentionally endanger our lives?" Briggs asked Walter.

"I don't know, but I believe you'll find the answers soon enough. It's Natalie who has more information than she knows."

"Me—I have information? What kind of information?"

"Knowledge about Homondiem and the homondie, of course."

"How could I have any information? This is the first time I've heard of any of this."

"That's something to worry about later. For now, we must concern ourselves with the matter at hand, the homondie."

"I still don't understand. How could everyone in this town be missing and the rest of the world doesn't even know we're stuck here?"

"The government has ways of keeping things secretive."

"I've had enough of you!" Briggs grabbed Walter's shirt and pulled him across the store. "The only thing that kept me from feeding you to the homondie is the fact that you may be useful to me. Time's up."

Walter grunted as he tried to jerk out of Briggs's grasp.

Briggs dragged Walter to the closet and stopped in front of it. "If you're not going to help us, you're going to be homondie meat."

As Briggs reached for the latch to open the portal, Walter shouted, "No, wait!"

CHAPTER 5

NATALIE WAITED TO see if Briggs was going to turn Walter into a homondie meal. Emily ran to Buster and held tightly to his neck.

Walter let out a whimper. "All right, all right, just please don't kill me. I'll tell you everything."

Briggs let go of Walter.

Walter straightened his shirt and tucked it into his trousers. He ambled back over to the other side of the counter and hoisted himself onto the rickety stool. It creaked as he spun around and started to explain. "Jameson and I had been working on research that tied us to the homondie world. As we conducted the experiment, Jameson discovered a portal forming in this town. These portals are a way to communicate and interact with beings from other dimensions. He told me to locate it and watch over it so I could calculate any fluctuations it might have. That's when Buster and I uncovered the first portal right here in this store. It's also when I stumbled on the owners, Abigail and Phillious, but it was too late."

Natalie shook her head in disgust. "You didn't!"

"No, they had already found the access when I arrived and they'd gone through the portal before I even knew what was happening. I never had a chance to explain it to them. That's when I found out that Buster can tell when the homondie are close by. He started barking right before they went into the storage closet, but it wasn't my doing. They were standing there when the portal enlarged."

"Didn't you try to save them?" Natalie asked.

"I did try to save them, and I almost got pulled in myself." Walter stared at the closet and pointed. "The homondie started to come out. They were trying to break free from their world. That's when I added the locking mechanism on the door and put the rope at the entrance so I'd know how far they can travel."

"What happened to the locals?" Natalie peered over her shoulder and out through the storefront window.

"Once the first portal opened, the secrecy of the testing was compromised, so the government took over and quickly engineered a cover-up. The next thing I knew, the community was fenced in and disconnected from the world, and all the townspeople were gone. They closed off all outside activity and phone lines. They even blocked cell phone service. When they seized this town, they decided to expand Jameson's findings to create an experiment. That's when they assigned military personnel and Operation ʤ commenced. Now there's a patrol outside the gates 24-7. Everyone involved was sworn to secrecy, and I wasn't allowed to leave. Since then, Jameson's been in a secret underground lab, while Buster and I stay here and guard the portals. I was told to wait and see what would come. But now the fears are real."

"What fears?" Natalie asked.

"Now they're trying to escape. We were afraid that might happen. Eventually, all the homondie will escape through those portals and into our world."

"Briggs, I'm not comfortable trusting him," Natalie said. "If you saw what he did to that couple who came into the store earlier, you would have doubts too." She turned to Walter. "What if I turn my back on you and you lock me in there with those homondie?"

"I had my chance." Walter leaned back and crossed his arms. "I could have pushed you all the way in and closed the door, but I pulled you out, didn't I?"

Natalie backed away, but she had to admit that he was right.

Walter's expression softened. "I know you tried to help them, but there's nothing we can do to save them now. But it might not be too late for the rest of us."

"I agree with Natalie," Briggs said. "How can we trust you after what you've done to us? You could have told the truth when we confronted you earlier, before my wife disappeared."

"I needed to make sure we could all work together before I let you in on anything," Walter said. "I want to get out of here as much as you do. Who knows how much longer I have before those homondie kill me too? I didn't want you to run off leaving me here to fend for myself."

"So does that mean you know a way out?" Briggs asked Walter.

"Yes, but it's not going to be easy."

"Tell us."

"I believe we can redirect a portal to open outside the town. That way, we could escape through that and into the woods where no one would see us."

Natalie threw up her hands. "Is that even possible? How do we know that we're not going to get sucked into the homondie world?"

"By using the portal detection device Jameson and I created. It's incredibly advanced technology. I found the portal here in this store with it and I can also detect others throughout the town. I know where they're all located." Walter reached under the counter. "Here, let me show it to you."

"A device?" Natalie could feel her curiosity growing. She gave her handbag a pat as it rested against her hip, wondering if it was safe to tell him what she had in there. Could she trust Walter?

Walter placed the device on the counter. It was simple in design with a small monitor attached to a handle—an exact match to hers.

Natalie leaned forward and studied both the device and Walter's reaction for a moment longer before replying. Maybe having her own device would give her an advantage, but she would need to understand how to use it. Would Walter show her how? There was only one way to find out.

"I have one of those in my handbag." She placed the bag on the counter and opened it. She pulled out the device and laid it next to Walter's.

"How did you come across that?" Briggs asked.

"I found it in a car, inside this handbag. I didn't think too much about it at the time but thought it could be useful, so I took it," Natalie said. "Walter, can you show us how it works?"

Walter turned his on, and it let out a short, high-pitched shriek. Quick, repetitive bursts followed, like a countdown to an explosion. Buster had taken off running across the store at the initial shriek, and Natalie watched him hide under the legs of an antique washing machine along the back wall. Natalie stepped back from the device herself, eyeing it warily. The device began to flicker, and the shriek faded as the screen slowly came into focus.

"Look at this." Walter waved them closer, holding the device out for them to see.

Natalie bent over the counter, pushing her chin-length bangs behind her ears. "Hmm, what are those dots?"

"Those are all the portals opening and closing around town."

"You can't be serious."

"Is there a way to stop them from opening?" Briggs asked Walter.

"It's possible. We should be able to control them with this device."

"*Should* be able to?" Briggs said. "You don't know for sure, and you want us to trust you to reopen a portal outside of town?"

"I can't be one hundred percent positive. I've never done it before, but I should be able to figure it out." He gazed at the device and tapped it. "That's not the end of our problems."

"Of course not," Natalie said, barely audible.

"Remember, I work for Jameson. It's Jameson that's in control of the portals, and we don't know how far he's going to take this."

"If we don't act fast, those portals are going to swallow the whole town," Briggs said.

"Watch this." Walter held the device up to the portal in the store and pressed another button. Suddenly, the dots disappeared, and the display flashed coordinates on the screen, revealing the portal before them.

Natalie could see the silhouette of the three trees, but the woman and the homondie were gone. "It's like having an x-ray machine into the homondie world."

Walter turned off the device and put it back on the counter. "I believe if we work together, we could at least try to reverse this mess and get as far away from here as possible."

Natalie straightened to relieve the tension in her neck and put her own device back in her handbag. She put the strap across her body and held the bag taut to her chest. She felt the need to keep it close. The device could mean the difference between life and death.

Buster, evidently deciding the danger had passed, extricated himself from under the washing machine and trotted back over to the others. He sat next to Walter, who patted the dog on the head.

"Before we even think about leaving," Briggs said, holding up a hand, "we're going to find out if there are survivors stuck in Homondiem. If there are, we'll help them escape. My wife might still be alive, and I'm not leaving without her."

"Mommy?" Emily grabbed her father's leg and sniffled.

Natalie stared at Emily and felt her cheeks flush. She thought about all the people who could be stuck in there with those monsters. She felt like her head might explode at any moment. She looked at Briggs; he looked back at her as he stroked his daughter's hair.

"If the homondie came into contact with the survivors, they'd have killed them immediately," Walter said. "Even if they didn't kill them right away, I'm not sure how much time they'd survive in there—or anywhere else."

"What do you mean?" Natalie asked.

"When we were conducting our experiment, our main objective was to try and access a higher dimensional space, but instead we tore through the fabric of our three-dimensional world. It's separating, and we've created pathways through these portals to Homondiem. Everything within it are becoming alive, and now the dead walk."

Often hearing a term like the dead walk only meant one thing: elimination. With their lives on the line, Natalie suspected they had to trust Walter if they ever wanted to get out of there. She whispered in Briggs's ear, "Like it or not, I guess we have no choice but to trust him. It does sound like he knows what's going on around here. Without him, we'd be lost."

"*If* he's telling the truth," Briggs whispered back. "We'll need to keep an eye on him."

Natalie needed a moment to process everything she'd heard. She drifted away from the group by the counter and wandered around the store, wondering if what was happening was meant to happen. *This could be the start of something new. Maybe our world would evolve into a better place for mankind*, she thought. But what did she know? She was just a college girl stuck in a mysterious place. It was the best she could do to cope.

"Now that it's separating, what's going to happen to them and us?" Briggs asked, gesturing toward the portal.

"Even though Homondiem is empty space, it still has the power to suck energy from our dimension into theirs," Walter explained. "This could go two ways. Either we'll disappear with it or we could shift into a fourth dimension. This internal rip in the fabric of space and time could cause this fourth-dimensional space to try to reconnect as a way of repairing our three-dimensional world. It's possible that during this repair, the fourth-dimensional mechanism, which has no boundary, could swallow up our world and destroy our dimension."

"If we can't survive, does that mean the homondie won't survive either?" Briggs asked.

"I believe no human on earth will be able to survive if a fourth-dimensional world takes over," Walter said. "However, as the homondie world evolves, it's breaking through ours. For now, the homondie can't exist outside their world, but as they feed on humans, they're producing a new breed. Once this new breed evolves and adapts, it'll be possible for them to enter our world, no matter the state of our dimension. At that point, they'll have full control over us as their world unites with ours."

"This is like the dinosaurs dying off," Briggs said, "except now we're going extinct."

"Yes," Walter replied. "Cosmic events cycle the same way human events do. They coexist as they repeat themselves throughout time. What happened thousands of years ago will ultimately happen again."

"Are you saying we went through something like this in the past?" Briggs asked.

"Most definitely. The past, present, and future have already happened. This world, our cosmos, everything happens over and over again, until the world doesn't exist anymore."

As Natalie listened to Walter and Briggs, she wandered around the store until she reached the closet. Buster had followed her. He stood next to her as she gazed at the closet for a lingering moment. Tearing her gaze away, she turned back to Walter and Briggs. "When did all this get out of control?" she asked.

"As soon as the government took over. They saw an opportunity to extend the research, and Jameson was on board, wanting to make history." Walter sipped his coffee then placed it next to his newspaper. "Now that the government's involved, Operation ʤ is all about opening up our three-dimensional world to the unknown. Even though we identified the dimensions by locating points of access just like the portal we have here, it wasn't enough for Jameson. He needed to take a more defined look into their world, to see what happens when life meets death. The only way he could fully understand it was to make contact with it."

"So what you're saying is that you deliberately allowed people to enter." Natalie hesitated. "For the benefit of your research?" She couldn't disguise the disgust she felt.

"I know that sounds awful, but we were fascinated with the discovery of this new life-form and we needed to understand them."

Natalie didn't want to believe that people could be so heartless. She closed her eyes and bowed her head. She clenched her hands together in anger. After she stood silently for a moment, she tried to clear her head of the confusion she felt. In her mind, she had already sentenced Walter and Jameson to life in prison for killing innocent people, but where would that get her? Not any closer to getting out of there, that was for sure.

Her anger dissipated enough for her to speak calmly. "So you decided to take matters into your own hands. Was it really worth it?" She didn't let Walter answer before continuing. "Not only did you make it worse by feeding innocent people to the homondie, but then you went ahead and got the townspeople involved. You didn't do anything about it, even though you know what they are! You know what they do!"

"You have to understand," Walter said, almost pleading, "our scientific study not only allowed us to witness the creation of life of the undead homondie but it also gave us the necessary tools to understand their world. Without our findings, we wouldn't know what they were capable of. Our research confirmed what would happen if they came into our world."

"You taught them to kill," Natalie said coldly.

"It was only a matter of time before they would have figured it out on their own."

"You don't know that," she yelled. "You fed the living to the dead and look what happened!" Natalie threw up her hands in disgust. "Don't you get it? We're all connected within the dimensions, but we're not supposed to be interacting with each other. Putting innocent lives in the mix only made it worse."

"If we didn't do these things, we wouldn't have realized how much of a threat they were until it was too late."

"You were the one who caused the threat," she shouted. "I bet you don't even know how many you created. You don't even know how many there are!"

"You're right, I don't know," Walter conceded. "All I can tell you is that they've become hungry for our flesh."

Walter seemed to understand that he bore the brunt of the responsibility for their current situation, but it didn't change the facts. Natalie shook her fists in rage. "Then why would you keep feeding them even after you knew what was going to happen? You know they're multiplying!" She watched the sweat run off Walter's brow. She could see he was unsure what to say next. "You still don't understand Homondiem and the homondie, do you?"

Walter reached into his pocket and pulled out his handkerchief. He wiped his brow then blew his nose before returning it to his pocket. He crossed his arms, leaned on the counter, and answered, "We've only scratched the surface of Homondiem and what the homondie are capable of. You must realize it's an unknown place and their level of evolution is far beyond our understanding, even as we've watched them become more human."

Walter pointed to the closet on the opposite side of the room. "You heard them trying to open the lock on that door earlier. They've never done that before, so they've already evolved to a higher level of intelligence. Those homondie may be stuck in there for now, but they will find a way to come into our world."

Walter bowed his head. "You have to remember, this is a government operation, and I did what I was told. Believe me, if we'd known about all of this beforehand, we wouldn't have opened the dimension in the first place, but I can't change the past. I wasn't thinking."

"Damn right you weren't," Briggs said, "but I hope you're willing to help us now." He picked up Emily and hugged her tight.

"Yes, of course." Walter stared across the room.

"If you try to deceive us, I'll kill you." Briggs eyed Walter, forcing the old man to make eye contact.

"All right, I get it," Walter said.

CHAPTER 6

NATALIE COULDN'T BELIEVE Walter and Jameson had done this. They had deliberately and with forethought caused this imbalance in the world. Whether their intentions were good or not, those creatures hadn't existed before, and now they were here, bloodthirsty killing machines.

Briggs interrupted Natalie's train of thought. "We could argue about this all day, but arguing isn't going to save the people in there. We don't know how much time they have left or if they're still alive. Our only option is to move forward and fix this mess. Now, Walter, think good and hard. Is there a way we can stop the homondie and reclose Homondiem?"

"I'm not sure," Walter said. "I believe the energy that's flowing into Homondiem is not only flooding their dimension but also the universe, and it'll continue on until we all die."

"So then what are we going to do about shutting this whole operation down?" Natalie said, unsure if there were a plausible solution to their situation.

"We're going to need help," Walter replied. "After we try to locate survivors, we'll head straight for the university where I work. There are a lot of scientists there. We may not be able to fix the tear in the fabric of our dimension, but we could probably slow it down long enough to come up with a solution. Then we should be able to stop the world's destruction." The old man paused and looked at Briggs. "As for searching for survivors in Homondiem, I have a map of the town." He pulled a worn map from under the counter. "We could pinpoint the portal locations and try to access it from the most secluded one. Maybe we can see if anyone is alive in there and try to rescue them."

"It's a start." Briggs set Emily down. She dropped to the floor and sat cross-legged next to Buster. Briggs took a look at the map and hefted the rope he'd been carrying onto his shoulder. "If we find anyone, we can use this rope to throw to them and see if we can pull them back out."

Walter turned the device back on. The resultant shriek caused Buster to cower behind Emily. He viewed the monitor and circled a spot on the map with his finger. "This one's perfect, but we're going to have to act fast before Jameson figures out our plan."

"What about the portal in here?" Briggs asked.

"The other location is better," Walter said. "It's more secluded, and there's no camera in that vicinity. If we rescue survivors, we could sneak them out easier from there. We wouldn't want Jameson to see us with people who'd gone into Homondiem. That would give our plan away." He paused and looked at the old grandfather clock. "It's going to get dark soon, and we can't risk trying to get to the other side of town since we don't know what might be out there. We should start in the morning." He placed a comforting hand on Natalie's shoulder and looked at Briggs and Emily. "I know tomorrow will be a stressful day, so for now, get some rest."

"Where?" Natalie couldn't see an inch of open space anywhere in the store, never mind room for four people to sleep.

"I have the perfect place." Walter patted Natalie on her shoulder. "I've spent many nights here, so I think you'll approve. Come this way, into the back." Walter led them through the cramped store. "There are a few vintage cots in the stockroom back here. I set up one for myself, but there are more you can use. They're not very comfortable, but it does the job—better than sleeping on the floor."

Natalie followed Walter as Briggs carried Emily, and Buster brought up the rear. "Aren't you scared they could get out while you're sleeping?" she asked.

"That's why I have Buster. He can detect the homondie." Walter flicked a switch on the wall. "Here we are."

A pile of old, torn-up cots were stacked in the corner of the stockroom.

"Find a spot and get some rest. We have a long day tomorrow." Walter pointed to a box on the floor. "There's food and water here if you want it."

Natalie grabbed a cot and set it up toward the back of the room, away from the others. Strangely, she had no hunger or thirst. Briggs put Emily onto her cot first, took a blanket from a pile and covered her, then plopped down himself.

Walter lowered the lights and put a hand on his own cot, guiding himself down. He settled with a grunt. "I think we can figure out a way to retrieve the survivors and escape before we all die. For the sake of our world, I pray we can get out alive."

With the possibility of dying firmly in mind, Natalie laid down, fully clothed and eyes wide open, fearful of what might come in her sleep. Restless, she watched Buster settle at the doorway. "Why won't Buster come in here?" she asked Walter.

"He has to stay there for our protection in case of a breach. If they do find a way to escape, he'll alert us." Walter yawned and began to doze off. "No more questions. You need to rest now. Don't you worry, we'll stop this, somehow."

Natalie lay silently on her cot. She stared at the water spots on the ceiling, watching the flickering light streaming in from the storefront. She listened to Walter's ragged breathing and Briggs's snoring. She began to think about the homondie world. Her mind clouded, and her thoughts wandered. She worried that she would never fall asleep, but her eyelids grew heavy all the same. She began to realize how exhausted she was. She ebbed into unconsciousness, succumbing to the darkness.

The grandfather clock chimed. It startled Natalie and jolted her awake. Exhausted from her restless night, she rubbed her eyes then blinked to adjust her vision. She had hoped to find herself lying in her own bed, sheets warmed by the morning sunlight streaming between the curtains that refused to stay all the way closed. But as she looked around, she saw only boxes surrounding her. *It wasn't a dream*, Natalie told herself, wishing it were.

She gazed around the stockroom, and the events of the day slowly came back to her. Emily and Briggs were still asleep. She searched for Walter and Buster, but they were nowhere in sight. Something was wrong.

Suddenly, Natalie heard Buster bark and Walter grunt. The noise filled the room. Instinctively, she knew they were in danger. Even though she was scared of what she might find if she left the stockroom, she knew if Walter and Buster were at the portal, they couldn't take on the homondie alone. There was no other option. She jumped off the cot, hoping she would find nothing out of the ordinary. She darted into the store to find Walter and Buster at the closet.

Natalie ran to the rope that she had knocked down yesterday. She felt an icy cold run through her veins as she watched scarred, decayed hands emerge through the crack in the door opening. The homondie clawed at Walter as he struggled to close the door. He kept a hold on the door and tried to reconnect the latch while Buster barked like mad.

"There are too many of them, Buster. I can't hold this door much longer. Be ready for anything," Walter shouted.

Walter turned and pressed his back against the door. He reached down to grab the lower latch, and one of the creatures clutched his sleeve. It rattled Natalie's senses as she watched the homondie grab and pull, almost causing Walter to slip and fall.

Natalie snapped out of her reverie and yelled, "Briggs, help!" She ran to Walter, placed her palms against the door, and pushed as hard as she could, but the homondie continued to yank on Walter's shirt. Buster moved in and bit one. He chomped down hard on its hand. The homondie screeched and retreated.

"Good boy, Buster, get them out of here," Natalie said. She leaned her shoulder against the door, and Buster jumped at another advancing homondie. One by one, the hands retracted back through the doorway, finally letting go of Walter. Briggs ran in, and the three of them gave the door a final push together. The door closed. Walter latched and locked it tight.

Walter wheezed and slumped forward. He moved away from the door and slid down the wall, then collapsed onto the floor.

Natalie watched the door as it rattled on its hinges. "Why did you open it without us? You should have woken us up."

"I was checking to see if I could control the portal with the device. I didn't see the homondie there and thought it was safe. I never thought they would be waiting for me," Walter explained. "They've never done that before. I may have underestimated them. They're getting more intelligent. They seem to be evolving by the day. Soon they'll have the ability to think like humans, and if that happens, any survivor in there is doomed."

"So we need to hurry before they start hunting the survivors," Briggs said.

Natalie stared at Walter. He sat on the floor, mouth hung slightly open. His skin, which had been flushed from the morning's excitement, had turned pale. After a moment of silence, he said, "How could they have known to be there at that precise moment when I opened the door? It seems impossible that they could have gotten to this point so quickly. Just yesterday, they didn't seem to understand, so what's the difference between yesterday and today? How could they become intelligent so fast?"

Walter huffed as he straightened his glasses onto the bridge of his nose. He got up with a grunt and paced the floor, then hurried off to a whiteboard at the store entrance. It rested on an easel and displayed the sale prices for a number of items.

Buster trotted alongside Walter with Briggs and Natalie following behind.

Walter half-wiped away the list with his sleeve and started writing equations in the blank space. He murmured, "How could they understand time?"

"What do you mean?" Natalie asked.

"Time is a way to measure our dimension. Our dimension is a direction. When space changes, so does time. Without time in our dimension, we don't exist. In a fourth dimension, having more direction could cause us sudden death if we were to appear in it. However, the reality of a fourth-dimensional world would be linked to a connection of a space-time continuum and wouldn't be noticeable at first. Past, present, and future would become one. I believe it's more plausible to say time is flowing forward, backward, and not at all consecutively. The problem is, we're currently only capable of observing it flowing forward. Look there." He pointed to the clock.

Natalie watched the movement of the hands as time seemed to slow down.

"It's only the arrow of time we perceive as an illusion of moving forward, but we've actually decreased the passage of time. We've made it go slower. I believe it's slipping away from us and being pulled through Homondiem and into the fourth dimension. Even though time exists in multiple dimensions, it's the difference of space-time that changes our perception. It may explain certain mysteries on the quantum level. That could only mean one thing."

"What's that?"

"Space is like a fabric, like a sheet. Space and time are warping as it produces these portals. As time evolves, it passes though the fabric of space-time and becomes infinite. Its density will fluctuate and inflate to the point of explosion. This will create the final split of the dimensions, causing space to expand while time passes. Therefore, our time is departing our world and entering theirs. In other words, as their world evolves, ours is dying as a new dimension is taking over. This will ultimately become the destroyer and creator of worlds."

"What should we expect if this new dimension does take over?" Briggs asked.

"Now that time is added to the mix, we could literally disappear into a fourth dimension. We wouldn't be dead, exactly, but we'd be unseen entities, like souls made of energy. However, if we could get back to our dimension before it ceases to exist, we could possibly reenter the bodies we left behind. So whether death exists or not, we could survive being thrown into another dimension if we were able to make it back in time, but we wouldn't know the outcome until it was too late."

Walter placed the marker on the counter and fled back into the stockroom. Natalie followed. Behind her, Briggs gently woke Emily.

Walter shuffled back and forth around the room, throwing flashlights, granola bars, medical supplies, and bottles of water into a pair of backpacks. He ran back to the counter and grabbed a handgun from under it, carefully tucking it into the waistband of his pants, and picked up the device.

"I thought there were no guns around here," Natalie said.

"This one is here for emergencies if the homondie get through it would give me a few seconds' head start."

He flung the backpacks over his shoulder and checked his watch. He glanced at Natalie and Briggs. "Are you coming? I want to get this started before we have nothing left of this world." Walter hurried toward the front of the store.

Natalie grabbed her sweatshirt and tapped the side of her leg. "Buster, come on."

Walter skidded to a stop. "I almost forgot. I need to lock the storefront. We wouldn't want anyone coming in while we're gone and accidentally let the homondie out." He pointed at Natalie. "I've got to get the keys and the map. Go to the car where we met. Do you still have the key?"

"I left it in the car."

"Okay. Run to it as fast as you can before Jameson catches you on the cameras and wait for me. I'll meet you there shortly."

Natalie ran to the car and let Buster into the back seat while Briggs and Emily stood outside. Briggs picked up his daughter.

"Aren't you coming with us?" Natalie asked.

"No, Emily and I are going to go back to the other side of town to tell the others about our plan."

"How will we find you?"

"I know where you're headed, and we'll get there as soon as possible," Briggs said. "If, for some reason, we don't make it, Walter has a map. We'll be on Oak Drive." Briggs ran off carrying Emily.

Natalie glanced up at the sky. A blackened haze seemed to hang over the store. She opened the car door and sat in the driver's seat.

What was that? She glanced through the rearview mirror and watched Walter lock the store then look up at the same dark sky.

Walter ran to the car. "Where's Briggs?" He snapped as he opened the passenger side door. "The portal seems to be expanding, and we need to get out of here quick." He tossed the backpacks on the seat behind them, nearly hitting Buster.

"He said he'll catch up with us later," Natalie explained.

"Then let's get moving," Walter said.

"Where should I go?"

Walter opened the map. "Back out and to the right." He ran his finger down the map's surface. "Take the next right and follow this route north to the end. There aren't as many cameras in that area."

Natalie started the car and raced down the street.

CHAPTER 7

NATALIE DROVE FOR a few blocks, while Walter peered through the windows. When they came to an intersection, Natalie asked, "Which way should we go?"

"Straight through to that path across the street." Walter pointed.

"That's not a road. I don't even think the car would fit."

"We need to hide the car, and this is the perfect spot," he said.

Natalie drove through the long dirt path, barely wider than the car. Tree branches and overgrown bushes slapped the sides and roof.

"Stop here. We'll have to walk the rest of the way." Walter lifted the device and scanned it across the woods. "Over there. We're going to make our way to that old abandoned farm through the cornstalks at the end of this path. Behind the barn is a shack. The portal should be in that shack." Walter reached into the back seat and grabbed the backpacks. He handed one to Natalie. She opened it and placed her own device inside.

Natalie opened the door and stepped out of the car. The air was crisp and cold. She grabbed her sweatshirt from the seat and opened the back door to let Buster out. Natalie looked up at the sky as she put on the sweatshirt. The now-familiar haze seemed to have expanded throughout the town, as if it was following them. A drifting light glimmered through the darkness, followed by a pulsating whoosh. Something wasn't right.

"Natalie, duck," Walter hollered from the other side of the car. "Don't move until I tell you."

Natalie crouched low, covering Buster with her body. A helicopter passed overhead.

As soon as it was out of sight, Walter called, "It's clear."

Natalie released Buster who ran to Walter.

Natalie stood and gazed over the top of the car at the partial path, barely visible through the overgrowth that led to the barn. Her eye twitched, and a chill coursed through her body. The air became heavy and still, leaving her with that same feeling she had in the store—an unnamed temptation. She couldn't understand why she all of a sudden wanted to get to that shack so badly. It didn't make sense. Logically she wanted to get as far away from it as possible, but something had changed. This desolate place had started to seem desirable, though there was a sense of foreboding that made Natalie uneasy. She shook it off and headed toward Walter.

Walter grabbed the two backpacks from the seat and rounded the front of the car. "Here you go," he said, holding out the backpack for her to take. "You don't want to forget this."

Natalie put on the backpack, and Walter handed her a holster fitted with a revolver and a sheathed knife. He dug deep into his own backpack and pulled out a box of ammunition; he poured bullets into her hand.

"For someone who says there are no guns around, you don't really mean it, do you?" Natalie asked.

"Some things need to be kept quiet," Walter said.

Natalie stuffed the bullets into her pocket and placed the belt around her waist. "Can they be killed? I mean for good?"

"I believe so."

"How do we do it?"

"First of all, you can cripple it," he explained. "Disabling its body so it becomes a useless corpse, but this would only allow you time to escape, as it's not fully dead. To exterminate them fast, the best way to deal with them is by cutting off their hunger. You could slice their throat or shoot them directly in the head. As long as you cause some sort of damage to their brain, they'll stop hungering for us."

Walter threw his backpack over his shoulders and started off down the overgrown path. Natalie followed close behind. It was eerily silent. Rays of sunlight forced its way through the darkening sky and shone down like a guide from above, directing them to the abandoned farm.

Natalie hiked to the end of the path and paused at the field, unable to take another step. She could see where the cornstalks had been broken off in the distance on the other side of the barn. The fence ran straight through the field and around the perimeter of the town.

"This would be a perfect spot to open a portal on the other side of the fence," Walter said as he began to stomp through the dry stalks.

Natalie stared across the field. She knew what lay out there: more homondie. Her heart hammered in her chest, and she began to sweat. A knot settled in the pit of her stomach; the anxiety was nearly overwhelming.

Walter turned around. "Let's get a move on," he said, hiking his backpack higher on his shoulders. "We don't know how much time we have left. Come on now, you need to do this."

Despite her fear, Natalie forced herself to follow Walter and Buster through the field. She noticed two tire tracks running through the middle and leading to the barn. As they reached the barn, she gazed up at the building, ramshackle from neglect. The silence seemed to grow the closer they got to the shack. "This doesn't feel right," she muttered.

"Now's not the time to back out." Walter's voice rose, then ended in a whisper.

Once the shack came into view, she paused and stood motionless. The door yawned open and swung slightly in the breeze. "Something's wrong. It's too quiet out here. There should at least be some birds chirping or something."

The building leaned sharply with pieces of the roof and siding littering the ground around it. The door hinges were falling off the rotted frame.

"Do you think someone's in there?" Natalie whispered as she brushed aside a few strands of hair that had blown into her face.

"I hope not." Walter shoved her gently from behind, and she took a step forward. As she rounded a bush at the corner of the barn, a high-pitched screech sent her reeling backward into Walter. Buster barked and clawed at the bush until a cat streaked across the field, still squalling.

Natalie crept toward the shack. Sticks snapped, and dry, brittle leaves crunched beneath her feet. She gazed around, having no idea what to expect.

Walter moved forward, putting Natalie behind him. He pulled out the handgun he'd tucked into his waistband. "Buster, come on."

Buster moved up next to Walter.

They crept closer to the shack until they were a few feet from the doorway.

Walter paused. "I guess the only way to do this is to go in and see."

Natalie stepped closer. As she was about to peek in, Walter grabbed her arm and guided her back. "Stay here. We'll go in first." He pointed to the ground next to the door. "Stand over there and be ready for anything."

Buster stopped just shy of the entrance and sat in front of the door. Walter gave him a pat on the head and held up his gun. "Buster, come on, boy." Walter yanked on the door. It creaked open, the sound deafening in the absolute silence.

Walter pointed his gun into the darkness. Buster slipped in through the doorway first, and Walter followed, leaving Natalie outside by herself.

The silence engulfed Natalie. She peered at the farm, the woods, and everything around her. In the distance she thought she could hear snapping tree branches and footsteps on dried leaves; the noises seemed to be getting closer.

Natalie grew fearful. *Could that be homondie already in our world?* She readied her gun. Her hands trembled as she tried to stay focused. She took to her sight, laid an eye down the barrel, and stared into the woods. She watched carefully for any sign of movement.

"Where are they?" she said aloud, her arms starting to shake.

All she could do was stand alone outside and wait. As the moments passed, fright began to obscure her vision, and she started to envision horrifying scenarios. Natalie began to fear for her life; she felt as if something was trying to reach out and extract her soul.

Unable to stand still any longer, she scurried to the door and placed her shaking hand on the knob, but paused and thought, *What if they got sucked in? What will happen if I open this door? Will I get sucked in too?*

She inched the door open. The door creaked, practically screaming in the silence. She could see nothing but darkness. The inside of the shack was as dark as the storage closet at the store.

She stepped inside, and the door slipped out of her grasp. It slammed behind her with a loud thud and shut tight. Startled, she turned to open it and leave but couldn't find the knob. She scratched at the door and whimpered in terror. Something grabbed her shoulder, and she screamed.

"Calm down, Natalie, it's only Buster and me here. You're safe," Walter spoke softly into her ear, comforting her as he shone a flashlight on her, then turned to illuminate the empty shack.

Natalie sat on an old wooden bench inside the doorway. She placed her elbows on her knees and rested her head in her hands.

"We're in no imminent danger," Walter said. "The portal's closed, so my guess is the homondie haven't escaped yet. I also searched the inside, and there seems to be no homondie here, so I'm going to have to find a way to open the portal." Walter held up his device and pressed a series of buttons. The first set of beeps were followed by a flash of light.

"Can't you open it?" Natalie asked as she walked toward Walter.

"With Jameson setting the program, I still don't have a full understanding of how this works, but it's only a matter of time until I figure it out."

"So how did you open the one at the store?"

"That one was already open. I didn't know how to use the device to close it. That's why I had to use the door to control that portal." Walter continued to press a multitude of buttons and paused. He put a hand to his chin and rubbed his bristly face as he watched a series of codes appear and disappear on the screen. "I have it," he shouted after a moment. "I figured it out. I don't know how he does it, but he's smart as a whip."

"Fantastic," Natalie said sarcastically. "We can give him a medal later. For now, we need to concentrate on the portal."

"Sorry, I got caught up," Walter said apologetically. "Using the stored data, I can reopen this portal." He showed Natalie the screen. "You see here, you press this button to close the portal, and then this one to open it." He pressed the button.

Natalie backed toward the door and held Buster tight while Walter activated the device. A loud crack rumbled, followed by a burst of light. Lightning shot from the portal, through the device, and up through the ceiling of the shack. The flash was so bright it could probably be seen for miles.

For a moment, Natalie was blinded by the light, but she heard the door swing open hard, almost pulling it off its hinges. The door slammed open and shut several times, smashing into the wall. She flinched and jumped out of the way, narrowly avoiding it.

She could feel her blood run cold and a chill strike her bones. Her body tingled as the hair on her arms stood up. She bent down and clung to Buster. "Walter, I can't look. Tell me what you see."

Buster barked. "What is it, Buster?" Walter asked. The dog lunged at something, breaking Natalie's hold on him. She opened her eyes.

Buster stood at Walter's side.

Natalie looked through the darkened hole. The darkness had a rippling effect; it looked as though someone had thrown a stone into the opening. The ripples expanded across the portal as the pulsating outer layer grew.

She inched toward it. The pressure tugged on her body. Suddenly, the darkness cleared, and she looked around, amazed. Though the entrance was dim, the landscape behind the thousands of decayed trees had a glow. This was not the simple glow from the rising morning sun but a spark that fed this new world.

"This is odd. It's nothing like when we were back at the store," she said. "Before, it was lifeless, but now it seems like life is emerging as their world grows—"

"Did you see that?" Walter interrupted Natalie.

"See what?"

"That flash. The light we had around us faded, like it's been sucked into Homondiem."

Buster barked.

The stench of a putrefied corpse filled the air. Natalie covered her mouth and stifled a cough. "That's not our only problem." She took in the sights of Homondiem and saw a figure, deformed and barely discernible. It lurched out from behind the dead trees and through the darkened backdrop. Overshadowed by the high tree limbs, it stumbled from the murkiness. Natalie tried to make out the figure as it drew closer.

"Could it be a survivor?" Natalie moved forward and leaned into Homondiem, just short of the dimensional pull. She viewed the figure coming toward the portal with interest. "Wait a minute, isn't that—Fred?"

Walter squinted. "Yes, the man from the store. But it . . . was Fred. Now he looks like a homondie."

"How could that be?" Natalie asked.

"They must have only extracted a portion of his life, rendering him a half-life. He's not living, but he's not dead either."

The creature flailed its arms and dragged one foot, missing a chunk of flesh. It tilted its head and sniffed the air. Its eyes remained unfocused until it caught sight of Natalie and Walter. It picked up speed and trudged toward the opening, moaning. Natalie screamed and pulled Buster back.

Walter scrambled for his gun. Natalie, too frightened to shoot, watched Walter sight down the barrel. He aimed for the creature, but before he could pull the trigger, there was a bang, and Fred fell.

Natalie eyed Walter's weapon. "Your gun didn't fire."

"Never mind that! Now we have the truth," Walter said. "Not only do those homondie extract our life, but it's also possible that we can become them. Just think, if you can survive the entry and them trying to eat you, you'll turn into one of those!" Walter stepped back. His hands shook and he almost dropped the gun. "So now we have to deal with two different things: those who used to be humans and those who are becoming humans."

Natalie murmured, "There must be a survivor in there. *Someone* shot it. Can you see anyone?"

All of a sudden, the sky darkened around the shack as the light grew brighter in Homondiem. It shone down on another figure in the distance.

"Wait, someone else is coming." Walter raised his gun and peered through the sight. "I-I think I see? Oh, yes, there's a survivor!"

"Can you see who it is?" Natalie asked. "Maybe Briggs's wife?"

"It's a survivor all right, but I don't know who it is." Walter smiled as he lowered his weapon.

Natalie's fear drained away at the thought of a survivor awaiting rescue. She ran to Walter's side, needing reassurance, and staked out the portal. "Well, I'll be damned!" She placed her hands on her narrow hips and studied the unknown man. She bit her lower lip and smiled inwardly at the notion of his survival. He had a few days of stubble on his face and his shirt was ripped, but at least there were no bite marks on him.

Natalie began to feel the pressure of the portal. It tugged at her body as if a hand were pulling her in. She backed up to where the tension was bearable.

Walter yelled to the man, "Can you hear us? We're here to help get you out of there. Do you think you can make it to us?"

The man stood in Homondiem and smiled at the pair. He nodded and spoke, but Walter and Natalie couldn't hear what he was saying. He tried to run to the opening, but he couldn't get close enough.

"What's the matter? What's wrong with him?" Natalie asked.

"He can't leave. The pressure is greater than his strength," Walter explained.

While the man struggled to move closer, Natalie wished she had taken Briggs's rope.

"Look around and find something for him to grab onto," Walter said.

Natalie plucked the flashlight out of her backpack and shone it around the inside of the shack. She glanced into Homondiem past the man. Lurking behind him was a pack of homondie, coming up from behind the trees and onto the path. They crept up on the unsuspecting man.

She watched the man turn to look behind him. The homondie paused and put their noses high in the air. They ran, rambling and disjointed, straight for the man. He aimed his riffle at the homondie.

She placed her hand over her trembling lips, trying not to scream. The man was in trouble.

Buster darted past Natalie and ran straight into Homondiem.

"Buster, no—come back!" Natalie was terrified. How would they get him back out?

Buster charged right at the homondie while the man unloaded his rifle. He ran up and bit each of the homondies' legs, temporarily subduing them, while the man delivered death blows, killing each one where they lay.

Natalie heard the click of an unloaded gun as the last homondie fell. "He's out of ammunition. We have to help him before anymore homondie find him. We can't leave him like that."

"We won't be any good in there, especially if we turn into one of those!" Walter's voice cracked. His hand quivered as he pointed at the homondie.

"I saw a thick vine growing on a nearby tree," Natalie said. "Help me get it." She turned and yelled to the man, "We'll be right back! We'll try to pull you out!"

The man signaled a thumbs-up that he understood.

Natalie ran outside but Walter didn't follow. "Walter, hurry up!" When Natalie ran back inside, the old man grabbed her arm as he was being sucked into the expanding portal. She held onto the door, but the rotted wood gave way, and the door flew off its hinges. She grabbed the doorframe as Walter's legs gave out. He released her arm and slid to the floor.

He clamped onto her legs with a tight grip. Natalie tried to hold his weight, but the strain on her legs was immense. She could feel her muscles ready to give way. "I can't hold on much longer," she said. "You've got to pull yourself to the doorway." Natalie felt around for a solid piece of wood to hang on to, but a chunk broke off, and her hands slipped down the doorframe.

Natalie hung on for Walter's sake, but his weight was dragging her in. Walter's strength diminished, and he slid into Homondiem.

With Walter's release, Natalie flew forward out through the door and onto the ground. She sprung to her feet and dashed back to the portal, but it was too late. The portal had closed with both Walter and Buster inside. Everything went dark. She could no longer see Homondiem.

Natalie pulled the device from her backpack and pressed the button to turn it on. She stared at the blank screen and waited for something to happen.

She held in her tears and forced her emotions down. She needed to stay strong and focus. She pressed multiple buttons on the device. Still nothing.

She knew she needed help. Briggs was her only hope. She gripped the handle of the device tightly and ran. She had no choice but to carry on alone.

CHAPTER 8

NATALIE PUSHED THROUGH the thicket and out of the field. She ran down the dirt road toward the car. At the car, she paused and plucked a few field thistles from her sweatshirt. She patted her pockets and felt a bulge. She pulled out the key, but it slipped from her trembling fingers. The ground was a pool of darkness, and she couldn't see where she'd dropped it.

In the distance, Natalie could hear a vehicle approaching. *Someone's coming.* She knew she only had seconds before they'd find her. She dropped to the ground and searched, feeling around with her hands. Her hand buried into the fine, dry soil, forcing a dust cloud into the air that obscured her view even more. She felt around for another few seconds until her fingers closed on the cool metal of the key, but it was too late.

Car lights gleamed through the path and onto her. Fast as lightning, she reached in through the open car window, grabbed the map from the front seat, and shoved it in her pocket. Turning to look behind her, she started to run when a plain white car screeched to a halt, narrowly avoiding her.

Dirt flew into the air and hovered around Natalie. She focused over the headlights, through the cloud of dust, and onto the two shadowy figures in the front seat. *Could that be Briggs, or is that the men that I saw the other night with the rifles?* she wondered. She didn't want to hang around long enough to find out. Her gut told her they hadn't been sent to help her. She had to find a way to escape.

"Don't move," a man's voice bellowed.

She froze. A flash of lightning crackled, followed by a rumble. The storm was getting closer, but it didn't matter. She wasn't giving up that easily. She knew what she had to do. It was time to make a run for it. Running through the woods during a storm wasn't her first choice, but it was the only one she had.

"She has Jameson's device. Get her," another voice yelled.

Before anyone could get out of the car, Natalie gripped the device so tight her knuckles turned white. She ran as fast as she could into the woods, away from the farmhouse. As she ran, she could hear the two men shouting to each other, their voices fading into the distance.

"We have to get her before she escapes."

"Where did she go?"

"She went east, over that way," one man shouted. "You follow her through the woods, and I'll meet you on the other side." She heard the car peel out as the other man gave chase.

Natalie's muscles strained, and her legs ached. Her mouth went dry as she panted and her heart pounded in her chest. She could hear the man behind her. She knew she couldn't outrun him, but she could outsmart him.

The trees towered above her with outstretched branches, the only thing giving her temporary cover. She focused as she darted and wove through the woods, making herself harder to track. The man was farther behind her now, and she hoped his legs would give out soon because she knew that even if she escaped this time, they wouldn't stop coming for her.

She broke from the woods and the protection of the trees. She stopped and stood in the middle of the dimly lit road as she monitored the sky. Only a few flashes of light flickered through the gray clouds to reveal a concealed path on the other side of the road. She might be able to make it to Oak Drive before the men find her, but she knew she'd be bringing a whole lot of trouble with her.

Natalie heard an engine rev and tires squeal. She watched a pair of headlights glint off a sign at the last curve. She peeked over her shoulder and listened to the crunching of leaves and twigs. The shadowy figure had edged closer, almost breaking the tree line. Closed in, with no place to go, she knew she had to hide.

Natalie ran to the path but paused when she heard the car come to a stop. She bent down and watched through the overgrown grass as the car door swung open. A tall, thin man dressed in a brown trench coat and khaki pants carrying a three-foot staff got out. His salt-and-pepper hair was clipped short on the sides, but the top was long.

She edged closer to see what he was doing.

The man spoke in a low, mellow voice. "Seth, where is she?"

"Sorry, Victor, she got away," a younger, stocky, sandy-haired man sporting a flattop answered.

"Go back into town and get everything in order for the takeover while I prepare things inside Homondiem."

"What about Jameson?" Seth asked.

"Let him try and stop us. Once he discloses his whereabouts, we'll be able to take care of him."

"I heard he might be located in a secret room where that homondie was brought," Seth said.

"We were in that basement. I didn't see any other access point besides the one set of stairs. Did you?"

"I remember there were pieces of plywood leaning against a wall next to the steel table. Maybe they were there to cover the doorway."

"He was hiding in plain sight all along. No matter, we have an agenda to deal with right now. We'll take care of him later," Victor said.

Steel table? Natalie thought. *I was in a basement with a steel table. Could Jameson have been there too?*

"In the meantime, what do we do about Natalie?" Seth asked.

"Don't worry, I've got everything under control. I know she'll come out of hiding when she finds out everyone in this town will be destroyed because of her."

"I hope you're right. I'm not sure if she's capable of human compassion," Seth said. "I guess we'll find out soon enough. We can't complete the takeover without her."

Human compassion? Takeover? Natalie thought to herself.

"Just go there and open the portal," Victor told Seth. "I'll send out the homondie, and you capture Natalie when she comes out of hiding. Make sure she doesn't get away this time," Victor's voice rose sharply. "After the homondie are released, check on the other portals and make sure they're expanding to the maximum. My men will stand guard and see to it that no one closes them, especially Jameson."

"Sure, but will you be all right in there by yourself, you know, without the Staff of Life working? You don't know how those homondie are going to react when they see you again."

"No need to worry. I'll be fine." Victor waved off Seth's concerns. "I've had enough time to study their reactions when we captured one, and I'll be able to handle them until we get that chip back." Victor spun the staff around and gazed at its empty orb. He flipped the top flap of the orb open, then shut. "I have confidence we'll find her soon, and it won't be long until I have this staff working." He reached into his deep trench coat pocket. "Here, don't forget this, and meet me at our town when you're done." Victor handed Seth a device, identical to the ones Natalie and Walter have.

"We'd never be able to gain access without them," Seth said as he grabbed the device from Victor.

"And it gave us the necessary information to give us the advantage to take control of this new world." A smile twitched Victor's lips. "What a sucker he was. Now get a move on. Wait for me at the rendezvous point of the invasion. It won't be long until we have full control."

Victor smirked, unnerving Natalie. *What do those people want from me?* she wondered.

"I'll be ready." Seth got in the car and drove off. Victor stayed behind and held up another identical device. He fiddled with a control, and with a flick of a switch, a loud crack rumbled, followed by a burst of light. The wind picked up and a portal opened. Lightning shot from it, through the device, and lit up the area. An access to Homondiem had opened. Victor stepped in and disappeared through it. The portal vanished.

Natalie couldn't believe her eyes. How could he have such control over a portal? He was able to come and go like it was nothing. It was as if he could control the entire dimension.

Footsteps through the woods behind her caused Natalie's ears to perk up. She turned to look but saw no one. *It can't be the men that chased me,* Natalie thought. Nevertheless, the noise grew louder. Natalie turned to run, but a hand grabbed her shoulder while another covered her mouth.

Natalie let out a muffled scream.

"Shh, it's me," she heard. The hands released.

She turned around, half-angry and half-terrified. "Briggs, are you trying to give me a heart attack?" she whispered.

"Sorry, I didn't want to make a scene. We don't know who could be lurking in the area."

"It's good to see you." Natalie gave him a hug on impulse. "How did you find me?"

"I was tracking a flash of light from earlier, thinking it must have been you and Walter. Then another one happened closer so I decided to track that one instead, and it brought me right to you."

"The flashes are portals opening," Natalie explained. "Walter opened one and we saw a survivor."

"That's great. That means my wife may still be alive." A glint of hope shone in Briggs's eyes. "Emily will be so happy."

"Where is Emily?" Natalie asked.

"I had to leave her with some friends to find you. There's someone causing trouble in the area, saying if we don't give up Natalie Thompson, we'll all die at the hands of the homondie. I don't know any other Natalie, so I figured that was you."

"Did you come here to give me up?"

"No, of course not," Briggs said. "I came to help you. There's mass hysteria in the town, but those people don't know who you are, and I have a place to hide you. Come quick." Briggs looked around. "Where are Walter and Buster?"

Natalie lowered her head. "In Homondiem."

"What?" Briggs gasped. "How did that happen?"

"The portal went haywire. I don't know if it was done intentionally or not, but I think either Jameson or this other pair of men were involved in their disappearance."

"Who are the others?"

"Their names are Seth and Victor," Natalie said. "They were after me."

"I don't know who's stirring up the townspeople, but it could be one of them," Briggs said.

"I listened in on their conversation. I'd say it's Seth causing the trouble. Victor went into Homondiem on his own. He can control the portals. From what I heard, Jameson is his rival."

"This is getting more complicated by the minute."

"We'll have to sort it out later. I don't know if Seth will be back here looking for me." Natalie scanned the woods and street for any sign of Seth. "Let's get to town and make sure everyone's safe."

Briggs led Natalie east through the woods to the back end of the street and crossed between a set of houses. They could feel a loud rumble on the ground followed by a gust of wind that blew through the streets, knocking down people in its path. Natalie and Briggs almost lost their footing.

"What was that?" Briggs yelled. "I've got to get to Emily!"

"You go to her, and I'll check on the townspeople," Natalie said.

Briggs ran back behind the houses, while Natalie kept to the street.

CHAPTER 9

TOTAL CHAOS FLOWED through the streets. People were running in all directions. Another rumble sounded as a gust of wind blew past Natalie almost knocking her to the ground.

"What's happening?" she asked a young passerby.

"You're going the wrong way," he hollered as he ran. "Run for your life!"

"Excuse me, miss." Natalie grabbed a woman's sleeve as she tried to run past.

"Let go of me!" The woman yanked herself out of Natalie's grasp, almost dragging Natalie with her.

Natalie couldn't get anyone's attention. It seemed like all hell had broken loose, but she didn't understand why.

She ran to the end of the street and saw Seth standing in the middle of an intersection with the device in his hand.

"Townspeople of Wells Springs, this is the last time I'm going to ask," he bellowed. "Get out here now and bring Natalie Thompson to me, or I'll destroy every living thing within this town. You'll never get out of here alive."

People came out of hiding and flooded into the streets. Natalie ran behind a tree to watch and listen.

"You know you can't get out of this town without authorization from government officials, so you better start cooperating," Seth said.

"We already told you we don't know anyone by that name," a man shouted as he hugged his wife. "Please leave us alone. We just want to go home."

"I've never heard of her either," another man hollered as he passed by the group and ran back into the house.

"You have one minute to bring her to me before all the people here are dead," Seth said, raising the device. "Even your children won't survive." He held the device above his head. "This device controls the portals you see popping up all over town. Once it's activated, I'll call upon the homondie and open their world to ours."

I have to stop this. Natalie ran toward Seth, intending to give herself up.

Seth lowered the device and pressed a series of buttons. A spherical, ring-shaped mass materialized next to him. Darkness consumed the interior as the rippling waves filled its core, and the outer frame pulsated.

Natalie screamed, "No, wait," but he couldn't hear her. She stopped running. The hairs on her arms rose as a chill came over her body. Everything went silent. It was too late.

Seth backed away from the portal. "Homondie, attack!"

The homondie ran from the portal, past Seth, and into the streets toward the crowds. The townspeople screamed and scattered.

Natalie took a final glance at Seth then at the charging homondie. *I've got to save these people,* she thought. *But how? I've got to find Briggs.* Natalie ran in the direction where she'd last seen him.

Once the last of the homondie were set free, they disappeared down the side streets. *Where are they going?* Natalie wondered. A burst of energy shot from the portal and reversed the wind. It began to suck everyone in.

Screams rang out as Natalie changed direction and ran toward the portal. "Everyone, out of the street," she pleaded. "Get as far away from here as you can!" She tried to direct them, but they were too frightened to listen to her.

Natalie looked up into the sky. The same mysterious blackened haze she'd seen at the store and the shack was gathering above the portal. It swirled overhead and started to engulf the whole town. The pressure of the portal's suction strengthened as it produced an overpowering vortex. The trees swayed, and leaves flew off the branches. The portal continued to expand, and she began to feel its pull.

Natalie ran, but was thrown to the ground and dragged back toward the street. Her hands scrabbled over the lawn. Dirt and grass caught underneath her fingernails as she tried to hold herself in place.

Natalie tried to keep a level head and think. Maybe there was a way she could stop the portal. She leaned to one side, hoping to grab the device out of her backpack, but was yanked onto the street as if someone had grabbed her legs.

The wind picked up and tree branches soared through the air. The wind roared so loudly she could barely hear the cries of the townspeople as they flew past her and into the portal.

The portal was ready to suck her in. She inched nearer and closed her eyes. All of a sudden, she stopped moving; everything went quiet and still. She opened her eyes—the portal was gone.

Natalie groaned in pain, clutching her side. She got up and looked around at the debris-scattered road, confused. She wiped the dirt from her clothing as best she could.

A woman lay beside her. "Are you all right?" Natalie helped the woman to her feet.

"Yes, dear, thank you," the woman spoke in a soft, flat voice.

Natalie watched a dark fog form around the street. Soon the mass hysteria had reappeared. The roads were dimmed by the haze, and the streets were flooded with people screaming and running. With limited visibility, they tried to drive away in cars, but they smashed into one another. One man jumped out of a car and bumped into Natalie as he ran in the opposite direction.

Natalie ran down the street to find Briggs when something caught her eye through the dense fog. She stared at the area where the portal had last opened. The homondie scrambled out of the fog and swarmed the streets. They chased the townspeople.

Natalie ran down the crowded road past the abandoned cars. She was about to pass a small ranch house but paused when she saw a young girl with braided hair. She stood in the hallway with her back toward the open front door. Natalie edged closer to the girl, who was wearing a pink flowered dress and snowy-white shoes. She couldn't be more than three years old.

"Daddy?" she cried.

Natalie crept toward the young girl, trying not to frighten her.

The young girl spun around, teary-eyed. Blood was splattered across her pretty dress, and drops of red dotted her shoes. Her big brown eyes focused on Natalie.

"Emily? It's me, Natalie. It's good to see you." Natalie hugged Emily. She closed the door behind her and locked it to avoid drawing attention to themselves.

"Where's your daddy?" she asked the girl.

"Daddy," Emily said as she pointed to the basement stairs.

Natalie set Emily back down on the floor. The little girl grabbed her hand and wouldn't let go. "It's okay, honey, I'll be right back," Natalie said, trying to reassure her with more confidence than she felt. "You wait right here, and I'll see where your daddy is." Natalie slid her hand out of Emily's tight grip and stared into the pitch-black basement.

She tried the light switch, but the electricity was out. She placed her foot onto the first step and heard it creak. She grasped the handrail with one hand and slid her knife out of its holster with the other. Her second foot touched the next step when she heard something fall followed by a grunt and the scuffling of feet. She heard moaning as she continued down the stairs.

Emily screamed, "Daddy! Daddy!"

Heavy footsteps began to climb the stairs toward Natalie. She sheathed the knife, turned around, and ran back to Emily.

"Shh, I need you to be brave for me, okay?" Natalie placed her hand on Emily's shoulder.

Emily nodded.

"Come with me." Natalie took Emily's hand and guided her down the hall and into the first bedroom.

"Where's Daddy?" Emily cried.

"I'll take a look in a minute, but I need you to be safe first," Natalie said. "So that means you need to be quiet, okay?"

"Uh-huh." Emily brushed her sleeve under her runny nose.

Natalie searched for a way to keep the door shut to the hallway. She took the chair from the desk in the corner and wedged it under the doorknob. She pushed the twin bed with ruffled sheets at an angle in front of the closet to act as a barricade, jumped over it, and guided Emily into the closet. Natalie sat Emily on the floor and placed her finger vertically across her lips, hushing Emily's heavy breaths.

"Stay in here and don't come out until I tell you." Natalie closed the closet door quietly and stepped around the bed.

A shuffling noise came down the hall to the bedroom. Natalie bent down and eyed the doorway. Shadows of feet were visible under the door.

Natalie carefully and, without making a sound, raised her knife from her belt and stepped closer to the door. The doorknob jiggled and spun. She heard a moan, followed by a loud bang on the door. Emily's muffled cries grew from inside the closet. The pounding on the door became louder and stronger. *What do I do?*

Natalie replaced her knife, lifted the chair from under the knob, and pulled out her gun. She opened the door, stepped back, raised her gun, and aimed at the opening. A massive bloodied body came barreling into the bedroom. Natalie had been ready to squeeze the trigger, but she paused and lowered her gun. "Briggs."

"Where's Emily?" Briggs growled in a deep, low voice. He stared at her with his large brown eyes and carried a blood-soaked kitchen knife.

"She's okay. She's in the closet."

"Thank God she's safe!" Briggs exhaled deeply as he sheathed his knife.

Natalie shook her head. "I almost shot you. Why didn't you say something?"

"I wasn't sure how many creatures were in the house, and I didn't want to draw any attention to Emily," he said.

"Well, banging on the door doesn't help!"

Briggs jumped over the bed and opened the closet door.

"Daddy!" Emily fell into her father's arms.

Tears were streaming down Briggs's face. He caressed his daughter's hair and hugged her tight. "Everything's okay now, princess."

"What happened to you?" Natalie took note of his bloodstained sleeve.

"There was a creature in the basement. It tried to kill me."

"Did you get bit?" Natalie stared at him wide-eyed.

"Yes, here on my arm, but I'll be all right." Briggs rolled up his sleeve where the homondie had ripped the skin, revealing a noticeable impression of teeth marks.

Natalie backed away.

"What's the matter?"

"All it takes is one bite for you to become one of them."

"Are you telling me I'm going to turn into one of them?" Briggs asked.

"Yes, well, sort of," Natalie muttered.

"How long do I have?"

"I don't know, but you'll have a fighting chance if we get you help."

"What do you mean?" Briggs asked.

"Do you have a car?"

"Yes, but the roads are blocked."

"I'll take care of that. Just show me where the car is," Natalie said.

Briggs reached in his pants pocket and handed Natalie his keys. "Where are we going?"

"We need to find Jameson, maybe he can help you."

"Jameson?" Briggs said, confused. "What can he do?"

"He created this mess. He must know what to do. It won't hurt to find out," Natalie said.

"We don't know where he's hiding."

"I think I do," Natalie answered. "I heard he may be in the house where this all started for me. We need to get to the other side of town, and the fastest way there would be by car."

Moaning sounds came from the hall, followed by a scuffle, as if the homondie were struggling to get to the room. Natalie closed the bedroom door and placed the chair under the doorknob. Briggs held Emily tight. The shadow of feet crept under the doorway and scratching resounded on the other side of the door.

"Let's go out through the window." Natalie opened the window leading to the back of the house and stuck her head out. "It's clear. You go out first, and I'll hand Emily to you."

"No, you go first. I'll take care of these creatures." Briggs's hands were clenched tightly into fists.

Their moans evolved into an ear-piercing shriek, and the scratching turned into pounding. They watched the door bend inward.

"I don't have time to argue with you." Natalie jumped out the window and held her hands out. Briggs sat Emily on the windowsill. The doorframe broke, knocking the chair out of the way.

Emily cried in fear, and her father dropped her into Natalie's arms as the door burst open.

"Die, you filthy creatures," Briggs yelled.

Natalie set Emily down on the ground and stood on her tiptoes, aiming her gun through the window.

Briggs stood in front of the door, stabbing each homondie that entered. Within seconds, everything in the room was splattered with blood.

Natalie squeezed off a few rounds, and some of the homondie fell, but more came in behind them. Briggs backed up toward the window.

"Come on! Just leave them there and get out! I'll have your back," Natalie yelled.

Briggs turned to Natalie. Blood was spread across his face, and a crazed look lit up his eyes. "Take Emily and get out of here," he said. "We're being overthrown, and I'm not going to let these things take over our world."

Emily clamped onto Natalie's leg, crying.

"Staying here is suicide," Natalie said and shot another advancing homondie. "You need to live, for your daughter."

"You're right, I'm coming." Just as he turned to jump out the window, the group of homondie grabbed him from behind and dragged him back into the room. They latched onto his body and bit through his skin. He howled in pain.

Natalie bent down next to Emily. She reloaded her weapon, grabbed Emily's hand, and ran.

"My daddy?" Emily asked through tears.

"I can't explain right now. Daddy wants you to come with me," Natalie said.

A pack of homondie came around the side of the house heading for Natalie and Emily. Natalie tightened her grip on Emily's hand and darted into the neighboring yard. She shot the homondie surrounding them as she ran, dragging Emily along with her. "There are too many," she said. They sprinted though the yard and into the woods behind the house.

A pack of homondie followed them through the woods and were about to surround them when Natalie backtracked and emerged on a side road. They hurried down the road and back toward Emily's house.

Emily began to drag her feet. Natalie paused for a moment so Emily could catch her breath. She knelt down and said, "We have to go back to your house."

"To get my daddy?"

"No, honey, and I'm so sorry."

"There's Daddy!" Emily pointed down the road.

"Honey, I don't think that's your daddy anymore." Natalie pulled Emily back as the creature shambled down the street.

"No, that's Daddy!" Emily broke from Natalie's grasp and ran toward him.

"Emily, stop!"

Emily kept running but stopped several feet from the advancing creature. "Daddy?"

The creature stared, a hunger in its eyes. It clawed at her, blood spilling from its mouth as it let out a moan.

Emily screamed.

Natalie caught up and pulled her arm hard. The creature leaped forward, almost grabbing the girl. Natalie pulled Emily away from what was left of her father.

Natalie ran around a house and hid behind bushes. She gave Emily a hug and stroked her hair until she calmed down. She glanced at the keys in her hand that Briggs had given her then gazed into Emily's eyes. "Emily, you have to be brave now. Can you do that for me?"

Emily sniffled.

"We have to go back to get the car and see if we can get out of here. There'll be a lot more bad creatures out there, and the only way I can protect you is if you stay right by my side. Don't wander off, okay?"

Natalie smiled and held out her hand for Emily to take.

"Okay." Emily sniffled and grabbed Natalie's hand.

Natalie raised her gun. Now she had not only the homondie to contend with but also the half-life humans while protecting Emily. She and Emily ran down the front of the adjoining house and cut back behind it to let the homondie pass. They edged their way toward the front. Natalie stopped at the corner of the house and peeked out. There was one car in the driveway. *That must be the one.*

"Emily, remember, stay with me and don't leave my side. We're going to have to make a run for it and get in the car quick. Ready?"

The girl nodded.

"Okay, on the count of three, we're going to run. One, two, three!" They took off running.

As they ran, the homondie staggered through the streets. They lifted their noses, then changed direction and went after Natalie and Emily.

Natalie stopped at the car, and let go of Emily's hand to open the driver's door. "Emily, get in, crawl over, and put your seatbelt on."

A moaning sound grew louder, and Natalie turned around. The creature grabbed Natalie, and Emily screamed. Natalie fumbled for her gun, almost dropping it on the ground. She struggled to get away. She pushed the homondie back, held up her gun, and shot it in the head.

Natalie turned back to Emily. She looked into the car, but Emily wasn't there. "Emily!" Natalie looked around frantically. Emily was gone.

Natalie searched, panicked, until she caught sight of Emily running back to where her father had last been seen. Natalie reholstered her gun and ran after the little girl. She caught up to Emily and grabbed her hand. She pulled Emily along and hurried back to the car.

Without warning, a blast from the portal shot across town and threw everyone to the ground. The force slammed the car door shut. The portal reopened, and the pressure began to build. Natalie clung to Emily's hand and helped her to her feet as she reopened the car door, but the suction of the portal became greater and forced them back to the ground. Natalie gripped the car door handle with one hand and Emily with the other. "Emily, get in the car," she said through gritted teeth.

Emily grabbed the side of the door and tried to pull herself in, but the suction of the portal was stronger than her ability to hang on. Emily was tossed from the car and collided with a lamppost. She managed to wrap her arms around it.

"Hang on, Emily. I'm going to come to you," Natalie shouted through the whirling wind.

Natalie gawked at the portal as it began to grow. The black space grew until it was large enough to sail a ship through. It flung the bodies of the townspeople in every direction and sucked in everyone close to it. The portal was out of control and getting closer to Emily. The closer it got, the more powerful the portal's energy grew, until it extended to the inevitable point of no return.

Natalie let go of the car and rolled toward Emily. She hung onto the post with one hand and Emily's hand with the other. Emily cried. The suction was far greater than her strength, and Emily was sucked into the portal.

"No!" Natalie stood clutching the post when a mailbox was torn from the ground, flung through the air, and slammed into the back of her head. Her body went limp, and she relinquished her grip on the post. She flew through the air, heading for the portal.

CHAPTER 10

NATALIE FLEW THROUGH the air and into the cool darkness of the portal. Not a sound existed between the dimensions. The hair on her arms stood up, followed by a full-body shiver as the essence of her being and consciousness compressed. Her body floated in midair for a moment. Breathing became difficult, but that only lasted for a few seconds.

Natalie struck a hard surface, and it knocked her fully unconscious. She drifted into dreams where she felt a cold surface beneath her. Her vision was cloudy, and darkness surrounded her. Only a dim light cast thin rays down from the top of the stairs. She tried to sit up, but straps held her hands and feet in place.

She wiggled her wrists and found that the straps were already loose. She freed her hands and feet then sat up on a stainless steel table. When her eyes adjusted and her vision cleared, she pulled up the sleeves of her sweatshirt and the bottoms of her jeans. She saw red marks around her wrists and ankles.

As she rubbed her wrists, she peered around the room. The walls looked to be solid concrete. A light hung overhead, and a small table next to her was covered with bloody scalpels, scissors, forceps, and used syringes.

She got up to walk to the stairs then stumbled. She lost her balance and fell backward, catching herself as she leaned on the table for support. The bloody instruments rattled, and a few fell to the floor. She placed her hand on her head and felt the ridge of a fresh scar.

Natalie woke and opened her eyes to find herself lying on her back in a wooded area, a foot away from one of the trees. The blackness loomed above her, and her ears rang from the explosion of the portal. She swiped her hand across her forehead and felt a bulge under her bangs. *What happened to me? Was the dream real?*

The thick air carried a rotting stench so strong it was difficult to breathe. She let out a cough and a grunt as she tried to move, but the pain was unbearable. *Where am I?*

The ringing noise overpowered her hearing as she tried to make out the sounds around her—the patter of feet, the slamming of doors, and the shrill voices, but they all seemed to be coming from a great distance. She could hear vehicles crash and horns honking. Within moments, the ringing subsided and the landscape started to make sense. Natalie could make out the streets, houses, and people swarming in mass confusion. She watched as they abandoned their vehicles and homes and ran through the streets. Then, suddenly, as if a plug had been pulled, everything was gone, and all fell silent.

She squinted as she gazed up through the decayed trees. The sky sent a faded light through the treetops; it alternated between dim and bright against the blackened haze swirling around the sky. Natalie rubbed the back of her head and looked around. She tried to sort through the cloudy mess surrounding her, but her vision was still distorted.

She rolled onto her side, and her eyes fixed on Emily lying silently on the ground. She crawled over to her and tugged on her sleeve. "Come on, Emily," she whispered. "We have to make a run for it." Natalie sat up and grabbed her hand; it was cold and clammy. "Emily, wake up," she said sternly. "Can you get up? It's okay to be scared, but we have to leave now." Natalie paused. "Emily . . ."

Natalie hung onto the little girl's cold, dead hand. She caressed it with her thumb, then let out a soft cry of anguish. "Emily, I'm so sorry." Natalie's eyes filled with tears. She stared at Emily and brushed her hair from her face. She gently let go of the girl's hand and placed it on top of her chest then caressed her cheek in a gesture of goodbye.

The sounds of moaning homondie filled the air as they scrambled about in the shadows. Natalie knew it wouldn't be long before they found her. Her pain seemed to disappear as she rose to her feet and reached for her backpack, then her gun; they were both missing. *They must have fallen off during the entry.* She searched the area. The dim light shone across the barren land and into the dead towering trees that loomed over her. She saw nothing but a death-racked world. *I-I'm in Homondiem.*

She glanced at the ground and the people lying around her. All dead. Battered bodies lay at her feet, limbs twisted grotesquely. Rivulets of liquid flowed under the corpses and pooled at her feet. She panicked and stepped back. She tripped over more bodies behind her. She fell to the ground, and something shiny caught her eye—an object glittered. It was a locket on a necklace sticking out from underneath decayed branches and underbrush. She reached over, grasped it tightly in the palm of her hand, and pulled, but it wouldn't budge. Natalie cleared away the crumbled debris and found it was still attached to a body, one upon which the homondie had feasted.

She carefully pulled the locket off its chain and opened it. Inside was a picture of a man and woman smiling. She'd never seen this brown-haired, blue-eyed man before with a muscular build. He was a few years older than the woman, whom she recognized from the driver's license she'd found. It was Natalie Thompson.

She dropped the locket and backed away as she held her hand over her mouth to stifle her cry, sobbing quietly as she listened to the homondie getting closer. Her head felt light as she stumbled and stepped backward, tripping over more bodies. Natalie regained her footing and fled from the heaps of shattered cadavers. She ran hard and fast, not knowing where she was or where she was going. She could see homondie in the distance as she fled farther into the unknown. She expected them to follow. She kept running as she waited for exhaustion to overtake her.

Natalie cried. She couldn't bear the fact that she had saved no one, not even Briggs or Emily. She slowed to a steady walk and panted with each step. She decided she wouldn't fight off the homondie if they caught her. She didn't deserve to live.

The homondie came out of nowhere. All of a sudden, they were just there. They cocked their heads, smelled the air, and groaned.

They sprinted toward Natalie and surrounded her. They advanced in a pack, a human leading them.

Natalie's instinct to survive kicked in, something she hoped her exhaustion would control. It took all her remaining strength to pull out her knife and pivot. She slashed it through the air, trying to ward them off as they closed in. She felt weak from fatigue, and the woods spun around her. She couldn't focus, and her body grew unsteady. She stumbled, veered left, then right, until she became dizzy, teetered back, and hit the dirt.

Natalie's eyes opened slightly, and she saw a human standing over her. He smiled and said, "My, my, who do we have here? Why, I can't believe my eyes. It's Natalie Thompson. I've been looking all over for you."

"You're that man from the portal." Her words were slow but steady before she passed out again. Her eyes closed and opened briefly. A couple of homondie carried her through the woods. She was being escorted somewhere.

When she opened her eyes again, she was tied to a table in an unfamiliar log building.

She looked around, confused. Candles lined the room, flickering, making it hard to see. "Where am I?" Natalie asked, still groggy. There were two humans with their backs toward her and a few homondie off to the side. The humans talked among themselves and ignored her while she tried to pull her wrists from the ropes.

"I was amazed she made it through," Natalie heard one man say. "She was the only one who survived."

"Thank you, Seth. Now go back and make sure the rest of the portals are opening at full capacity while I take care of Natalie."

Seth? Natalie tried to focus on the men.

Victor turned around and faced Natalie as he fiddled with a few knives on a table, lifting up each one as he examined them.

"You're not going to kill her, are you?" Seth asked.

Victor turned to Seth, pointing a blade at his chest. "Are you going soft on me?"

"No, I'm just saying there's no need. She may die anyway, so you don't need to kill her to take it."

"I won't have you dictating to me," Victor said, his voice sharp. "You can either take her place or go tend to the homondie and check those portals. I'll take care of Natalie any way I see fit."

"Fine." Seth left, not saying another word.

Victor leaned over and examined her. "Natalie, you're awake. It was so good of you to bring yourself to me. We've been searching all over for you. I was getting a bit concerned."

"You're concerned about me?"

"Well, not too concerned." His lips curled into a smile. "I do want you dead, but I'd like to torture you a bit first."

"You don't even know me," Natalie said. "Why does it matter if I'm alive or dead?"

"Oh, I know you all right," he said in an icy tone.

"How?" she asked.

"You don't remember? I'm Victor Bernard. I met you in the basement with Jameson. Then when I saw everyone dead in the rubble, I feared the chip could have been damaged and you might be dead as well. I must say, I'm glad you made it here alive. At least I know the chip is all right." A mischievous look filled his eyes.

"I don't understand. I woke up in a basement alone," she said. "What chip are you talking about?"

"Don't act so innocent. The chip Jameson put in your scalp at the temporal ridge." He tapped on the scar at the side of her forehead. "I gave him the chip to use with his experimental dimensional research. I was there when Jameson gained access to the homondie world and also when he experimented on one particular homondie. Once we found out that the chip began to sync with the dimensional world, that's when I fashioned the Staff of Life to hold the chip, giving me unlimited control over the homondie. When I arrived to retrieve the chip from Jameson, it was gone. He hid it from me. Not only did he steal it, he made you a part of it. Now it's you who has *my* chip, and I want it back."

"I've never heard any of this before," Natalie said, her head clearing. "I've never met Jameson, and I think I'd know if someone put a chip in my head. I have no idea what you're talking about."

"Don't play stupid with me!" Victor slammed his hand on the table. "I know you're working with Jameson to keep it, but it's not going to work." He took a long deep breath then spoke in a soft voice. "It doesn't matter. You possess something of mine that I need back, and in return, I have something special waiting for you, Natalie. Wait until you see. You're going to love it!" He snickered.

"Humor me and tell me what's going on," Natalie said, stalling for time. "It's not like I'm going to be able to tell someone, but at least give me the satisfaction of knowing why you want me to die."

"I guess I can tell you." Victor sat next to her, arms crossed. "When Jameson began the dimensional split, all the information was recorded in that chip stored in your head. That chip *is* this creation. Without it, I'll never completely be in control of this new world, and I won't have you or anyone else stand in the way of that happening."

"So you're the one responsible for killing everyone in town, and eventually the world?" Natalie asked. "How can you live with yourself knowing what you're doing?" She wrenched her wrists, trying to break free.

"There, there. Don't you worry your pretty little head," Victor said. "You won't be alive for long either."

"You're insane," Natalie shouted. "Let me go!" She wriggled frantically, trying to loosen her restraints.

Victor leaned over and tightened her straps.

"You're not only killing the people inside our world but the whole world itself just to create Homondiem for yourself? This isn't evolution. It's regression," she yelled.

"You can call it whatever you want, but this world is mine to rule." Victor touched her face. His fingernail scraped along her cheek. "I can't wait to show you what's waiting for you."

Natalie turned her head to the side and caught sight of the staff and knife beside her.

"I can see from your face that you've figured out my plan."

"This has nothing to do with me," Natalie cried. "How did I even get involved? I'm no scientist or government employee."

"You should know. Maybe you have a bit of amnesia. You did take a big hit when crossing through, so I'll humor you, for now. You're a part of this whole world, and your connection to Homondiem is more than just superficial. It goes much deeper than that."

"You mean the chip has something to do with my connection?"

"Your connection has to do with far more than just the chip. However, without that chip, you'd be dead by now. That's the only thing that's keeping you alive."

"What do you mean the chip is keeping me alive? Are you saying someone else tried to kill me?" Natalie asked.

"Don't you worry about the past. You're not going to be alive for long anyway," Victor said, fairly taunting her.

"Yes, you've mentioned that already," she said angrily, "but I don't understand. How did I almost die? I don't remember any of that."

"You don't remember? Hmm, well, that's a shame," Victor said. "Let's just say it was an experiment gone wrong when you were lying on that surgical table. That's when we found out the live chip kept you from dying, and I must say it did work, don't you think?"

Natalie, wide-eyed, stared at Victor. "How do you know all this?"

"I don't want to spoil the whole surprise," he said, an evil grin creeping across his face. "I think I'll leave some things a mystery for now." Victor scoffed then said, "You'll find out once the chip is removed."

"I don't believe anything you're saying, and for you to think I'd believe a chip is keeping me alive, you're crazy!"

"You don't believe me? Here, I'll show you." He picked the knife off the table and, without preamble, stabbed Natalie straight through her heart.

Blood spewed out of her chest and splattered in all directions. Natalie gasped as she choked on her own blood. Her eyes widened as her head tilted to the side. She lay motionless for a moment until the blood stopped oozing and her wound closed. She regained consciousness. She coughed up the remaining blood and glared into Victor's eyes as she tried to discern what was happening to her.

"That should make you believe you hold more than just a simple computer chip."

Victor was telling the truth. She must have that chip implanted in her. How else would she have lived through that?

With the thought of dying and seeing what that chip could do, she knew she couldn't allow Victor to take it. There must be a way to stop him. She squirmed as she tried to think of a way to escape.

"You might as well stop fidgeting, Natalie. Escape is futile. Just be patient. It'll be over in no time, and you won't feel a thing." Victor chuckled. "Of course, you'll be dead."

"Do you really think I'm going to lie here and let you cut into my head?" she asked.

"Doesn't seem like you have much of a choice." Victor gestured to the homondie grouped together in the corner. "Come here, my homondie, hold her down."

"Don't you let those things touch me," Natalie screamed.

The homondie gripped her arms and legs with cold, decomposed hands. Victor held up the bloodied knife, slid it across her forehead, and down the side of her face, leaving a trail of blood in its wake. Using the knife to move her hair away, Victor revealed a slight bulge under her skin.

"Ahh, there it is. At last, I'll have my chip." Victor sneered.

Natalie wiggled and felt the tension on the straps loosen.

"Now it's time to take back what's rightfully mine." Victor smirked at Natalie. "Not only do I plan on extracting the chip, but once it's in place, I'll call the homondie forth to witness your death. You'll be a good example to show them I mean business. I'll prove to the homondie that I'm the one who can give them what they need to become alive. I'll be the first to expand their world and restore their faith in humans."

Victor stood over Natalie and recited an incantation in another language. Natalie turned away and closed her eyes. She wouldn't give Victor the satisfaction of seeing her in anguish.

The ground quaked, and wind howled through the doorway. A cold shiver ran through her body as the chip connected inside her mind. Natalie thrust her head back and forth as she felt the energy flow throughout her body and into her subconscious. She couldn't comprehend the connection the chip had on her, but her uneasiness subsided with every word of Victor's chant. She realized that she had begun to understand what he was saying.

"Now I can have complete control of this dimension and all within it," he bellowed.

The surge of energy forced Natalie's eyes open and fixed on Victor's knife. It seemed the chip knew she was in danger. She twisted her wrists and searched the room.

Victor raised his knife to her forehead. Natalie's chest fluttered with uncontrollable breaths. She was desperate to escape but was mesmerized by the cold steel that glistened in the flickering candlelight.

The final hymn ended and faded from his lips. Natalie realized they were the last words she would ever hear and knew her time had come. She closed her eyes and awaited her death.

CHAPTER 11

A PORTAL OPENED WITH a burst of light. A man jumped out and whistled. His soft curls wafted in the breeze.

Buster barked and took off running. Walter yelled, "Buster, get back here! Don't you leave me alone!"

"Over here, this way," the man shouted to Walter.

"Jameson, is that you?" Walter approached him, and the two men shook hands. "It's good to have you here with me. I don't know how much longer I'd be able to survive alone."

"It's not that bad," Jameson said. "Look around, there's a beautiful world flourishing here. Enjoy it."

"Enjoy it? How can I enjoy it when there are things in here that want to kill me?" Walter asked.

"You always were the worrywart of the group," Jameson said. "Come on, let's find Natalie before Victor gets to her first."

"How did you know I lost her?"

"I saw you get sucked in with Buster, then Natalie met up with the townspeople. Now that everyone's dead in Wells Springs there's nothing left to watch on TV, so I thought I'd come in and join you." Jameson slapped Walter on the back and started walking. "You missed the exciting part where Seth opened a portal and sucked in the whole town. Maybe there'll be a rerun for you to watch later." Jameson snickered.

"Wait up," Walter called. "You're going the wrong way. I've already come from there."

"You were always bad with directions," Jameson said, condescension in his voice. "Think about it: you came in from the west side and I came in on the east, which means Natalie's somewhere north between us."

"We can't just stroll around these woods," Walter said. "It's hard to see the homondie lingering around here."

"Don't worry," Jameson assured him. "I have a rifle, a couple of handguns, some knives, and a backpack full of ammo."

"If we run into a pack of homondie, all that ammo could be gone in seconds."

"Did you not hear me say knives?" Jameson asked, smirking.

"You've got to stop kidding around. This is a serious place to be if you want to stay alive."

"There you go again. Stop being an old fuddy-duddy, Walter. Enjoy life. You don't have much of it left, old man." Jameson chuckled and cleared his throat. "On a serious note, we have to check everywhere Natalie may be. I'm not running all over hell's creation to end up going in circles. The shortest distance between two points is a straight line."

Jameson marched through the underbrush and between the trees as Walter and Buster followed.

"Always taking chances, just like your father. God rest his soul."

"Yes, but I'm not looking to die anytime soon."

"You'll be the death of me if you keep this up," Walter said. "If it wasn't for your father asking me to watch over you, I wouldn't be stuck in here right now."

"Stop pretending, you're loving this," Jameson said. "If it wasn't for me taking risks, we'd never get a chance to see a world evolve before our eyes."

"That would have been fine with me." Walter huffed several times as he pushed through the thicket.

"Try to keep up. I want to find Natalie before Victor does." Jameson picked up the pace.

"I'm trying. This world puts too much strain on this old body of mine," Walter said, breathing heavy.

Jameson didn't slow down even as they went deeper into the cadaverous, primeval forest of Homondiem. Walter was forced to keep up, tripping over branches and stumbling on the uneven ground.

"You were a handful growing up. I don't know why I thought you'd grow out of it." He caught up to Jameson and tugged on his sleeve. "Don't you think this is getting out of hand? I don't have a good feeling about this."

"Relax and stay focused. I'm not stopping. If you want to survive, stay close to me, and everything will be all right."

"I think you're taking this further than your dad expected when you took over his research."

"I promised my dad I would finish what he started." Jameson met Walter's eyes. "He'd be proud knowing what I've accomplished that he never could."

"Your father was doing it to save humanity, you're doing it to destroy it," Walter said. "I don't think he was trying to eradicate mankind with his research."

"Don't think of it as eradicating mankind." Jameson waved a hand dismissively. "With the special serum I've created, we'll have no problem designing the perfect mix of human and homondie. We'll revive our world as we create a new breed to undo all the injustices caused by our governments. No one can make changes to our world as long as they constrain us."

"You can't predict what will happen. It's possible to survive," Walter said.

"All the countries have already set up troops along their borders, missiles ready to launch. Our world is in crisis, and if we leave it up to the governments, nothing will be resolved. World War III is upon us only days away. Do you want to go back there? I don't."

"I understand it won't be easy to restore our nation," Walter said, "but do you actually believe that creating a master race would truly wipe out the inferior ones? I don't think so."

"I only want to eliminate things that are destroying our cultural identity and nationalism. We need to break free from the stranglehold held on us by the governments in order to expand our world and bring back an age of prosperity. If it leads to the liquidation of our population, so be it."

"We know a lot of what the governments were planning. Why don't we resolve this and take it to the media?" Walter asked.

Jameson scoffed. "The media aren't any better. They're controlled by the government, and they're up to their necks in this as well. They know our world's coming to an end, but have they told the world's population? No. No one stepped forward and told the truth. They force us to watch and listen to what they want us to as they hide the real situation from us."

"What you're doing will be far worse than you initially thought," Walter said, resigned.

"Our world is at the breaking point. We have no choice but to take control of things now. We'll control Homondiem as our new territory expands. Only then can we live free and become self-sufficient. Any remaining survivors will be the people of our future. They'll settle on this land and make it whole again."

"The government officials are going to put a price on your head," Walter said. "They thought if all else failed, we'd provide them with an alternative destination of another dimension. Not only did we lie to them, but we also took their chip, the only live AI in existence."

"I'm not worried about them. I'm just upset that Victor found out where we hid the chip."

"The chip is no good to us if we can't find the Staff of Life," Walter said.

"I'm sure when we find Victor, we'll find the staff." Jameson paused, then said, "When we meet up with Natalie, you better not say a word about any of this to her. I can't have her knowing our plans, especially when I'm not even sure how much she'll remember."

"Lucky for you, she remembers nothing."

"She told you that?"

"She did."

"She doesn't remember the real Natalie, what happened between them, or what she was before?" Jameson asked, incredulous.

"Nothing at all," Walter said. "She has no knowledge of you or the chip you placed inside her. She only remembers the memories you programmed into it."

"That's fantastic." Jameson could barely contain his excitement at the news.

The pair pushed through the last of the dense thicket and into a barren stretch of land. Jameson took off across it, walking unafraid.

"Hold on. Jameson, over there." Walter pointed to the sky. "Did you see that flash on the horizon? It added light into this world."

"Possibly a portal," Jameson said. "Let's head that way. Natalie could be there."

Jameson ran through the dimly lit forest, Walter huffing and wheezing behind him. Jameson hesitated for a moment, raised his device, and scanned the area. "I think this is it. Natalie should be around here somewhere." Jameson stomped through the dead underbrush and hollered, "Oh, Natalie, there are some gentlemen here to see you!"

"Please, could you keep it down a notch?" Walter pleaded with his hands clasped together. "You're going to get us killed."

"Buster, come boy," Jameson bellowed. Buster ran to him and sat at his feet. "That's a good boy." He patted the dog on the head. "Now go find Natalie. Go on, boy!"

Buster ran ahead, Jameson and Walter following him at a distance. As they moved, darkness set in, and shapes seemed to form at their feet. They stumbled over a firm but pliable surface. Something lurked beneath them in the shadows of the rubble.

Walter stopped abruptly. "Something just brushed against my leg." His voice rose as he jumped. "What are we stepping on?"

"I don't know." Jameson took out his flashlight. The bulb blinked a few times then went out. He banged the side of it against his palm. "Do you have a flashlight? The batteries are dead in mine."

Walter took a flashlight out of his backpack and shone it onto the ground. He let out a whimper. "Do you see what I'm seeing?"

"Sure am," Jameson said, unbothered.

Walter closed his eyes. "What do you see?"

"A massive amount of dead bodies, covered in bite marks, their chests ripped open, limbs missing, and half-eaten faces." Casually, he added, "Most of them probably died of heart attacks, maybe scared of being eaten, before they would have died from their wounds."

"What do we do?" Walter lifted his feet, unsure where to step.

Jameson nudged a corpse over with his foot. "My advice to you is to be careful where you step. Rigor mortis hasn't set in for all of them. Could make them twitch. Their nervous systems might still be active." Jameson dug deep into his backpack and found a new pack of batteries. He popped out the old ones and replaced them with the new. He shone the light in Walter's direction.

Just as Walter stepped over a corpse, it twitched. He scrambled away as fast as he could, trying to find a clear place to land his feet. Heedless of where they were stepping, Jameson and Buster trampled over anything in their way.

"Finally!" Walter stepped onto an open path and exhaled in relief.

Buster barked.

"I hope it's not a homondie." Walter looked in every direction.

Jameson shone the flashlight at Buster, who had buried his nose in something. "Buster, what did you find there?" Jameson asked. He hopped over a corpse, blood oozing from the open gashes. He reached down and picked up what Buster had found and held it up. "Look here, Walter, it's a backpack."

Walter inspected it. "That's mine. I gave it to Natalie. And here's her revolver." Walter plucked it off the ground and handed it to Jameson. "Here, hang on to this."

"So, I was right. She was here, but not anymore." Jameson tucked the revolver into his belt and put the backpack over his shoulder. "Where did she go?" He shone the flashlight around the area. "It looks like the whole town is here."

Walter stepped into the light. "Yes, it's all rubble. What do you think happened?"

"My guess is, the portals aren't doorway-sized openings anymore. They're expanding at an exponential rate. They seem to be extracting whole towns now and disintegrating upon entry."

"What about us?" Walter asked.

"I think only living things can pass through, but whether they survive or not is a different story, and if we have these inanimate items on our possession," he said, holding out his flashlight, "they must be able to break through intact."

"Everything we left behind will be gone in a matter of hours." Walter searched the skyline. "It's getting lighter again."

"That's because Homondiem has expanded again," Jameson explained. "My assessment is that our world is falling into darkness. It's on the verge of dying."

Jameson stepped over some of the dead while Buster barked and sniffed at an object on the ground. Jameson walked over. "Wait a minute. This looks familiar." He picked up an open locket, stared at it for a moment, then looked at the corpse lying on the ground beside it, half-exposed, and pinned under a pile of debris. "Never in my life did I think I'd see this again."

"What is it?" Walter asked. "You're looking a little pale. Are you all right?"

"Here, take a look at this." Jameson threw the locket at Walter.

Walter caught it in midair, and it snapped shut. "It's a locket. So what?"

"Not just any locket. Open it and see who it came from." Jameson pointed to the corpse at his feet. "Turns out, she lived a little longer than I expected."

Walter pried the locket open. "Oh my, it's Natalie. Sorry, Jameson." Walter snapped the locket shut and tossed it back to him. "Are you going to keep it?"

"I think I'll leave it right here with her. She was more emotionally attached to these things than I was. She can have it." Jameson laid it on the corpse's chest and stepped away, emotionless.

Walter stared at the corpse. "It's surreal, seeing her here like this. It puts everything in perspective—what this whole experiment was supposed to be about. But now, it's literally tearing everyone apart."

"We have to finish this, Walter. We've come this far. You can't back out now."

"Well, how about Natalie?" Walter asked. "Was it worth it to see her suffer, all for an experiment?"

"Get a grip! You're not going to fall apart on me now, not after all we've been through," Jameson said, his voice steely. "Just remember what she did. She tried to destroy my experiment."

"I think she saw it as stealing a device to stop your experiment and save the world."

Jameson reached out and grabbed Walter's shirt, twisting it with his fist. "Don't go soft on me now," he said menacingly. "Keep your mind on the task at hand and remember where your loyalties lie, or there'll be consequences. You're in as deep as I am."

"I got it." Walter choked. "I'm sorry. I won't mention it again."

Jameson let Walter go. Walter straightened his rumpled shirt.

"Now think. We need to find Natalie and get this over with." Jameson looked around. "We didn't run into her, so she must have fled south." He patted Buster on the head. "Buster caught her scent on the locket and the backpack. I guess it's up to him now. Buster, where'd Natalie go? Come on, Buster, find Natalie!"

Buster whimpered. He tilted his head and raised an ear.

"What is it, Buster?" Walter asked. "Is it Natalie?"

Buster ran as Jameson and Walter jogged behind him. They hastened down the path, once more lit by a break in the sky's darkness.

CHAPTER 12

JAMESON AND WALTER continued to run as the sky grew brighter. They wove erratically through the woods trying to keep up with Buster. Abruptly, Buster stopped and smelled the ground then sat.

"Buster, what's the matter?" Jameson jerked his head up as he heard a creak and a crackle, then a loud bang rang out and echoed through the woods.

"What was that?" Walter asked.

"I think something big fell. It came from over there." Jameson pointed to his right. "Follow me." They took off in the direction of the sound.

"Now it sounds like knocking and homondie moaning," Walter said.

Jameson hid behind a clump of dead underbrush and peeked through the dry leaves. Walter crawled up next to him. Buster sat between them.

"What's this? I can't believe what I'm seeing," Jameson said.

"It's a town . . . in Homondiem?" Walter said.

Jameson gazed down the dirt road into the small town and took in the sight of a clan of homondie who looked to be constructing something. "Homondie . . . building? How can that be?"

"It looks like the ones with chains around their necks are still wild. It seems they're being trained to chop down trees."

"See how that one is different from the rest?" Jameson pointed. "He's more upright, and he walks a bit straighter, almost like a human. There's intelligence mixed in this pack of homondie, like a chain of command exists. The upright ones still have the features of homondie, but you can vaguely see the human side beginning to break free."

"That's not good," Walter said. "I noticed that in the store when the homondie almost got out. We hoped they wouldn't become intelligent so fast."

"Well, it didn't help when Seth opened the portal to the whole town," Jameson said. "They had an exceptional feast on their hands. At least we were slowly adding life to the mix. In this case, I think Victor wanted them to grow faster for his own use. I hope we have enough time to get this world under control once we get our hands on that chip."

"With this new breed of intelligence, they might be harder to take over, and they'll definitely be harder to kill," Walter said.

A human voice rang out. "You've interrupted me for the last time!" They watched a man storm out of a building with a large, bloody knife in his hand.

"That's Victor," Jameson said.

"Victor Bernard, the Head of D-III. I can't believe he's been able to train them so fast," Walter said as he stared intensively. "He couldn't even train his own men to listen to him. I guess that's why he replaced them with homondie." He chuckled.

Victor advanced on the homondie, the knife menacing in his hand.

"It looks like he may already have the chip. We need to get closer to find out if Natalie's still alive." Jameson unloaded his weapons and placed them in a pile with the backpacks. "Walter, stash your things in this thicket. We'll only take our knives. If we get caught, we wouldn't want to lose everything we have." Jameson covered the bundle with branches.

Buster let out a muffled whine. Two homondie shuffled past about twenty yards away. "How are we going to avoid the stragglers?" Walter asked. "We don't know how many there are. Victor could have them scouting the area."

"Buster will alert us." Jameson scurried off, forcing Walter and Buster to catch up.

Together, they crept close enough to listen in.

Victor roared at the head homondie. "What's going on out here? How many times do I have to tell you not to interrupt me? Keep these creatures chained and quiet! I have a delicate surgery to tend to."

The homondie stared at Victor.

"What are you waiting for? Can't you see there's still a straggler? For the last time, if you can't control these beasts, I'll have you killed, and someone else will take your place."

The homondie gave an unfocused stare and shuffled backward.

"Get that one over there. Put another chain around its neck, tie it to the stake, and show it how it's done!" Victor pointed the homondie in the direction of the others who were chopping down trees.

The homondie spoke to the others in a strange language.

"Did you see that?" Walter asked. "They can understand our language, but they speak to each other in their own."

"It looks like they're learning our language fast. It must have something to do with human life absorption. Maybe our DNA has a language code imbedded in it and they acquire it as they feed on the living," Jameson posited.

Two homondie held a third steady as the leader placed a chain around its neck and pulled tight. Once the chain latched, the head homondie tugged on it and drew it closer. It attached the creature to a ring at the end of a stake set into the ground, next to a group of trees.

Victor sheathed his knife and stepped up, grabbing an ax. He held the ax in front of the homondie. The homondie darted toward him as it screeched. The head homondie grabbed its whip, lashed the creature, and knocked it down. It got back up, groaned, and charged again until it stretched the chain tight. It bit the air and chomped down, almost biting Victor's arm.

"Teach it a lesson! Break it so it knows who's boss," Victor shouted.

The homondie whipped it again, but it still tried to attack Victor.

"You need to control it! Here, let me show you how it's done."

The head homondie backed up sluggishly.

Victor spun the ax around and delivered a bone-crunching smash to the creature's kneecap with the handle. He kicked it in the face as it fell to the ground and broke its teeth while it tried to bite him. It was still trying to attack, so Victor dropped the ax and pulled out his knife. He grabbed its straggly hair, scalped the top layer off its head, and flung it onto the ground. The creature moaned in agony as blood oozed from its head and ran down its cheeks.

Victor picked the ax back up and swung it at the tree where it stuck. The creature, dazed, stood and stared at the ax before approaching it. It took hold of the handle, wrenched it from the tree, then it started to chop. Victor turned and walked back toward the building, past another group of homondie. "You there, get moving," he bellowed. "It's not going to build itself." The other homondie went back to chopping, notching, and fitting logs together.

"That was amazing!" Jameson stared in awe.

"Where's he going now?" Walter asked, not taking his eyes off Victor.

"I don't know, but we have to get closer and see. I want to know what's going on here." Jameson checked to make sure the coast was clear, then moved forward, waving two fingers in the air to signal for Walter to follow.

They crept through the dried underbrush and around the trees to see where Victor was headed. He came to a stop in the center of the town and paused. They stopped to listen to him.

Victor raised his arms and his rhythmic incantation echoed through the woods. It pierced the homondie's ears and their heads cocked sideways. They moaned and scuffled to follow Victor's voice.

Jameson was impressed to see the homondie swaying. They seemed to be soothed by Victor's song as they obeyed his every command.

The head homondie stood before Victor. "Now watch the woods carefully," Victor said. "The stragglers will be coming soon."

The homondie bowed.

"What's he doing?" Walter asked.

"My guess is he's calling them in to work," Jameson said.

Victor stormed back into the building, leaving the door slightly ajar.

"We've got to find a way to get to Victor's building to see what he's up to before the homondie arrive." Jameson surveyed the woods. "Quick, let's go around this way." He pointed to a path between the thickets.

Walter followed silently as Buster brought up the rear. Jameson led them farther out and circled the town to get closer. Buster whimpered. Moans and the shuffling of feet echoed from the woods and toward the town.

Jameson stopped. "We can't get any closer. There's a lot of activity around here." He realized they were heading straight into a pack of homondie leaving the woods.

"It sounds like hundreds of homondie are on their way here. I don't think we can hold off that many." Walter's voice sounded calm, but he looked panicked.

"Then we're going to have to make sure they don't find us." Jameson eyed the building Victor had entered. "At least we should be able to hear him from here."

Jameson shuffled around, searching for an angle that would allow him to see inside. He moved closer to the path into town and gazed toward the building. "Natalie! Victor has her!"

"Is she alive?" Walter asked, a glimmer of hope in his voice.

"Yes."

Walter peered over Jameson's shoulder. "We may still have a chance to get that chip back."

"All right then, let's get in there and save her before it's too late," Jameson said. "We know what Victor has planned for her."

Buster took off running.

"Buster, come back," Walter called faintly so as not to draw attention to himself, but Buster kept running. "He's never done that before," he said to Jameson. "Something's not right."

Jameson felt for his knife, ready for action.

"We have to get out of here." Walter crouched down and backed away.

"Get back here! We're not leaving until we have Natalie and Victor's staff." Jameson bent down and scurried to catch up to Walter.

Walter shuffled across the ground. The homondie screeched and pointed in their direction, having caught sight of him.

"Uh-oh." Walter stopped moving.

Jameson looked back toward the town and spotted Victor standing over Natalie. He had the knife poised over her scalp when a couple of homondie posted at the doorway tilted their heads and smelled the air.

"Now what?" Victor scoffed.

The homondie pointed in Jameson and Walter's direction.

"Oh, I see." He snapped his fingers. "Intruders are near." Victor let out a whistle. "Seize them and take their weapons!"

A swarm of homondie headed straight for Jameson and Walter.

"Get ready, Walter. You're going to need to fight." Jameson slid his knife out of its sheath and rose off the ground. A homondie staggered toward him. When it got close enough, he jabbed his knife straight through its eye and out through the other side of its head. Blood flowed down its face. The homondie let out a small grunt as Jameson twisted the knife and pulled. He popped out its eye, stuck on the tip of his knife, and flung it to the ground.

Walter stabbed a homondie yelling, "There are too many of them! I don't know how long I can fight them off."

Jameson ran to Walter, who wearily kicked at an advancing homondie. He grabbed the closest one and stabbed it multiple times. It fell, groaning, in a pool of its own blood. He turned around and slit the throat of another as two others crowded around, clawing at him.

Jameson drove his knife deep into the creatures without batting an eye, moving out farther with each kill.

Walter killed two of his own and hollered, "They just keep coming. I can't hold them back!"

Jameson retreated to help Walter. He pulled a homondie off him before Walter got bit and punched it in its face. He knocked it back and cleared some space around the old man. Another attacked.

He thrust forward and stabbed it in its open mouth. It gurgled on its own blood and fell at his feet.

The homondie surrounded them. Victor pushed through the horde and approached Walter and Jameson, stepping over homondie lying in pools of blood. "Jameson, I thought you'd be dead by now. I didn't think you had it in you."

"Let Natalie go," Jameson yelled.

"You of all people should know I can't do that. I know you need her as much as I do." Victor grinned devilishly.

"She doesn't understand what's going on!"

"Perhaps it's because you forgot to clarify some things with her," Victor said.

"She doesn't need to know," Jameson muttered.

"Ahh, so you *didn't* share any information with her. I thought she was lying this whole time," Victor's voice rose. "No matter if she knows or not, I still need that chip. I was just about to take it before you rudely interrupted me."

So he doesn't have it yet, Jameson thought. His poker face was a good one. Now it was time to up the ante. Jameson knew Victor's knowledge would give him an advantage. "We've seen you with those homondie, controlling them somehow. How could you have taken control without the chip?" he asked.

"We waited for you to access Homondiem first, making sure we understood the homondie fully so we could control them once we entered," Victor explained. "You showed us that they're always waiting and wanting more life. So we worked with what we knew. As long as we feed them, they'll do us no harm, and they do what we say. The more they feed, the more intelligent they become, and the more they can be controlled. Right now, it's easy to control the smarter, human-type homondie. With the less human ones, I only have limited control, so I use brute force, but that's only temporary. Once I have the Staff of Life in full working order, I'll be in total control and become their leader."

"I don't understand," Jameson said. "You shouldn't have access to Homondiem so easily. Entering a portal without one of my devices is almost always a death sentence, and I know Seth has the one I gave you. How can you pass through freely?"

"You mean a device like this one?" Victor pulled it out of his pocket and twirled it around in his hand.

"How could you have more than one?" Jameson asked.

"Oh, I just helped myself when you were busy with Natalie in the basement. Now I have full control of the portals and can come and go as I please." Victor laughed darkly. "Thanks to the both of you, not only do we finally have interdimensional travel, but a breach to release the homondie is exactly what we wanted. This new breed has formed better than I could have imagined. We couldn't have done it without your help—and Natalie's, of course. If you didn't have that breakthrough, we never would have gotten access to this dimension ourselves."

"You call yourself the law keepers?" Jameson said. "All government agencies are alike. Stealing people's ideas and taking control of whatever you can get your hands on. You suckered my father into believing he was working with you for the good of humanity, but I see right through you." Jameson's voice was choked with rage.

"If you had only given up the chip when I asked for it, you wouldn't have been involved," Victor said, "but you had to be greedy too, and look where you are now. You know we can have only one leader, and I'm not good at sharing."

"I don't know what you're talking about," Jameson yelled.

"Don't pretend to be innocent," Victor shouted. "If you didn't steal my chip, we could have worked things out."

"You shouldn't have tried to kill us off. Then maybe we could have made a deal."

"You almost defeated me, until Seth happened to run into Natalie."

"Seth?" Jameson looked around. "Where is your sidekick anyway?"

"Oh, he's back at the portals, using your device to expedite the openings. I never was a patient man." Victor glanced at the device in his hand. "You did a fine job creating this. It's a magnificent device, but the small talk is over. Now it's time." He called to the homondie, "Take them to town and secure them tight. You'll have their life force soon enough."

The homondie stepped forward and grabbed Jameson and Walter by the arms.

"I have some important business to attend to with Natalie and you'll have front-row seats." He leered and chuckled. "No hard feelings. It's just business." Victor flicked his wrist in the air and turned toward the town. A few of the homondie staggered along behind him while the rest guided Jameson and Walter.

The homondie pushed them through the dead vegetation. Walter stumbled over a rotted tree.

Jameson leaned over and whispered, "Don't try to break free. This is a perfect opportunity to get into town and rescue Natalie. We'd never be able to get this close without being led in."

"What if they kill us before we can get her out of there?" Walter asked.

"Don't worry, there'll always be a way for us to escape."

"How can you be so confident?"

"Because we have a higher level of intelligence," Jameson said. "That's like asking how we'd escape if an ape held us prisoner."

"But these aren't apes," Walter said. "Some of them are on the verge of being human and quite intelligent, while the others are irrational and deadly."

"Look on the bright side. If we don't make it, at least once we're dead, we'll technically be ancestors of the new modern humans. That's a fascinating breakthrough. Just think of it. How many lifetimes would it have taken to be able to see human ancestors?"

"Sometimes I wonder about you, Jameson." Walter shook his head.

They turned and walked down a gentle slope as the homondie led them the short distance to the town.

CHAPTER 13

JAMESON AND WALTER were led past a couple of buildings, when Jameson slowed his step and whispered to Walter, "Look, over there." He pointed to the one with the open door.

"Where did all those boxes of food and water come from, and how did he get all that in here?" Walter asked.

"I don't know, but Victor sure didn't waste any time."

The homondie pushed to keep them going.

They passed other groups of homondie with limited rationality. They were chained to stakes and had been tasked with chopping down trees. They were clearing multiple areas for other homondie to use to assemble buildings. The irrational ones swarmed toward Jameson and Walter as the men came closer.

Still brainless, and slightly mad, the homondie moaned and chattered their teeth; they were hungry for their life. They rushed Jameson and Walter as their instincts kicked in. The force almost yanked their stakes from the ground. Once they reached the limit of their chains, they were flung back, their heads snapping on their necks.

Walter jumped and tried to hide behind the homondie beside him. The homondie guides growled at the oncoming feeders and drove them away, back to their work.

"I don't know how long it'll be before we end up as their dinner," Walter murmured as he squirmed. "It may be sooner than we think."

Without further incident, the two men were tugged along as the homondie shoved them toward the town square. Suddenly Walter gasped.

"What's wrong?" Jameson asked.

"See the three trees clumped together over there?" Walter said.

"Yes, what about them?"

"I watched a single tree from their undeveloped dimension turn into those three trees right there. As the tree split, their dimension grew and took on the life from our world."

"Are you sure they're the same trees?" Jameson asked. "It seems too far away from any portal opening."

"I'm sure of it," Walter said. "I'm one hundred percent positive they're the same ones. I remember when I found the portal and I watched the store owners get sucked in. I'll never forget it. Those are the exact trees that split from the single one when this all began. It was also where Natalie and I watched a woman be taken. The trees cast shadows over her. She was lying on this same dirt path when she was eaten alive."

"If you're saying you saw this same cluster of trees from the store, then that means Homondiem has expanded at an alarming rate. The dimension should be completing its final transformation soon," Jameson said.

"It shouldn't be long before our world is gone for good." Walter pointed. "Look over there. The trees are coming alive!"

Jameson watched leaf buds form as the branches extended. "We're running out of time. If we don't get that chip out of Natalie soon, she'll become one with it, and there'll be no controlling Homondiem."

The homondie pulled Jameson and Walter in front of the building where Natalie was being held.

Victor stood outside and commanded the homondie. "Tie them up here. I want them to witness my victory once I place the chip into the Staff of Life and govern this land."

The homondie yanked the two men to the ground, pulled their hands behind their backs, and lashed them to the cluster of trees in front of the building.

"We're going to die in the same place this all started," Walter said.

"Stop it!" Jameson hushed Walter.

Victor walked past them and set off into the building, leaving the door wide open behind him.

Jameson stretched as much as he could to examine the room. "Our knives are right there on the table next to the door."

He looked up at the three trees above and followed their shadows as they crossed the door and fell on Natalie tied to a rectangular table. Candles surrounded her. She lay helpless. "Look what's next to Natalie," Jameson said.

A tiny sliver of light caught the reflection on a blade of a long knife sitting on top of the table next to Natalie. Next to the knife was a familiar-looking staff.

"There's the Staff of Life," Walter muttered.

"I see it. I knew he'd have it close by. We don't have much time. Try to twist your wrists to loosen the ropes just enough to slide your hands out."

Victor ranted, "The time has come, my homondie. We've retrieved Natalie just in time. The sun is rising on schedule. The alignment of our dimension is in place, as shown by the shadows of these three trees. It's time to take back what is rightfully mine." His face glowed with satisfaction as he tied a cloth over Natalie's mouth.

"Can we stop him?" Walter asked.

"It's not too late, not yet," Jameson said.

Victor chanted and lifted the knife above Natalie. She turned to Jameson and stared at him, pleading silently with her eyes frightened and full of tears.

"Hurry, Walter, we don't have much time!"

"I'm going as fast as I can. Those things sure can tie a mean knot."

Jameson twisted his wrists. "I can't get out of mine either." All he could do was watch and wait.

All eyes were on Natalie making it possible for Buster to slip through without being seen by the homondie. He crept up behind Jameson and Walter and chewed the knot binding Jameson's wrists. Buster bit and pulled at the rope, setting him free.

"Good boy, Buster." Jameson pretended that he was still tied up.

Buster ran away along the side of the building.

"For a moment there, I thought we were goners," Walter whispered.

"I could have eventually escaped on my own, you know." Jameson smiled.

"Yeah, right!"

Once freed, Jameson paid attention to where all the homondie were located as he reached over and untied Walter, keeping his movements to a minimum. He knew they would have to move quickly.

"We need a plan to get Natalie out of here," Walter said as he looked around.

Jameson showed Natalie his freed hands.

Natalie gazed back with hopeful eyes then turned to Victor. Her eyes grew large and round at the sight of the blade, and for a moment, Jameson expected her to scream.

Jameson glared at Victor. Victor's eyes and snarling face were ready to deliver judgment. He grasped the handle of the knife and pointed the blade at Natalie. When his final chant came to an end, he began to lower the knife.

Natalie grunted and jerked her head from side to side.

"Homondie, hold Natalie's head still and don't allow her to move. This needs to be precise so I don't damage the chip."

The homondie's dry, brittle hands grabbed the sides of Natalie's head and held her still. Her eyes never wandered away from the knife. She struggled to move, but the homondie held her like a vise. With death mere seconds away, she began to tremble. The blade started its downward motion. Natalie squeezed her eyes shut and waited. As the knife got closer, Victor's coat sleeve momentarily obscured Jameson's vision.

With only seconds before the knife made contact with Natalie's flesh, Buster ran in ahead of Jameson and Walter.

"No plan. Just run," Jameson said. He charged into the room behind Buster, and Walter followed.

The tip of the knife made a small incision. Blood trickled down the side of Natalie's forehead.

Buster jumped and bit Victor's hand. Victor howled and dropped the knife, clutching his bleeding hand. Buster barked and growled at him, nipping the air with his teeth. He backed Victor up to the wall.

Walter grabbed one of his knives off the table as he entered the building and slashed the neck of the homondie that had held Natalie down.

Jameson untied Natalie. "Nice to meet you, Natalie. My name is Jameson Walker." He helped her off the table, pulled out a knife hidden in his boot, spun around, and stabbed a homondie in the head as it grabbed Natalie's arm.

Natalie removed the gag from her mouth. "So you're Jameson." She snatched Victor's knife off the floor. "I've heard so much about you. Duck!"

Jameson ducked, then said, "Good things, I hope."

Natalie threw the knife into the face of a homondie coming through the door. "No, not at all." The homondie dropped where it stood.

"I think it's time to leave." Jameson escorted Natalie out the door.

Natalie paused, stepped on the homondie's face, and pulled out the knife.

"Great move. You've killed before?" Jameson asked.

"Just thinking of what I'd like to do to you right now," she said.

"That hurts," Jameson said.

Walter threw his knife at Victor, missing him by an inch. The blade stuck in the wall. "Damn, that one was my favorite."

Victor tried to grab the knife from in the wall, but Buster bit him. He fell to the floor, grunting as he held his leg.

"Buster," Jameson shouted.

Buster growled at Victor one last time then ran to Jameson and Natalie.

"Homondie, attack the outsiders," Victor yelled.

Walter picked up the staff. "Thanks, Victor, this will come in handy." He hurried to the door and grabbed the rest of the knives from the table before exiting the building.

The homondie scurried after the group.

"Walter, look out," Jameson hollered.

Walter turned around and shoved the staff into the homondie's chest. The creature tumbled back into the others and dropped to the ground. One of the homondie lurched forward and clawed at him, trying to grab his leg as he fled, but missed.

Walter caught up to Jameson and Natalie while Buster barked at the oncoming homondie. As they passed the cluster of three trees in the center of town, Natalie stopped in front of them.

A homondie leaped at Natalie. Buster jumped and bit the homondie as Jameson grabbed Natalie's arm and pulled her along. "Snap out of it, Natalie!" Jameson steered her around a building toward Walter, who had ducked behind it. They broke into a run while Jameson whistled for the dog. Buster caught up, and they ran through the woods together.

"Over this way," Jameson said. "We need to grab the backpacks and weapons we ditched." He uncovered them, handing Walter his.

"For a town that had no weapons, they sure do multiply," Natalie said.

Walter gazed up toward the trees as he threw his backpack over his shoulder, avoiding eye contact.

Jameson picked up the other backpack. "Here, Natalie, I found this. And you dropped this too." He held out her revolver.

"Thank you." Natalie stared at Jameson. "You look familiar, but I can't remember where I've seen you before." After studying him for a few moments, Natalie said, "Oh, I know."

"You do?" Jameson felt sweat break out on his brow. He couldn't have her learn what he did. How much could she remember? He thought she wouldn't be able to access that information. *I'm sure I wiped that part of her brain. Maybe I placed the chip too close to her cerebrum and it's somehow allowing her to recover her memory.*

"Your picture was in a locket among the dead. Was that your girlfriend who passed away?" Natalie asked.

Jameson let out the breath he'd been holding. "Oh, that, yes. Sad she had to go in that fashion," Jameson said but didn't sound very convincing.

"I'm sorry for your loss." Natalie hesitated, then added, "If that was your girlfriend, how did I end up with her license?" Natalie took the license out of her pocket and handed it to Jameson.

"You don't remember?" Jameson glanced at the license then placed it in his pocket.

"No."

"She was your friend and you were cold so you borrowed her sweatshirt. The license was in the pocket," he told her.

"I don't remember knowing her," Natalie said, "and why do I have the same name?"

Jameson let out a nervous giggle. "Yes, what a coincidence that is, huh?" He shot Walter a glance.

Walter called, "Natalie, remember the cluster of three trees you talked about earlier, the ones you saw through the portal at the store?"

"Yes, what about them?" she asked.

"I figured it out. That's where it all began. One single tree split into those three trees in Victor's town. They're the same trees we saw at the portal entrance in the store."

"That's why I got hung up on looking at those trees," Natalie said. "Curiously, a soothing tranquility came over me, but I couldn't understand why. It must have sparked a memory."

Jameson pointed toward the town. "Listen to that crazed man still going at it." He chuckled as he watched Victor ranting and pacing around the town, hollering at the homondie.

"Yes, and his homondie aren't very bright either. They're still trying to figure out what to do," Walter said.

"Get them, they have Natalie and my staff," Victor roared as he marched through the town square. "Get off the ground and get them, and retrieve my staff." He kicked one in the ribs. "Hurry, they're escaping! Kill them but bring Natalie back to me. I need her!" He stomped past them. "I won't risk ending my reign over a couple of fools. I worked too hard to create this world, and no one will take it away from me!" Victor stormed back into the building.

CHAPTER 14

JAMESON LED THE group north through the woodlands and away from Victor's town. "We're heading downwind, so the homondie won't pick up our scent anytime soon," he said to Walter.

As they walked, Natalie rubbed the dried blood off her face with her sleeve. "I'm not going to let Victor get away with this! I won't allow any more innocent lives to end up here, dead, or worse, as one of those creatures. The bloodshed ends today!"

"You're right, no more blood needs to be shed," Walter said as he twirled the staff between his hands and stared at the empty orb.

Natalie turned to Walter and indicated the staff he carried. "What do you think you're going to do with that?"

"I couldn't just leave it there. If Victor had it, he'd just try to get you back again. It's best to keep it as far away from him as possible," Walter said, sliding the staff through his belt.

"I hope you're telling me the truth, Walter. I wouldn't want to think you have it out for me as well," Natalie said warily.

"Come on, Natalie. I'd never do anything to harm you."

Jameson interrupted. "It's good to see you're recharged and ready to go. Let's get out of here before it's too late." He tugged on Walter's sleeve to get him moving.

"This isn't over for either of you," Natalie shouted as they walked away.

"Wait a minute. Look over there." Walter pointed. "Remember there was a stream flowing through the woods on the other side of the fence around the town?"

"It's identical," Jameson said. "Looks like we've passed the point of the town and it has extended farther out. Who knows how far the portals expanded?"

"We should explore it and see how far it goes."

"No time now. The homondie caught up with us. Run!" Jameson whistled for Buster.

They ran through the woods for half a mile, but with each step, Walter faded farther behind.

"Come on, Walter. You can't stop now." Jameson turned around, slowing to a jog to allow Walter to catch up.

"Remember, I'm a bit older than you." Walter puffed. "I can't believe I've lasted this long."

"Just a little farther, Walter, then we can stop for a break," Jameson said.

Walter staggered along, desperately trying not to be a burden.

A moment later, Jameson stopped. Walter nearly crashed into him. "I think this is good enough for the moment." He surveyed the area while Walter rested against a tree.

"We only have a moment before they catch up to us," Natalie said, scanning the forest. She turned to Walter. "Are you going to be all right?"

"I just need a little bit of rest." He bent to sit on the ground at the base of the tree.

"Sorry, Walter." Jameson grabbed his arms and pulled him upright. "There's no time for resting now. They're out hunting for us."

"You can't expect me to keep running all over Homondiem," Walter said. "We need a plan." He bent over and put his hands on his knees.

"Don't you think we need to do something about the end of the world?" Natalie asked.

Jameson walked away.

"Don't run off on me, Jameson." Natalie gave chase. "You've started something, and we need to take care of it."

"You don't need to tell me what to do," Jameson said, his gaze fixed on the forest ahead.

Walter heaved himself up and followed behind. "Great, I can't even rest for a bit and now I have to listen to the two of you bicker on top of it."

"Someone around here needs to take control," Natalie said, arguing with Jameson. "Between you and Victor, there's a battle for this world, and neither of you are going to win. You have to make things right and get our world back to normal."

"You don't have a clue what's going on," Jameson said dismissively. He kept walking.

Natalie quickened her pace and fell into step beside him. "Then enlighten me. All I know is what Victor told me."

"I don't know what you're talking about."

"He told me you stole the chip from him to keep it for yourself."

He wasn't sure how to tell her what he had done without revealing too much information. It didn't seem necessary to go into detail. Besides, why bring up something that might never be noticed?

"Victor is going to lie to you so you'll side with him," Jameson said. "You should know that."

"Don't give me that. Why would Victor lie to me when he was going to kill me anyway? He doesn't need me on his side. He was just going to take the chip by force. And what *about* the chip?"

"I don't understand." Jameson kept walking, refusing to look at her.

"Victor said the chip is alive. You put a live thing inside me? How could you do that?"

"Okay, I can explain that one," Jameson said.

"So explain."

"I had no choice."

"That's it?" Natalie said, aghast. "Because of that chip and my involvement in this whole ordeal, I just had to live through Victor stabbing my chest and then he tried to take the chip. How do you think I feel? He could have killed me! And speaking of dying, I heard I almost died once before. I don't know if you had something to do with that, but whatever you're involved in could have gotten me killed!"

"The chip *did* save your life."

Natalie shook her head. "I can't believe you got me involved in all this crap."

"I thought you'd be excited that you have extra abilities," Jameson said.

"Excited? Excited about what?" Natalie's voice rose, on the verge of yelling. "You think everything's all right because I have some kind of superpowers now? Are you saying I'm some sort of machine?"

"I wouldn't go that far," Jameson said, "but haven't you noticed anything different?"

"What are you talking about?"

Jameson stopped and stared at Natalie. "How do you think you could fight so well all of a sudden? I bet you've never done it before Homondiem opened up. That's a skill that has to be learned."

Natalie's eyebrows crinkled, her lips puckered, and she stared at Jameson. "I don't know." Her voice faded, and she looked at the ground. "I guess I didn't think about it until now." She paused, then asked, "Beside my new skills, what was so important that you needed to hide a chip in my scalp?"

Jameson realized that Natalie wasn't going to stop asking questions. He was going to have to reveal some information to satisfy her, but hopefully he could hold enough back. "Let me start at the beginning. Walter and I began working on an experiment at Wells Springs University when Victor and Seth arrived. They showed us their badges, there was a strange D-III symbol on them, and they said they were from some branch of the government called the Department of Interdimensional Invasion Intervention. We're not sure what part of the government they report to. I'd never heard of them before, but they claimed to be responsible for overseeing interdimensional travel. Something about them being the law keepers?"

"I've never heard of them either," Natalie said.

"They said they'd worked with my father up until he passed away and asked if we could continue his work with their interdimensional travel research. We agreed, and they gave us some highly classified information that I don't think we should have had. Then they handed us the chip to store our data and left."

"Go on." Natalie motioned for him to continue.

"Walter and I created a device to open an interdimensional access and inserted the chip to record the data. Each time we added data to the device, the chip seemed to change somehow, kind of . . . growing in response to the knowledge we fed it. It would process our information and add to it all on its own, like it was thinking and reasoning. We put it under the microscope, and we could see things moving in there. It constantly fed on our information, and it seemed to be evolving right before our eyes. That's how we found out the chip was alive. It was beautiful. We'd never seen anything like it. One thing led to another, and we found ourselves knee-deep in something we weren't ready for, and that's when we decided to hide the chip from Victor."

"It would have been nice if I were involved in the decision," Natalie said.

"I didn't have the time to explain," Jameson said apologetically. "Things happened so fast, and I had no other options."

"So your intentions were for the good of humanity from the very beginning?" Natalie asked.

"Yes, of course," Jameson said. "We knew we couldn't give it back to them, not the way they wanted to use it, and not after what we discovered, but we also couldn't destroy it."

"How did Victor and Seth take that?" Natalie raised an eyebrow.

"They were angry, of course. When they arrived and brought the Staff of Life to use as the chip's host, they demanded we hand it over, but we had already hidden it where they would never find it . . . or so we thought."

Walter added, "I'll never forget when the device created the very first portal and opened an access to the homondie world. Once the separation process began, we could see into this place filled with creatures we'd never encountered before. These creatures were in some sort of suspended animation. They were dormant and unalive. But the chip began to sync with the device, and it seemed to summon the homondie. They became curious about our world as we exposed them to life. It made them want to hunt and kill so they could become alive. Once they started trying to escape, we had to stop them. We needed to separate the chip from the device, but we also needed another host to control it. We were out of options and out of time. There was only one thing we could think of."

"It's strange that I can't remember anything," Natalie said, unconsciously touching the small scar at her hairline. "I wonder if that chip changed my memory in some way."

"Natalie, I'm so sorry for getting you involved in this," Jameson said, appearing genuinely regretful. "I didn't know what else to do. I never thought any harm would come of this. I thought I'd have this whole thing wrapped up before you even got involved. But once things started down the wrong path, I tried to mend the wrongs with rights."

"Well, obviously, something did harm many people, and nothing has been right since," Natalie yelled. She turned on her heel and walked away, Buster following. Jameson and Walter watched her go.

Jameson called after her, "Natalie, wait. Who could have predicted what would happen? I want you to know we'll never let Victor get his hands on that chip, not ever!"

Natalie didn't stop or look back.

"Come on, Walter." Jameson jerked the old man's shirt. They followed Natalie as she walked off through the forest. "Damn you, Victor," Jameson mumbled.

CHAPTER 15

JAMESON KNEW IT wasn't the right time to make Natalie angry. If she got too upset, she'd ruin all his plans. He couldn't lose her, not when there were so many critical objectives hanging in the balance. So how could he get away with something so devious? No matter what, he had to stick to the plan.

Jameson jogged to catch up and fell into step beside her. "Natalie, we got off on the wrong foot. Let's start over and make things right."

Natalie kept walking and ignored him.

"Natalie, please stop."

She turned to him. "What?"

"You want me to say it? I will. We need you, Natalie. We can't do this alone."

"What do you want from me, Jameson? You want that chip back? Well, you're not getting it. Victor said it's the only thing keeping me alive, and I'm not ready to die yet."

"We don't have to remove it," Jameson said, waving his hands. "I bet you could access it through your brain and give us the information we need to restore our world back to normal."

"This should have never happened in the first place." Natalie shook her head and put her hands on her hips. "You should have known better. How could you let this happen?"

"Sometimes I get carried away with my research," he said.

"Might I add . . ." Walter began but was cut off abruptly by Natalie's glare. "Sorry. I didn't mean to upset you."

Natalie gave them both a lingering stare. Her eyes twitched. Jameson watched a ray of light flash within, then expand across her eyes. It added a slight reddish tinge to the already unusual color palette.

Her hazel eyes fused with the colors of green meadows covering the amber forest floor, followed by golden speckles scattered throughout. When the light reached its end, it exploded and burst into a blooming flower on a warm summer day, then flickered and faded away. Her pupils contracted, then dilated to cover her irises. They darkened to the blackness of a midnight sky encircled by rings of fire.

Natalie smirked at Jameson and Walter, then turned around, and walked away.

Walter elbowed Jameson and whispered, "Did you see that?"

"Whoa," he murmured in response, his face blank.

"That scared me," Walter said. "I couldn't maintain eye contact with her. I thought she was going to kill us."

"That's a bad sign," Jameson muttered. "It looks like the chip has activated, and it's uniting with her inner self."

Natalie turned back around. The rings in her eyes had grown brighter. "Is this funny to you two?"

Jameson stared at her, mouth agape. "Natalie, I think you need to calm down." He put his hands up.

"Don't tell me to calm down." Fire blossomed in Natalie's eyes.

"Then just listen to me and relax a little bit." Jameson stepped back. "I'm trying to be honest with you. I wouldn't intentionally try to destroy our world. I'm not like that, but I am trying to fix my mistake. You think I like being stuck here?" He opened his arms in a gesture of supplication. "So what do you say? Will you help us, please?"

Natalie shot one last glare at Jameson and Walter. The old man stepped back.

Natalie's eyes returned to normal. "All right, Jameson," she said. "I'll give you the benefit of the doubt. Let's make this right."

Walter sighed in relief.

"Strange." Natalie looked around.

"Oh, I see it." Jameson watched the darkness break at its highest point in the distance. The daylight hung around the trees and washed the night away.

"I see it too," Walter said. "I noticed something odd when I first came here. In the beginning, only small particles of light came through the portals from our world, then it came to a point where wildly energetic particles had been unleashed. That was when I could see light coming through the shadowy trees. The rest of Homondiem was still in the dark. Now, I see it's becoming daylight throughout more of Homondiem as the world is growing and expanding." Walter held out his wrist for them to see. "Take a look at my watch."

Jameson and Natalie leaned in.

"When I first arrived, the hands moved every which way. There was no organized time, but now it's slowly returning to normal."

"Why is that?" Natalie asked.

"It's because the portal is warping the fabric of space-time, including light, and entering here," Jameson explained. "Once the portal relinquishes its hold, it's recreating our world in this one."

Walter glanced up. "It doesn't end there. When I first entered this world, I could easily figure out my exact location by the areas length and width. Now, every time we move from one location to another, it takes longer, and the calculations are constantly changing."

"What do you mean?" Natalie asked.

"At first, the only true danger was that my life expectancy was getting shorter. In the beginning I was getting weaker, and I knew I could die at any moment. I thought that humans couldn't survive in Homondiem. But soon after, I felt something different. My life expectancy started increasing steadily. The evolution of the dimension continued, and that's when the trouble started. Homondiem got wider. Even using the device, I had a difficult time finding the portals. They kept changing locations as Homondiem grew. During this time, the number of life-forms had doubled, even quadrupled here. That's when I had to keep running so they couldn't catch me."

"You've been running since you got here?"

"That's the only reason I'm still alive," Walter said.

"You must be tired of running."

"It's not so bad. It's kind of like home once you figure out how to avoid these homondie, only you can get eaten alive while you sleep." Walter smiled involuntarily.

Jameson held up his device. "Look here. This spot right where we're standing will continually change locations while this world expands and ours contracts, until this world sucks every last ounce of energy from ours, like a vampire. Everything is shifting into place and will continue until this world is complete."

"How could it happen so quickly?" Natalie asked.

"The portals are made of two parts. As the outer spherical ring expands, increasing its pull, the inner portion narrows, decreasing its pull. Once the expansion ends and our dimension is completely destroyed, the outer section will stop widening. The force of the inner area will apply tension onto the outer casing and draw the two sections together until it closes up for good, leaving us stuck here. Once that happens, day and night will cycle just like they do back home."

"So we don't have much time before our world is gone and we'll have nothing to return to." Natalie's voice cracked. "So how do we get out of here?"

"Even if we could escape, we can't leave, not yet," Jameson said, shaking his head.

"Are you saying we're stuck in here?" Natalie asked, panic edging her voice.

"For the time being," Jameson said. "We need to take care of these portals first. I believe Victor sped them up, and we need to slow them down enough to be able to reverse them until they close altogether. It'll be much easier to do this from the inside."

"But how can we do that?" Walter asked. "The pressure of the dimension will keep the portals open until our world's end."

"I've been working on the coding through the device. I believe I've figured out how to close them for good," Jameson said. "If my equation is correct, we can create a pressure of inward motion through the portals. In turn, that'll successfully close them and guarantee the reversal of the dimension." He put his device away and held out his hand. "Let me have your devices and I'll recalculate them with my new formula."

Natalie handed Jameson her device. "So you want to build up the pressure until this world implodes?"

"Technically, yes," Jameson said as he flipped the latch and opened the panel at the back of the monitor, exposing the circuits and wiring. "Once the pressure is at a maximum, the expansion will subside here while our world expands back to its full capacity."

"What about us? Where will we be when it blows?" Natalie asked.

"We'll be at the very last portal," Jameson explained as he fiddled with the wiring. "Theoretically speaking, the pressure will force our bodies out of Homondiem and back into our world as time restarts itself."

"What will happen if the portal closures don't work or we run out of time?"

"If the portal closures fail, it'll factor into the equation, and our world will need to end as it reconnects here. This world will become the dominant dimension, ruled by the homondie."

"So we'd be stuck in here forever?" Natalie asked.

"I'm afraid so." Jameson pushed the panel back into the device until the latch clicked, then handed it to Natalie and took Walter's.

"So let's get moving before it comes to that."

"It's not that easy," Jameson said as he popped open the panel of Walter's device.

"But we have the device you made," Natalie said, scratching her head.

Jameson closed Walter's device and handed it back to him. "Turn around and take a look. Does anything look familiar?"

Natalie looked around, her brow furrowed. "It changed. We're in a totally different area."

"If you take a look at my device," Jameson pointed at the screen, "we're here and that's where the last location of the portal existed before the increase of land. Every time this dimension expands, the portals shift their position. It'll be difficult to track them, even with the device, but somehow we need to shut down each one."

"In theory it sounds great," Natalie said, "but it also sounds futile. What if we're heading toward one, then it disappears? How can we deal with that?"

"Don't forget, new ones could also appear as well," Walter added.

"And we still have the homondie and half-life mutated humans to deal with," Natalie said.

"At least Buster can alert us." Walter patted the dog on the head, reached in his pocket, and pulled out a handful of dry dog food; holding his hand out for Buster to eat.

"The homondie can sense us as well," Jameson said.

"How?" Natalie asked.

"As we begin to travel, they'll be hidden until our life drifts through the air," Jameson explained.

"They'll smell our life?" Natalie asked.

"Yes," Jameson said. "They're attracted to it. They'll be drawn to us no matter where we go or how much we try to hide." Jameson attached his device to his belt, pulled out some ammo, and reloaded his rifle.

"It's possible that Buster may sense them first. Dogs do have a keen sense of smell," Natalie said.

"That's true," Jameson agreed, "but you have to understand the homondie. Their only purpose is to find life. Those creatures will lurk in the darkest shadows of your nightmares, living without a conscience, waiting silently to attack and feast on us."

"Is there a way to outsmart them?"

"Sure. As long as they remain brainless and irrational, we can outsmart them. Right now, they act like wild animals in search for food. The less human the homondie are, the easier they'll be to kill."

"Don't you think we should start moving now?" Walter turned to leave.

"I'm not finished." Jameson grabbed Walter's collar, tugging him back.

"Make it quick. I have a bad feeling." Walter stumbled over his words.

"You must watch them carefully as they attack because they move at different speeds to retrieve their prey. The more life they extract from the humans, the faster they become, and they'll tear apart anything they come into contact with that has the essence of life," Jameson said.

"Now can we get moving?" Walter asked.

"Yes, Walter."

"Where to?" Natalie's gaze wandered through the woods and back at Jameson.

"Right here." Jameson pointed to the screen of his device. "We should head northeast. After you." He stepped back and allowed Natalie to lead the group through the decayed woodlands.

Walter tugged on Jameson's sleeve, pulling him farther behind Natalie without her noticing. "What are you doing?" he whispered. "Do you mean what you said? We're going home?"

"Of course not. I told you we're not backing down."

Natalie turned around, and Jameson hushed. He sped up, but before they reached their portal destination, he paused to scout the area. They stood below a massive, ominous tree; its shadow hung heavy over them.

CHAPTER 16

NATALIE PEERED UPWARD and viewed the monstrous dead mass towering over them, taunting her with its clawlike branches attached to twisted, disfigured limbs. She felt helpless and scared. Why had she been sent into this place of torment? She dropped her head.

Jameson nudged her. "There's the portal."

As they began to move closer, Buster growled softly to alert the group to danger.

"Wait, something's coming," Natalie whispered.

"It's the homondie," Jameson muttered.

"They're coming straight toward us," Walter moaned.

"We have to take them out," Jameson said.

"Isn't there a way to go around them?" Walter asked Jameson.

"No, they're too close to the portal. If we let them go, they'll just get in our way. We're going to have to get rid of them before they charge us. It's the only way to make sure we'll have enough time to close the portal."

Weapons ready, Jameson ran out first with Buster right behind. Walter led Natalie out with a battle cry as he charged the homondie. Natalie rolled her eyes at his offensive screech and ran out shooting.

Jameson was first to reach the homondie. One of the creatures licked its thin lips and chomped its teeth as it headed straight for him. He lifted his rifle and shot it straight through its forehead. Its neck snapped, and it fell to its knees.

Buster barked. A bloodcurdling scream left a homondie as it dragged its shambling body in Jameson's direction. Natalie raised her gun, aimed, and fired. The bullet went straight through its head, and it fell.

Jameson turned around. "You're a natural at this."

Natalie shouted, "Walter, look out!"

As the creature got closer, Walter spun around. "That's Abigail! She is or should I say she was the owner of the store."

The half-life cocked its head to the side and gave Walter a disturbing glare with its black eyes. Blood was splattered across its body and face. Salivating, it moaned and lurched forward. Walter raised his hands in front of him and backed up. "Abigail, it's me, Walter. Don't you remember me?"

It staggered toward Walter and attacked. He ran backward as it ran at him, screeching.

Natalie pulled out her revolver and fired multiple shots at the creature. Walter's body jolted, and he ducked. His knees bent, and he put his hands on his head. It twitched and jerked. Natalie fired over Walter's head until she knocked it down.

Walter rose to his feet. "That was impressive," he said, barely audible. He brushed himself off.

Natalie stood next to Walter as he leaned over the half-life that had once been Abigail. "Sorry, Abigail, I didn't want to hurt you." It twitched once more and startled Walter. He jumped back, pulled out his handgun, and unloaded a final shot to the head.

"I thought you didn't want to hurt her." Natalie chuckled.

"Ha-ha, very funny." A smile twitched Walter's lips. "All right, Jameson," he said, sticking his gun back in his belt. "I don't see any more homondie coming. Let's get this portal closed. I hope your device works and your theory is correct."

"Watch out. I'm not sure what's going to happen when I put this into reverse, but it might be worse than opening it." Jameson stepped back a few feet. "Whatever you do, don't stare directly into the portal, or you'll go temporarily blind." He held up his device and readied his stance. He looked around once more and pressed the button.

A loud crackle rumbled around them and pierced the air as lightning shot from the portal and into his device.

A slight breeze blew across Natalie's face, and an explosion sounded in the forest. She closed her eyes just in time, but the blast made her senses vibrate. She covered her ears as her eardrums throbbed and her body shuddered. She could feel the flash through her eyelids as she knelt on the ground and hid her face in her hands.

Natalie opened one eye a crack and saw the portal had enlarged and daylight extended. "What did you do?" Natalie asked Jameson.

"I tried to close the portal. I don't know what happened," he said.

"It doubled in size," Natalie yelled. They stood back and stared into the massive hole. "Wait a minute." She saw a familiar sight through the portal. "Is that our home, our world?" She moved forward to look closer.

"Hold on." Jameson grabbed her arm and stopped her. "Can you feel that?" He forced her to step back. "The portal just shifted. It feels like we're going to get pulled in."

"That's a good thing, right?" Natalie asked.

"For later, yes. We have to finish closing off the other portals first or we'll end up right back in the same situation."

Their feet started to slide across the ground as if on a frozen lake. A few dead trees uprooted and flew through the portal.

"This isn't good." Walter moved backward. "It's still expanding."

They scrambled to get away.

"Keep going until we can't feel the pull anymore," Jameson said.

Buster barked. Walter fell to the ground and pulled the others with him. They stopped just shy of a batch of homondie staring at the pulsating portal.

"It's still unstable here." Natalie watched the trees sway.

"We can't fight off these homondie here. We could get sucked into the portal," Jameson said. "I don't see it closing anytime soon. We'll have to try and go around them."

Several more homondie appeared. "I'll get the ones on the right and you take the ones on the left," Natalie said. "Swing around, and we'll meet back at this spot." She took off, Buster following.

"Just be careful not to get caught up in the portal," Jameson yelled, running in the opposite direction. Walter backed up and fired shots at the advancing homondie.

Natalie approached the creatures and picked off each one as if she were playing a carnival game.

She tried to keep an eye on everyone else while staying safe. She noticed that Jameson and Walter were farther apart than she was comfortable with. "We have to stay together," she hollered, but they kept moving apart, trying to put more distance between themselves and their targets. There were too many homondie to fight off. As they surrounded her, Buster barked wildly. Natalie's eyes met Jameson's. She could see that he wanted to reach her, but it was too late. He, too, was surrounded by multiple homondie.

Natalie backed up even farther until she lost sight of the others. Her instinct was to run. She continued to shoot as she ran backward through the woods, the homondie right on her heels. One came up behind Buster and launched itself at him. It moaned and knocked Buster down—its sharp teeth chattered and went straight for his neck.

Natalie aimed but couldn't get a clear shot. She ran to Buster and pushed the homondie off, but the scuffle placed her between the dog and the creature. The homondie sank its teeth into her flesh. Blood spewed from her leg immediately. The homondie released Natalie and turned to Buster.

Natalie's scream echoed throughout the woods. She could hear in the distance, "Hang on, we're coming!"

She kicked the homondie off Buster and shot it in the head. Blood splattered over Natalie as Buster ran up behind her and leaped to knock another homondie down, biting deep into its decomposed flesh.

Natalie scrambled backward on the ground. "Come on, Buster, this way." She got up and limped, blood soaking through her jeans, as she put some distance between them and the remaining homondie. She moved far enough away for Walter and Jameson to finish them off as they ran toward her and Buster. She sat on the ground and held onto her leg, trembling, unsure what to do.

Jameson leaned over her and looked down.

Natalie sobbed. Her wound throbbed, and her jeans were drenched with blood. Her body trembled, and her voice quivered. "Shoot me! Just shoot me now! I don't want to become one of them!"

"Don't worry, they can't harm you," Jameson said as he took her hand and helped her up. She leaned on him for support and hobbled, keeping pressure off her leg.

"I got bit," she said. "I've seen what happens when someone gets bitten. If they survive, they turn into one of them."

All of a sudden, the throbbing stopped. She applied pressure on her leg and stood upright. She looked down at the bloodstain. Curious, she pulled up the leg of her jeans only to see that the bite mark was gone; so was the pain. The blood that had been seeping down her leg had dried on her skin. "What's happening to me?"

"You have healing capabilities," Jameson explained. "You're the giver of life. As long as that chip is inside you, you'll be healed. Even a homondie's bite won't harm you, but the rest of us need something more." He smiled as he pulled a syringe out of his backpack.

"What's that?" Natalie asked.

"I was working on an antiserum to counteract their bite so we don't turn into one of them."

"What happens to us when they come into contact?" Natalie asked.

"Their bite alters our DNA sequence as it damages the cells that are exposed to it. If it goes unrepaired without the antiserum, the damaged cells that contain our genetic makeup are replaced by new, homondie-mutated ones. Cells can be replicated independently, so how much of the homondie DNA was absorbed will determine how mutated each human becomes."

"How would you even know where to start to make something like that?" Natalie asked. "They just began to come alive, didn't they?"

"Well . . ." Jameson trailed off, and Natalie clearly noticed him weighing his options on how much to tell her.

"I guess you could say we had a homondie in our possession and we took samples so we could make an antibody transfusion."

"You mean you actually captured one and brought it into our world?" Natalie said, shock marring her face.

"It wasn't that hard," Jameson said. "We tied a rope around Buster and threw a loop onto the ground inside the portal. Then Buster lured one in our direction. It stepped into the ring, and we hauled it in."

"So basically you used him as bait. How could you put Buster in danger like that?"

"We had to—it was in the name of science," Jameson said.

"In the name of science? What kind of scientist do you think you are?" Natalie asked. Her eyes squinted and lips puckered.

"I'm a theoretical physicist by nature, but I also hold degrees in biology and genetics and I've made several medical research discoveries in the past."

"That was a rhetorical question!" Natalie let out an exhausting sigh. "Every time I think I've heard it all, something else shocks me. I hope there's nothing else you've hidden from me."

"No, that's it, honest," Jameson told her. He searched through his backpack, pulled out more ammo, and reloaded his guns.

Natalie crossed her arms. She wasn't convinced she was done with Jameson's surprises. Even though he came off as confident, there was something about him, something evil just beneath the surface.

"Let's get to the next portal before another swarm of homondie comes through," he said.

"What about this one?" Natalie asked.

"There's nothing more we can do here. We'll come back to it later."

CHAPTER 17

JAMESON HEADED WEST toward the next portal while Buster trotted close behind. Natalie and Walter struggled through the ever-growing forest to catch up. They weren't in the same desolate woods they had first encountered.

The branches extended into their path and made it difficult to make progress. Leaves formed, and some began to flourish. It was the sign Jameson had been waiting for. He knew it was only a matter of time before the homondie world would finally be his.

Natalie passed Jameson with quick, impatient steps. She kept a few paces in front of him as Walter noisily tried to catch up. She pushed through the branches and flung them out of her way, allowing them to whack Jameson in the face.

Natalie turned around, and Jameson watched her focus on the movement of a shadow when a noise from some distance away caught his attention.

"I feel strange. Something's not . . . right?" Natalie's voice quivered.

Jameson felt a slight breeze, and a chill ran through his bones.

"I've never seen this before. It's . . . cold?" Jameson stared at his frosty breath and eyed the trees. The buds that had formed into leaves had begun to wilt.

"I believe this homondie world is now acquiring the traits of our world as it's taking over our dimension," Walter said. "It's no longer a dead place. It's now full of life."

As suddenly as it had come, the cold passed, and the leaves revived. The towering dead trees had faded away into maples, pines, and spruce trees. Birds were chirping, and a squirrel ran past.

"I'm not one to pull rank, but our time here is over," Walter said, his face pale and eyes glassy. "Ammo is scarce, and the homondie will be here shortly."

"You're right," Natalie said. "We have to find the quickest way to the portals and with the least amount of homondie. Jameson, where's the next one?"

Jameson swiped the device through the air. He watched Natalie close her eyes. When she opened them, Jameson could see them twitch as a light formed. The light ran from one eye to the other, then burst when it reached the end, signaling that the chip had been activated.

"I can see where the homondie are," Natalie said, her head bobbing in all directions. "I have some sort of radar that can sense movement in the area." She sounded surprised, unsure of what she was seeing. "I think you may have unlocked some sort of extrasensory perception in my mind when you planted that chip."

"It unlocked more than that," Walter said, just above a whisper. Natalie didn't hear him, but Jameson did.

How many times do I need to hush that man? Jameson elbowed Walter in the ribs and gave Natalie a sly smile as if nothing happened. "In that case, I believe you're in charge, Natalie." Jameson gazed at the device screen and pointed. "I see a portal a little north of here."

"Okay, let's get moving." She fled into the woods as the men followed. She veered off the path and directed them out even farther.

Jameson began to worry. "Where are we going?"

"This way," Natalie said, her voice tinged with bitterness. She slapped branches out of her way while Buster ducked underneath them.

"This is the wrong way," Walter said, readying his gun. "We're heading back where we came from." He stomped through shrubs and small trees forming new undergrowth on the forest floor. "Why don't we follow the path?"

Natalie paused, and Jameson stopped short, narrowly missing colliding with her.

She spun around, her eyes once again darkened to the blackness of a night sky with rings of fire encircling her pupils. "Either follow me or don't, it's up to you."

Walter took a step back and asked nervously as he stuttered, "What about the homondie? Aren't we going around them? I can hear them out there."

"This is the way with the fewest homondie," Natalie said, turning and continuing on her way.

They sprinted through the woods. Jameson ducked several times to avoid getting caught by one of the branches in Natalie's wake. "I haven't been around here before. Wait a minute." He hesitated and squinted. "I see where you're taking us, but it looks like we made it back around." He picked out the signs of an old battle. Crumbled debris littered the area as both dead homondie and humans littered the ground.

Natalie stumbled across the rough terrain and slowed to a stop. "I tried to go around the homondie, but there's no way. There's a wall of them waiting for us at the portal. They must know we're on our way there."

"What do you suggest?" Jameson asked.

"We don't have an option. We're going to have to go through them," Natalie said, her voice flat and resigned.

Walter clutched his hand to his chest. "I can't take too much more of this. Come on, Natalie, let's just follow Jameson. He knows the way."

Natalie stared at Jameson and Walter, and her eyes returned to normal. "I've seen where to go. This time, you'll have to trust me." Natalie fled. Buster pranced into the lead, seeming to anticipate her movements. Jameson and Walter followed hesitantly, unsure where they were being led.

"Natalie, don't get too far ahead," Jameson whisper-shouted.

Buster growled. Natalie stopped and ducked as the others caught up and knelt beside her.

She pointed and whispered, "The portal is there. We only have to get to the other side of that ridge."

Jameson mumbled, "There's that smell again."

"They're coming up fast," Natalie said.

Jameson inched past her and crawled through the underbrush while Buster and Walter took up the rear. "I don't see them yet."

They peeked through the ever-changing landscape, the world now familiar. The trees had flourished, almost reaching their maximum growth. The skies boasted wispy clouds, and mountains rose in the background. A few birds flew past, chirping. A cat ran by Buster, but he made no attempt to follow. He remained at Natalie's side.

A crowd of homondie emerged from the opposite direction, blocking access to the portal.

"There are more homondie on the other side of those trees," Natalie said.

"It's best to avoid them," Walter spoke quietly. "Let's head back."

"Walter, you know we can't avoid them, and even if we could, we're trapped. We don't have any more time left. We're going to have to go straight through. The faster we get to the portal, the quicker we'll be out of here," Jameson said.

"Then what are you waiting for?" Walter asked.

"Just wait a minute. I need to concentrate." Jameson turned to Natalie. "Natalie, where's the weakest area? We'll have a better chance if we go through the smallest number of homondie."

"To the right, just ahead," Natalie whispered and pointed. "Just beyond that group, but I think we'll have a better chance if someone draws them away and loses them in the woods. That way we have more time to close the portal."

"Who are you suggesting might do that? Don't think I'm going to do it." Walter folded his arms.

"I wouldn't expect you to. I'll do it." Natalie smiled with a confidence Jameson hadn't seen before.

"That's not funny," Jameson said.

"I'm not trying to be funny." Natalie stood.

Jameson's eyes narrowed and lips pursed at Walter, pointing to Natalie, silently pleading him to reason with her.

Walter broadened his shoulders and stood tall. "Natalie, I'll do it. I don't want you to wander off like that."

"Don't worry about me, I can take care of myself." She walked away.

"Natalie, wait," Walter said.

She reluctantly stopped walking.

"We need to stick together."

"Don't worry, I'll be back for you," Natalie said.

"How can we be sure?" Jameson's voice rose with slight panic.

"Because I need to keep an eye on you two."

Jameson was bothered by the possibility of Natalie escaping. He straightened up and stood beside her, putting his arm around her waist and pulling her down. "Get back down before someone sees you."

She squatted next to Jameson.

"I don't want you to be alone out here," he told her. "I know we've had our differences, but this isn't a joke. Victor may find you again, and next time he'll take that chip and you'll be dead."

"Don't worry about me," Natalie said. "I have an uncanny feeling that the homondie aren't going to hurt me. Besides, I can outrun the two of you, and I can definitely run faster than they can. You just worry about getting to that portal, and I'll meet you there once I lose them."

Jameson glanced at Walter and realized he had no choice. He had to let her go. He knew she wasn't going to change her mind, no matter what he wanted her to do.

"Then I guess we have a plan." Jameson pointed in the opposite direction. "You run to the right and sweep the surrounding area. We'll meet at the portal."

Natalie pinned Jameson with a knowing gaze. Without another word, she ran, firing her gun into the air. She hollered, "Come on, try and catch me if you want my life!"

Jameson patted Buster on the head. "Buster, go with Natalie. Go on, boy. You keep her safe." She had more courage than he'd once thought, which was bad news for him. How could he refuse to let her leave without revealing his plans?

"You're not actually going to allow her to run off like that, after we just got her back from Victor?" Walter asked. "You know he's out there waiting to nab her again."

"You can see that we can't stop her," Jameson said, gesturing in the direction she'd run. "She would only ask questions. We have to let her go or she may figure out what's going on. We know she has the best shooting skills, exceptional speed, and the ability to see where the homondie are. All that gives her the advantage, so I know she'll be safe."

"What if something happens to her and she injures that chip?" Walter asked. "Where would that leave us? If that chip gets damaged, we can't control the homondie, and we'll be sitting ducks, waiting for our turn to die!" Walter wheezed, and his cheeks flushed.

"She'll be fine and the chip will be fine," Jameson assured him. "As long as she has that chip, she can't die, and she'll be back."

"What if she tries to use the device to escape back to our world?"

"I recalibrated all our devices," Jameson said. "They're set to only expand the portals, not contract them. The suction begins as if we're about to enter back into our world, but then it reverses. That's why we needed to get away from that one before Natalie noticed."

"Oh, that's why the portal enlarged."

"We need to stay ahead of Victor and control the portals ourselves, and when the time is right, I'll get Natalie to hand over the chip willingly." Jameson chuckled at his newfound success. "We found this world, and I'm not going to let Victor take it from us. We'll be the ones in control, not him. All I need is that chip, then we'll rule this land together."

"You are an evil one, aren't you?"

"I've got everything under control. Don't worry so much." Jameson stood. "Come on. We've got to get moving so we can find her before Victor does."

Jameson ran off shouting, "Come on, Walter, and don't look back! Just keep running! Head toward the portal so we can get her back as soon as possible!"

As they ran, a loud wave of thunder rolled across the sky, and the ground quivered under their feet, almost knocking them over. They came to a halt.

"What was that?" Walter asked.

"That's our world dying, and we don't even have the chip yet," Jameson said.

"We have to hurry and find Natalie. We can't predict how much time we have before the homondie are out of control," Walter said, panic rising in his voice.

"There's the portal right there." Jameson pointed. The pressure began mounting. "Come on, let's keep moving."

"The pressure's getting worse. It's hard to move," Walter said. "The closer we get, the harder it is. How much farther do we need to go?"

"Just a little bit closer. We don't know if Natalie's watching."

"Damn it, there are homondie coming this way."

The homondie forced Jameson to take an alternate route farther out. He stopped, and they hid behind a cluster of trees, ready to circle back to their rendezvous point.

"I can see the portal from here," Walter said, "but where are Natalie and Buster? They should be on their way back by now."

"She'll be back soon, just give her a minute," Jameson said.

"You don't know if we have another minute," Walter's voice rose. "You might as well just finish off the portal expansion and get it over with."

"I'm not going to risk it. I could jeopardize our whole operation if she ends up walking right into its path, and we'll lose the chip for good."

"But the homondie—"

"We only had that brief encounter. Maybe if we wait until they pass, they won't catch our scent."

"There are plenty more out there," Walter said, "and I'd like to get out of here before they return."

"She'll be back."

"Maybe she lied. She wanted to leave us earlier."

"The one thing Natalie is not is a liar," Jameson said. "In fact, I think she's incapable of lying. If she said she'll be here, she'll be here." He watched the homondie come closer. "Walter, did you notice something?"

"What's that?" Walter's eyebrows drew together.

"The pressure of the portal isn't affecting them. See that? They're walking straight through."

"I never noticed that before."

Jameson and Walter watched as the homondie limped by and stopped. One raised its nose high into the air. Its head shuddered, then cocked in their direction.

Suddenly, a loud rumble shook the ground and rocked the trees. The portal sounded off with a boom. A dust cloud burst as bodies flew in through the portal and knocked down the passing homondie. They piled up around the portal. The portal began to expand away from Jameson and Walter, but the expanding portal hadn't stopped the homondie.

"There's more homondie coming. We're trapped," Walter shouted over the rumbling portal.

Jameson spotted more trouble approaching from behind and said, "Now, Walter, stay perfectly still . . ."

He glanced briefly at Walter. The old man's face was a mask of worry. Then he did something that surprised Jameson. Walter pulled out a large serrated knife and ran.

"Walter, no. Don't do it," Jameson said, though he couldn't yell to draw attention to himself. All he could do was watch.

The homondie sniffed the air and caught the scent of Walter's life passing by. It dragged one leg across the ground as it tried to keep up. Walter kept one step ahead but stumbled. He collapsed to his knees and crawled, his fingernails clawing at the dirt as he scrambled to get to his feet. As he struggled, another homondie separated from the pack and chased him. It seemed to increase its speed as it became more human.

What's he doing? Jameson asked himself. He stared at the old man trying to lose the homondie in the woods. *He's going to get himself killed.*

Jameson was tired and thought maybe all this wasn't really necessary. The fun was over. Had there ever been any fun at all? Yes, a little in the beginning, but not now, not anymore. No matter, he had to finish what he'd started and find out what had happened to Natalie. He should have listened to Walter. If something happened to her, they were doomed. Jameson was through with the games. He pulled a machete from his belt. Now was the time for action.

While Walter circled back, Jameson ran in the opposite direction to cut off the homondie.

Jameson's and Walter's eyes met as they closed in and forced the homondie into a group with nowhere to go.

"Let's get this over with," Walter yelled, panting, exhausted by his run.

Jameson went straight at the homondie, gazed into its hollow eyes, and smelled its rotting body. He rushed in and attacked, charging full force, filled with an energy he hadn't felt before. He moved swiftly and steadily toward the depraved, vile creatures, then slowed and waited for the homondie to catch up.

Jameson raised his arm, and the first homondie jerked its body forward, groaning and snapping at its supper. He swung the machete in a clean pass. Blood spewed from the homondie's neck as he severed its head from its body. He moved on to the next one, spinning around and chopping the machete into its side, then spinning back as the blade lodged in the face of another. It fell. He pulled the blade free and jammed it into the throat of the next one. It lay gurgling on its own blood.

He heard another homondie edge up behind him. He kicked it then plunged his knife into its brain, and it dropped. He placed his foot on its head, pulled out the weapon, spun, and stabbed another in the chest. He looked over his shoulder to see Walter running toward him. He stepped over the last homondie, blood still oozing from its chest, and toward the old man.

Walter caught up and said, "I told you. I knew something's wrong. Natalie should have been here by now."

"I guess we should go find her," Jameson said, "but first, I want to get the last of the portals connected in time for the final expansion to complete." Jameson locked onto the portal with his device as he got closer.

"You know there are more homondie coming this way," Walter said as he followed Jameson to the portal.

Jameson stopped a cautious distance away. He held out his device and aimed. "Here we go. I hope Natalie is nowhere near this when it goes off."

Jameson pointed the device at the portal and pressed the button. An explosion rocked the ground and uprooted the trees. They fell, and the blast shook the device out of Jameson's hand. The portal expanded with nothing to control it and sucked the neighboring portals into itself.

"I had no idea how large these things would get," Jameson said in awe. He picked up the device and brushed himself off.

The wind picked up, and they stepped back, slowly at first, then with greater urgency.

"If we don't get away from this portal now, we'll be killed. Look how much it has expanded since we've been here," Walter said.

"Time to find Natalie." Jameson glanced at his device, but the screen was blank. "It's not working." He waved it around.

"You must have broken it when you dropped it. Here, use mine." Walter pulled his out of his bag and turned it on. "Mine's not working either." He slapped the side a couple of times. "There must be some sort of interference with that last portal explosion, and Natalie's nowhere in sight. What do we do?"

Before Jameson could answer, another roar boomed across the land and jolted them where they stood. They took a few steps back from the force.

They kept moving backward, getting farther away as they watched the portal expand, filling Homondiem with a strange glow in every direction. When the rumble subsided, the glow turned into a massive burst of light and swallowed the remaining existence around them almost instantly.

The portals were linked and were expanding faster. The wind picked up and knocked over the trees as it created a massive dark hole.

They glanced through the hole into their world. A rotating column of air whipped up homes and cars. It damaged trees and leveled buildings. As the objects neared the portal into Homondiem, everything disintegrated into dust and debris. Nothing but living things and plant life stayed intact as the portal consumed everything in its path.

Wild wind unleashed the dust throughout Homondiem and went in every direction; it was far more powerful than they could handle.

Jameson and Walter clung to trees. A massive swirl of dust formed around them. They had to shield their eyes. It flung them off their feet and threw them far away. They landed with a hard thud.

"That hurt," Jameson said, standing up with a grunt, "but I'm grateful we went farther out and not into the path of that thing." He tousled his hair to shake the dirt loose then smoothed it back into place. "At least it drops the debris in the vicinity of the portal. It pretty much stays with it as it's expanding, so we're already out of harm's way. We're safe here." Jameson brushed the remaining dirt off his clothing.

"How are we going to find Natalie now?" Walter asked, readjusting his suspenders and wiping his glasses with his shirt to remove the layer of dust.

"I don't know," Jameson said. "With that last burst, I'm sure we've all shifted in different directions."

"What if she was in the path of the portal when it exploded?" Walter asked.

"It's best not to think about it," Jameson said. "No time to worry about what might have happened. Let's get out there and search for her and Buster."

"We don't know which direction to go in, and we can't use our devices to see where we are!"

"Don't worry, we'll find her," Jameson told him.

"If we don't, all our experiments will be for nothing! You know Natalie is the key to this whole godforsaken world," Walter yelled.

"I know. You don't have to remind me."

"Damn it, Jameson, I told you not to let her go!"

CHAPTER 18

JAMESON AND WALTER trudged through the woods opposite the portal. "All of this is unfamiliar. This place has grown tenfold since we were last here," Jameson said.

"Where are we going?" Walter asked. "She could be anywhere by now. We don't even know how big Homondiem is after this much growth. We could be walking for days, and I'm already exhausted." Walter lowered his head as he walked alongside Jameson. "We're never going to find her."

"We're going to keep searching until we do." Jameson paused. "Wait a minute." He pulled Walter down, and they hid in the underbrush. They ducked out of sight as a group of homondie ambled by.

Jameson watched with narrowed eyes as the unsuspecting horde passed. "They're out of sight." He stood and quickened his pace.

Walter trailed behind, falling into step a moment later. When he caught up, he pulled on Jameson's shoulder. "Looks like another town destroyed upon entry."

Jameson assessed the damage. Rubble covered the landscape.

"Everything is totally destroyed. It's like a tornado went through here." Walter ran his hand over his balding head. "I was hoping to find something besides a pile of dead bodies."

Jameson walked over the mound of debris and something caught his eye. "Look at this." He rolled the dead over and found weapons. He continued to search through the bodies and found they were all armed. He went through their pockets and found extra ammunition.

"I've never seen people in here with weapons before," Walter said. "The world must know these homondie are alive and are trying to take over their world or World War III has begun."

"Either way, it's great for us." Jameson picked up a weapon. "This one's loaded. Walter, take any weapons that have ammo, leave the others." Jameson shoved the bodies around like logs and picked through to find more weapons and ammo. He scavenged everything he could find and threw them into a pile.

"We hit the jackpot!" Walter scrambled across the ground. He picked up a few replacement guns then yelled, "Jameson, look at this!"

Jameson strolled over. Tucked between a pair of bodies was a large serrated tactical knife.

Walter moved one of the bodies, all chewed up and bloodied with its intestines hanging out, then wiped his hands on his pants.

Jameson grabbed the second body with two hands and flipped it over to reveal the knife strapped to the dead man's waist.

"I don't know how you can touch them like that." Walter reached down and took the knife gingerly from the man's belt. "Now this will come in handy." He swung it around.

"Shh, get down quick, hide," Jameson whispered. "There's homondie right over there."

Ammunition and weapons in hand, they dropped to the ground. Jameson hoped the stench of the dead bodies would cover their smell. As he'd hoped, the homondie set off away from them, but seeming to follow the direction of the other horde.

"Where are they going?" Walter asked.

"They could be after Natalie. I think we should follow them," Jameson said.

"Follow them? Usually they chase us, we don't chase them," Walter said.

"They wouldn't be heading out like that unless there was a reason," Jameson said, "and if that reason is Natalie, we have no choice but to follow them. Just wait until they get a little farther away."

As they were about to get up, Walter signaled Jameson and whispered, "I hear something. They're coming back."

They ducked back down and heard a man say, "They went in that direction. Hurry, go through those dead and see what you can find before they come back."

"There are weapons here with no ammo," a woman's voice said.

"People, human people?" Jameson whispered. "I thought only device bearers could survive entry into Homondiem."

"That's great," Walter said. "We could use some help getting rid of Victor."

"Yes, but we have to play this one carefully. We don't know who they are," Jameson said. "Follow my lead."

Jameson shouted, "Hey, you there, we're like you! Don't be alarmed. We're coming out." He and Walter stood and stepped out, hands up above their heads.

"Don't come any closer." A broad-shouldered man scrutinized them. He sported a short crew cut and was dressed in camouflage. His clothes were bloodstained, and he clutched a rifle. He glared at them down the barrel, trigger finger extended through his cutoff glove. He kept his weapon high in his steady hand.

"It's so good to see other people in here." A woman approached Jameson and Walter.

"Caroline, stand back."

"Nonsense, they're like us, Wade." Caroline motioned for him to lower his weapon then turned back to Jameson and Walter.

"You would hold a grudge too if you were left stranded by this one." Wade pointed at Walter. "He was outside the portal with a woman, and they said they were going to help me, but instead they disappeared and left me stuck in here."

"As you can see, I got sucked in too," Walter said.

"I didn't see you," Wade said.

"The portal must have shifted and thrown me to a different location."

"I don't want to hear that scientific crap," Wade grumbled. "You had the chance to get me out before you got sucked in."

Jameson noted that Caroline was no more than a few years older than Natalie. Her blue eyes gleamed with shock, and terror marred her face. *Strange, she has no weapons.* She came closer, and he noticed she had been roughed up a bit. Her short blonde hair was mussed, and her face bore bruises and a swollen lip. She wore dirty khakis and a white blouse stained with more dirt than blood.

"I apologize for his rudeness. He never acted like this before. He's a bit distraught right now, that's all. We're so glad to see other human faces. I count my blessings that you found us like this." Caroline's composure didn't last long. Her eyes teared up, and she said, "I don't know how much longer we can survive here, wherever *here* is."

Jameson turned his attention to the man. "I see you've done some killing." He walked closer, lowering his hands.

"All there is to do around here is killing." Wade raised his weapon again. "I told you, don't get any closer."

"We're not here to cause trouble," Walter explained. "We can help you if you'd like."

Wade chuckled. "You, help us? I'm a soldier, and I think we're in over our heads. How could you help us?"

"We know how to get out of here, for one thing," Walter shot back.

"Really? You can get us out?" Caroline said, hope in her voice. "Oh, that would be wonderful."

"Don't get too excited," Wade said. "We don't know them. This could be a trap. They might rob us of our weapons and leave us for dead."

"I don't know you either, and you've helped me," Caroline said.

"Yes, but I got my reasons, same as the next man who comes around." Wade put his rifle across her chest to prevent her from stepping forward. "You're not going anywhere."

"If the lady wants our help, she's going to get our help," Jameson said, raising his own gun and catching Wade off guard.

Wade tried to bring his rifle back around on Jameson.

"Whoa there, Wade," Jameson said calmly. "Point it at the ground or I'll shoot."

Wade lowered his rifle, and Caroline whimpered.

"I just want to talk for a minute. There's no reason for any impulsive actions. I don't want anyone hurt," Jameson said.

"There's no need for that," Wade said, slinging his rifle over his shoulder.

Jameson lowered his rifle but kept a watchful eye on Wade as his finger twitched. "Have you seen any more of us around here?" Jameson asked Caroline.

"Yes, there are others back at our camp," she said.

"You don't need to be telling these strangers that," Wade said. His eyes narrowed, and his lips clenched.

"You have a camp?" Jameson asked.

"Yes, we can take you there if you want," Caroline said. "It's not too far from here."

Wade adjusted the rifle over his shoulder as he glared at Caroline.

"It's not like they're going to hurt us or anything," Caroline said. "They would have done it by now. We have to stick together to get through this."

"Maybe you have to stick to a group, but I don't." Wade reached for the handle of his knife.

Jameson dove forward and snatched the knife from Wade's fingers as he began to draw it from its sheath.

"I think we'd be safer together." Walter aimed his gun at Wade while Jameson took the rest of his weapons.

"Give those back to me." Wade lunged, and Jameson pushed him back.

"Stop it and cooperate with them," Caroline cried. "Why are you acting like this? We need all the help we can get!"

"Whose side are you on?" Wade asked, staring her down.

"I'm on our side, the human side, and I think I'd rather have them by my side than be outnumbered by those creatures out there."

"Give that stuff back to me, or else," Wade yelled at Jameson.

"Or else what? You're not in a position to be trying to settle a score with me right now. You'll get it back when I say you'll get it back. But you're taking us to your camp first." Jameson slid Wade's knife into his waistband and slung his rifle over his shoulder.

Wade said to Caroline, "What did I tell you about blabbing our business?"

"I'm sorry. I didn't mean to get everyone fighting. I've said too much." Caroline's voice cracked. She stepped back, away from Jameson and Walter.

"Don't be frightened, miss," Jameson said to her. "We can give you and your friends some assistance if you want it. We're not going to hurt anyone as long as everyone is civil and cooperative." He grinned at Wade. "Now why don't you show us where your camp is? I'm sure we can help in some way."

"Over that way." Caroline pointed toward the east side of Homondiem. "Come on, I'll take you there."

Jameson and Walter followed. Wade trailed silently behind.

"I noticed you have a lot of guns and knives on you. Are you in the military too?" Caroline asked.

Jameson saw Caroline staring at his belt full of knives, along with his collection of guns. "No, but I've hunted back home, so I have some experience with both guns and knives. You can't survive here on guns alone—now it's more about the knives. You can never have enough when you run out of ammo. Unfortunately, it seems that in here, they're purely for killing homondie."

"Homondie? I didn't know they had a name," Caroline murmured.

Jameson realized he had said too much and needed to change the subject before too many questions arose. "So how long have you been in here?" he asked.

"It hasn't been too long, not sure exactly. With these crazy days here, it's been hard to get my bearings," Caroline said.

"Is your camp much farther?" Walter asked.

"No, it's just over that way." She pointed. "It seems secure after the last flood of refugees came barreling in. They heard our voices and were so pleased that we welcomed them into our camp, but then they brought a bunch of those creatures with them. They didn't know they were being trailed. We heard the creatures coming and were able to get rid of them quickly out in the woods and away from our camp before they attacked the group. Luckily, no one was harmed. Since then, we haven't seen anyone else."

"What have you been doing here since you set up camp?" Jameson asked.

"Myself and a few others go out each day to hunt for supplies. We lost some people on our hunts, but now, most of them are too weak to go. The remaining ones are too tired and need to rest after walking for so long without food and water."

"Where do you look?"

"We scavenge about in search of the dead and rummage through their bodies," Caroline said with slight waver in her voice. "There aren't many of us that made it through alive. Those of us here were lucky to make it. Most who were carried into this world died upon entry, and there seems to be a new pile of dead every day. Today we were out in hope to find not only weapons and ammunition but also food and water as well. Our main concern is to try and get everyone well enough to fight if our camp gets overrun by those creatures. Here we are." She stopped talking as they entered a thick patch of trees where the camp was hidden on the other side.

Their camp comprised about thirty feet of cleared land with bushes and trees surrounding it for cover. Jameson watched as the group of eight people glared at them. He could see the devastation in their eyes. The makeshift camp was in shambles. Clothes from the dead had been tied together and placed across the trees for shelter as survivors sat on the ground. A pile of empty water bottles and food wrappers sat in the corner of the camp.

"You're here. Give me back my weapons." Wade reached for his rifle, and Jameson knocked his hand out of the way.

"A deal is a deal." Jameson handed them over grudgingly.

Wade tucked the knife back into his belt, flung the gun strap over his shoulder, and set off to check on the rest of the group.

A thin young man jumped up from the ground. His clothes were stained with blood. He couldn't have been more than sixteen. His eyes were bloodshot from days without rest, and his hair was shaggy and matted.

"There are more of us?" he asked anxiously. "I didn't think we would see any more of our kind. Welcome, have a seat." He patted a large boulder, signaling that Jameson should sit.

"Thank you." Jameson approached him. "What's your name, kid?"

"Zack," he said. "I want to apologize, we have nothing for you to eat or drink. We were just discussing our next trip out to search for food and water. You don't happen to have any, do you? Some of us are close to starvation."

"Sure, Zack," Jameson said, unzipping his backpack, "but you'll have to ration it among yourselves."

Jameson pulled two water bottles from his bag while Walter stuffed his hand deep into his backpack and pulled out a handful of granola bars. They handed Zack the food and water to pass around. They each took a sip of water and a bite of a granola bar before they zipped their backpacks and placed them over their shoulders.

"You're going to have to share it. Only sip a small bit of water and pass it on to make sure everyone gets some. Same thing with the food. As long as things don't get out of hand, we have no problem sharing with all of you, but we have to ration everything we have. Until we can find more, we'll only have a scrap of food and a few sips of water a day," Jameson said as Wade left the group to sit alone.

Jameson knew they had enough food and water to go around. He knew how much Victor had in his town. They could always sneak in and grab some supplies if things got bad. On the other hand, if the group knew how much was available, they could have a problem. He didn't want to start a revolution with the group making off with all the goods.

"If this is all you have, we won't take it. You can keep it," Zack said.

"Don't you worry about it," Jameson said, waving him away. "I'm sure we'll find more sooner or later."

"Don't get your hopes up," Caroline said. "I think we've already gone through it all. We haven't found any more dead to scavenge."

Zack took a sip of the water and broke off a piece of the granola bar. "Thank you. We appreciate it."

"It's tough to live under these harsh, primitive conditions where food and water are so scarce," Caroline said.

Zack went over to a girl sitting on the ground, her back against a tree. She looked to be his twin. "Here, sis, this will help." He placed the water bottle to her lips. "Savor every last bit, Zoey. We're not sure when we'll have more."

"Thank you, Zack," she spoke softly, dry-mouthed, and took a sip. She swished it around in her mouth, savoring each drop, swallowing a bit at a time.

Zack placed the small ration of food into the palm of her hand. "Eat up. You need to build up your strength. You'll feel better in no time." He patted her on the shoulder and sat by her side.

Zoey swallowed the rest of the water and nibbled a few bits off the granola bar. "We've heard those creatures were dead, but now they're coming alive."

"Yes, it's true," Jameson said, holding his weapons on his lap, eyeing the still-angry Wade.

"Do they really want to hunt us?" Zoey asked.

"I'm sorry to say they do," Jameson answered.

"Not all of us have encountered the creatures in person yet, but we know if they're out there waiting for us, we're bound to come into contact with them sooner or later, and we aren't going to last much longer once they catch up to us," Zoey said.

"Have you seen them?" Zack asked.

"Yes, it's not a pretty sight," Walter said.

"I've heard the creatures are drifting up from the south, so you may want to avoid those places," Zack added.

"The homondie are everywhere, not just the south," Jameson said.

"Homondie, is that what you call them? We've been calling them feeders," Zack said. He looked at Jameson. "Do you know what's going on here?"

"What do you know about this place, Zack?" Jameson asked.

"All I know is that a black hole grew in the middle of our town and everything got sucked into it. We tried to run, but it showed up so fast that it sucked us up too, and we ended up here."

"Well . . .," Jameson said, "we don't have time to explain everything, but that hole was a portal into this world called Homondiem, and our world is about to be taken over by the homondie."

"What about these portals eating up our towns? Is there any way to stop them?" Caroline asked, joining the conversation.

"We're trying to find a way to close the portals and reverse the dimensional shift," Jameson explained.

"What will happen if you can't?" Zack asked.

"The portals are spreading out across our world. If we don't close the portals and stop the expansion of this world soon, eventually our world will be gone and this will be our only place to live from now on."

"I don't think I could get used to this," Caroline said. "What do you think we should do?"

"Why are you asking him?" Wade hollered. "Haven't I been taking care of this group? I'm the one who's kept you safe."

"Sure," Zack said, conceding the point, "but he seems to know an awful lot about this place." He gestured to Jameson.

"Yes, maybe too much." Wade squinted at Jameson and Walter. "Doesn't it seem strange to you that these two guys just strolled up, all decked out with weapons, food, and water? You ask me, it seems like they knew what was going on and had plenty of time to prepare. I think they had something to do with this."

"How could they possibly have done that?" Caroline asked.

"I think there's more to this than what anyone's saying," Zack said, holding up his hands to stop the argument.

"What do you think happened, Zack?" Jameson asked.

"Back home, I heard rumors about World War III, but nothing was confirmed because the government and all media were shut down right before this happened. A riot started, and then the portal opened. I think this is all because the government tried to open a dimension for themselves to hide. They were going to leave the rest of us to fend for ourselves," Zack said.

Walter leaned in and whispered to Jameson, "You're going to have a lot of government officials putting a price on your head. You better hope they don't find you."

"You're in this as much as I am," Jameson shot back.

Wade met Jameson's eyes. "I see you're not going to let us in on how you stumbled upon this information about Homondiem and the homondie." Wade crossed his arms.

"We overheard it as we were coming into this world." Walter stumbled over his words.

"Who was your contact?" Wade asked.

"A government official by the name of Victor Bernard," Walter blurted.

"I'd like to meet this Victor Bernard, see if he really exists," Wade said, "but I'm sure he's not around."

"He's closer than you think," Jameson said.

"Let's set aside the blame here and get to the point," Caroline interjected. "You said you could take us home, right?"

"I'll try my best," Jameson said.

"Can we go home now?" Caroline asked, looking around at the exhausted and hungry group.

"No, not yet," Jameson said. "Natalie hasn't come back, and we can't leave without her."

"Natalie?" Caroline said.

"Yes," Jameson answered, "Natalie Thompson."

Caroline's face contorted into a mask of shock. "Natalie Thompson?"

"Yes," Jameson answered impatiently. "Do you know her?"

"She's alive?" Caroline teared up, and she covered her mouth with a shaking hand. "I'm so thankful she's alive."

"Well, I hope she is, anyway," Jameson said. "We seem to have lost her."

"What happened?"

"We were out scouting the portals when we got separated. We were looking for her when we met you. How do you know Natalie?"

"We met at a pit stop on Highway 903. I was coming back from a business trip," Caroline said. "She was sitting alone, and it looked like she'd been crying. I went over to her and started talking to her, but she wouldn't tell me what was wrong. The funny thing was, we found out we were from the same town, and I even went to the same grad school she's in now. I only graduated last year." Caroline smiled briefly. "She never told me where she was going, but I was concerned about her driving in that condition, especially during a storm. I gave her my number and told her to call me when she was back in town, but I never heard from her again. I didn't know what happened to her. Shortly after, we'd heard that people were missing, like Natalie. To think that it's always been this world sucking us in. I don't think I would have believed it before." Caroline choked up and her voice broke. "Until now, I thought we were the only ones who survived the entry into this place."

"She may still be in danger," Jameson said. "We have to get back out there to find her."

"Get over it," Wade said. "There are other people out there besides this Natalie. Why don't you care about them?"

"Mind your own business," Jameson hollered at Wade.

Walter took off his backpack and rummaged through it. "Never mind him, we're running low on ammo," he told Jameson. "We need more before we take on all those homondie."

Jameson placed his bag on the ground at his feet and counted his ammo. "This isn't going to work." He passed a couple of rounds to Walter. "We're definitely going to need more before we head off to find Natalie. Caroline, do you know where there might be more around here?"

"You took my weapons, invaded our camp, and now you want us to help you?" Wade marched toward Jameson.

"Wade, that's enough," Caroline cried. "I can't take it anymore!"

"*You* can't take it anymore?" Wade said. "What about the rest of us? All you do is whine and cry all day long, and we've got to sit here and listen to it."

"I'm sorry if I'm having a hard time adjusting," Caroline said. "I didn't ask for this." She took a deep breath. "What we need right now is to cooperate and work together to help each other. I'm not going to stand around and let you bully these men any longer."

CHAPTER 19

WADE STORMED AWAY from the others, while Caroline whispered to Jameson, "In the beginning, there was no trouble finding the dead, but I think we plucked all them dry." She paused, then said, "There might be one more place. I remember seeing it."

"Where is it? Is it close?" Jameson asked.

"Back where we met you. I saw some dead lying on the side of the path. We were going to backtrack and check them, but we got held up by some of those . . . those things, the homondie. We haven't had a chance to get back there, but they're bound to have something on them."

"Could you show us the way?" Jameson asked.

"Sure." Caroline scowled at Wade as she led Jameson and Walter out of the camp and into an unknown section of woods.

They hurried through the trees and came to a bend in the dirt road. "Which way?" Walter asked.

"That way, to the right." Caroline pointed.

Jameson inspected the darker path. "Are you sure?"

"Yes, I remember this road. It leads to the three towering trees clumped together that I saw in the distance. I remembered it because it gave me an eerie feeling. I couldn't forget them if I tried."

Walter whispered to Jameson, "We're heading back to Victor's town again. We can't have them see all that food and water there. We need that to survive."

"A town . . . here?" Caroline asked, having overheard. "What about food and water?"

Jameson was livid. Walter had blown it.

"Why didn't you tell us back at the camp?" Caroline asked, her eyes narrowed and teeth clenched.

"Because it's too dangerous to go there right now." Jameson tried to calm her. "We gave your people enough to hold them over until the time is right."

"You still should have said something," Caroline said. "What else are you hiding from us?"

Walter frowned as Jameson glared at him. "We're not hiding anything from you," Jameson said.

"Take me there," Caroline said, planting her feet and crossing her arms. "Take me to this town."

"It's dangerous," Jameson said. "There are homondie crawling all over that area."

"I heard you say the name Victor," Caroline said. "Are there people there too, real humans?"

"Not the kind you want to meet."

"Why?" Caroline asked, but neither man responded. Instead they turned and walked down the path. She had to run to catch up.

Walter and Caroline followed Jameson silently for a few moments. Walter glanced at Caroline and said, "You don't have anything to defend yourself with. Take one of my knives. We're getting into homondie territory here."

"No thank you. I'm fine." Caroline put her hands up and backed away.

"What happens when you get ambushed?" Walter asked.

"I never wander out alone, and there are plenty of people here who have weapons."

"I strongly advise you to carry one," Jameson told her.

"I'll take my chances. Thanks anyway." Caroline hesitated for a moment. "I recognize this area. The dead were over there." She pointed to the right.

"Let's be quiet, just in case there are homondie there." Jameson remained in the lead as they got closer, hoping to find ammunition or weapons before they were noticed.

"Get down and let me take a look." Jameson's voice softened as their feet snapped some twigs. "What happened here?" He looked around at the carnage, a pile of corpses lying on top of one another. "Obviously, someone killed them."

"Was there a war here?" Caroline peered over Jameson's shoulder.

Suddenly, the sound of men's voices could be heard in the distant woods. The small group stopped and hid.

"Stay out of sight," Jameson said to Caroline. "Walter and I will get closer and see what's going on."

Caroline crouched down as Walter and Jameson got as close to Victor's town as they could without being detected. Once there, they peered through the woods and saw a bunch of homondie surrounding Victor and Seth as they were leaving the town.

"What are they doing?" Walter whispered.

"I don't know. We need to get closer so we can hear what they're saying. Maybe we can find out where they're headed. We wouldn't want to end up in the same direction they're going." Jameson edged closer.

Their shouting got louder. Jameson and Walter hid behind a group of trees and saw a homondie pawing at Seth. Seth knocked it back, stormed toward Victor, and pushed him.

"It doesn't look good, whatever's going on between them," Jameson said. "Let's get a little closer. Maybe we can hear what's going on." He crept toward a cluster of bushes and peeked around.

Walter followed and sat next to Jameson.

Victor was lashing out at Seth in anger. The homondie began to surround the pair.

"What are they arguing about?" Walter asked Jameson.

"I don't know. I can't make it out."

"Never mind them for now. They're preoccupied. Let's get out of here before we're seen," Walter said.

Jameson gave a slight nod then hurried back to Caroline.

"Come on, Caroline, we're leaving."

They ran from the town and came across more dead. "This is it," Caroline said.

Walter stopped short. "I can see where a town got sucked in. There are imprints of the streets on the ground. It was probably a flourishing town once."

"It looks like a portal opened here and our people tried to fight off a horde of homondie." Jameson raised an eyebrow.

Caroline stepped around Jameson and toward the bodies. "It looks more like a massacre. What's happening around here?"

"I don't know, but let's not stay long enough to find out," Jameson said, keeping an eye on her.

"Do you think the homondie escaped into our world and they're waging war there?" Caroline's face paled.

"It's a possibility." Jameson wasn't going to tell her what he really thought. "We don't have time to worry about what's happening out there right now. Our only concern is finding Natalie and closing the portals before we have nothing left to go home to."

Jameson knew all too well what was happening in their world, but he didn't want to reveal too much to Caroline. He knew Homondiem had already covered most of it, and with the portals combining and expanding, their world had to be almost gone by now.

Jameson stood, surrounded by a swarm of lifeless, rotting bodies. He bent down and started to dig in. "Look, this human has bullet wounds."

"That means one of our own kind shot him?" Walter asked.

"Looks like it."

"I don't understand what's going on." Caroline backed up, eyes wide, her hand covering her mouth.

Jameson continued to scavenge the bodies, collecting weapons and placing them in a pile.

Walter rummaged through another pile of dead. "They aren't just our kind. There are homondie in here as well."

Jameson turned over another body. A homondie had been pinned underneath, left by some outsiders. It snarled and tried to wriggle free. "This one isn't quite dead yet."

Walter backed up.

"I got it," Jameson said as he watched the homondie snarl.

Walter moved out of the way while Jameson watched the homondie squirm and try to grab him. He glanced over his shoulder as Caroline step closer. "Just go around it, you'll be okay. It can't go anywhere."

"What if it escapes?" Caroline asked. The homondie snapped its teeth at her as she passed.

With one swift motion, Jameson stabbed it in its head. The homondie went limp. "You don't have to worry about that anymore." He pulled out the knife and returned to digging through the pile.

Caroline started to dry heave as Jameson disturbed more rotten corpses and the stench filled the air.

"Are you all right?" he asked as he continued to dig through the bodies.

"I feel a little weak, and my stomach aches a bit," Caroline said, then dry heaved again. She regained her composure and picked up some ammunition lying at her feet. She held it out for Jameson to take.

"Why don't you bring it back to your camp and give it to the others?" he said.

"Please take it. I want to make sure you have enough to rescue Natalie. You're going to need every last bullet." Caroline held it out. "Just in case."

"Thank you." Jameson took it and smiled.

Walter placed everything he'd pilfered in a pile on the ground before them. "There we go, and there's plenty to go around for everyone at the camp too."

"Shh," Jameson said, motioning for Caroline and Walter to listen.

Nobody spoke. All they could hear were the groans from the homondie in the woods. It was a haunting sound.

"It's all right, we'll be safe here as long as they don't get close enough to smell our life."

"Smell our life?" Caroline asked. "What kind of creatures are these?"

"Dead ones who come alive by devouring our flesh and blood as they suck the life out of us," Walter explained.

"Is that what they're after?" she asked.

"Yes," Jameson said. "Now come on. Let's take these weapons and get out of here before they return. We have everything we need."

While they walked toward the camp, Jameson eyed Caroline, who kept looking over her shoulder. "What's the matter?" he asked.

"I'm just checking to see if anyone is following us. I have this strange feeling I can't shake. It feels like we're being watched."

"You would hear them," Jameson said. "I think we're all right."

As soon as they arrived back at the camp, they heard a gunshot in the distance. Wade stepped out from behind a bunch of trees, but Jameson paid no attention to him.

"Do you think that's her?" Walter asked.

"Possibly." Jameson glanced in the direction of the sound.

"What do we do?"

"It sounds like it's far away." Jameson listened to the echoes. "Let's go."

"Is there anything we can do to help?" Zack asked.

"If you help them, you're not staying here anymore," Wade said. "I've had it. Bad enough she's gone off with them." He gestured to Caroline. "I don't need the rest of you unraveling. We need to stick together if we all want to survive."

"If we help them, we can all work together to get out of here," Zack said.

"That's a bunch of bull. They can't get us out of here. I don't trust them, and neither should you." Wade's face grew red, and he stormed off.

"You all stay here and decide what you want to do," Jameson addressed the group. "We'll find Natalie, and when we return, you can either come with us or stay with him."

Caroline tugged on Jameson's shirt as he started to walk away. "Do you really think you can get us out of here?" she asked, hope flashing in her eyes.

"We'll do our best to get you back home," Jameson answered and gave her a brief smile. "We don't have much time," he said. "We're battling time as we speak. Be quick and sharp-witted, and keep out of danger. Our world is dying and becoming one with this world, so stay safe and save as many lives as you can. We'll be back soon." He tossed some extra knives and weapons on the ground. "Use these."

"Thank you," Caroline said, grabbing Walter's arm as he passed. "Whatever you do, just bring Natalie back alive. I'm so scared for her being out there all alone."

"We will." Walter patted Caroline on her shoulder.

"Let's get a move on," Jameson said. He shot one final glance in Wade's direction and walked out of the camp. "I can't wait to find Natalie and Buster and get this over with," he said to Walter.

"Let's just hope Natalie's safe."

"She's strong-willed and levelheaded. I think she'll be fine," Jameson said.

Walter mumbled, "I hope so. I guess we'll see soon enough."

"Come on, pick up the pace. It's time to get moving."

Jameson started to jog, and Walter struggled to keep up. Another gunshot rang out. Jameson ran full speed in the direction of the noise.

"Tracking her down will be like finding a needle in a haystack," Walter said, huffing along behind Jameson.

Another gunshot went off.

"Not if these shots keep firing." Jameson was glad they had a sound to follow but upset to know that Natalie could be in danger. But it was the only thing they had to go by.

As they ran on, Walter slowed down, panting. "We haven't seen any homondie around for some time now, and I haven't heard any more gunshots. Do you think it's too late?"

They stopped running and listened to the silent woods. Walter bent over and placed his hands on his knees, panting and sweating profusely. "Can you hear anything?" he asked. "Twigs crunching, homondie grunting, anything?"

"No, it's all quiet." Jameson took stock of the area. "Where did the homondie go? I hope they're not all after Natalie. She could never take down that many."

"I think the worst may have happened," Walter said.

“I think she was captured and taken back to Victor again,” Jameson said calmly, not wanting to upset Walter further. “We have to get back to the town.”

As they ran toward the town, a loud boom echoed across the land. Jameson saw a flash of light in the distance. “That has to be Natalie. She could be trying to close a portal.”

“I hope we’re not too late.”

“Hurry, this way,” Jameson said and ran.

CHAPTER 20

THE GROUND QUAKED violently, almost knocking Natalie off her feet.

"Keep moving, Buster." Natalie dodged a few homondie, weaving in and out of the trees. "I have to save ammo for when I really need it." She rested against a tree and paused to catch her breath. Buster sat by her feet, tongue hanging out as he panted, staring up at her.

She pulled a bottled water out of her backpack and poured it into her cupped hand for Buster to drink. As he drank, she peered through the woods, watching the homondie head straight for them. There were so many of them now. *They're everywhere.* It looked like every homondie in Homondiem were after her. *I bet Victor's behind this.* She placed the bottle in her backpack, still having no need for it.

Grunting sounds grew louder as the homondie approached. Natalie peeked around the tree and saw a pile of dead humans who hadn't made it. She searched the corpses and found a shotgun and ammo. She picked up the gun. The magazine was as long as the barrel—definitely military. She pulled out the magazine and loaded it, then placed the remaining ammo in her pocket, still watching the homondie closing in. "Come on, Buster. We need to keep moving so we aren't surrounded." She patted her leg, ran off, and Buster followed. She headed back to the portal where she'd left Jameson and Walter.

Natalie wove through the woods. She rounded a large tree and paused in disbelief. She gazed at the portal. "I never thought it would get that big," she mumbled and scanned the area. "Now where did they go? I hope nothing happened to them." Natalie wondered if Jameson and Walter had been sucked into the portal. There was no sign of them. She didn't want to believe that she was alone in this strange world. She shook her head to dispel the thought. *They must have panicked and ran off. They couldn't even wait. I guess it's up to me to close the portal.*

Natalie pointed the device at the portal. "Buster, back up a bit. I don't want you to stand too close." She waved her hand and gestured him.

Natalie's device sounded off and illuminated the area, but nothing else happened. "I hope Jameson set this thing correctly," she murmured as she watched the light grow against the darkened backdrop of the horizon. The portal began to expand at an alarming rate, sucking in everything from the world she'd once known.

Before she could figure out what happened, it was too late. Branches snapped as a horde of homondie came upon her quickly, probably drawn by the light. "Run, Buster, run," she screamed.

Natalie ran hard and fast, not wanting to see what was behind her. She could hear Buster panting when the homondie came out of the woods in every direction, surrounding them. Natalie tripped and dropped her shotgun.

Buster barked, jumped at the homondie, keeping them at bay and away from Natalie while she picked the shotgun up off the ground. She raised it at the creatures, finger on the trigger, but hesitated when she heard a voice say: "Well, well, who do we have here?"

"Victor," she shouted.

"Why so frightened? You know they won't harm you, don't you?" he asked, stepping out from behind a group of ravenous homondie.

"They won't?"

"Of course not," he said.

"Why?" Natalie mumbled as she felt the chip guide her thoughts. She stared at the homondie, trying to understand. She couldn't take her eyes off them.

Victor gave no reply.

It must have something to do with that chip. Victor must be playing with her mind, confusing her and setting the chip to control her thoughts. No matter if Victor was telling the truth, she realized she was seeing the homondie in a different light. Her mind raced backward, like a video rewinding. The chip showed her the way.

Natalie could feel a strange tingling sensation throughout her body as the chip connected to her brain and communicated to her from inside, information she'd never been privy to before. It revealed pictures of them changing and growing into humans as it showed her the ways of the homondie—a life they had never known until they were exposed to it.

She suddenly felt a connection to them, as if she understood what they were going through. To think they had changed and evolved because of the dimensional tear. Not only were the homondie coming alive, but the chip was as well. Natalie could feel the life pulse inside of her as the chip grew. It would expand and create as it fought to stay alive.

Now she could see the homondie's transformation, their sunken black eyes taking on color. Their movements, once sluggish, had become more upright and stable, and their bodies and facial features became more human. The actions and appearance of these creatures, as they developed greater intelligence, didn't worry Natalie. She embraced it.

Natalie felt a sense of ease for the first time. "I can feel it. My mind is connected with the chip. I *am* one with the creation before me."

Victor sung his black magical hymn and stepped through the crowd of homondie to face Natalie. He snatched her shotgun from her hands and searched her. "Where's my staff?" he yelled at her as Seth appeared beside him.

"I don't know," Natalie answered.

"Of course, you know. You steal my chip and now my staff? I want them back! The homondie may not harm you, but I will!" The vein in Victor's forehead swelled and his face reddened. "We need that staff before the merger of the final portal is complete. We have to take control of this world before that happens and our worlds become one."

"I swear I don't know where it is," Natalie said, frightened of Victor's wrath. She recognized the danger she was in but didn't know how to get out of it.

"You there," he said, addressing the closest homondie, "grab her and hold her down. Seth, go out and find my Staff of Life. We're taking the chip out of her here and now!" Victor's eyes were alight with fury.

The homondie grabbed Natalie as Buster barked.

"Kill that dog!"

"Victor, wait and think this over," Seth said. "There's no need to harm him."

"Why is that?"

"Killing the dog won't change anything, and we don't have much time. We need to focus on Natalie and the staff. The chip is useless without the Staff of Life, and we don't know if it can survive without a host. Besides, we can't go running around Homondiem wasting our time not knowing where it may be hidden when these portals are about to blow at any minute."

"Don't you think I know that?" Victor snarled. "I know there's nothing I can do until I get that staff back, but I'm not going to have her lead us on a wild-goose chase all over Homondiem," he bellowed. "We're better off getting the chip out and trying to find the staff on our own."

"Buster could find it," Natalie said, desperation in her voice. "He has a keen sense. I know he could take you right to it."

Victor approached Natalie, his face inches from hers. He glared at her. "This better not be a trick."

Buster stood at Natalie's side.

Victor glanced at the dog with disgust. "Well, what are you waiting for? Send him off."

"I have to go with him," Natalie said. "I'm the only one who can direct him."

"You don't know what my homondie are capable of. They're getting quite intelligent now. Look how easily they found you." Victor raised his arms toward the creatures.

"Didn't you think that making them intelligent could backfire? Aren't you worried they'll become so intelligent they won't listen to you anymore?" Natalie asked.

Victor scowled at her. "That's nonsense. They know I created them. I brought them life and created a paradise for them to live in."

"Paradise?" Natalie let out a cruel laugh. "This is what you call paradise? They're bloodthirsty killing machines in a death-racked world. That's not my idea of paradise."

"To each their own." Victor leered at Natalie. "My patience has grown thin." He sneered. "Take her to town and kill the dog!"

"No," Natalie screamed.

"Tell me where the staff is," Victor yelled. "Tell me now or I will kill him in front of you and I'll find it on my own."

"I lost it in the woods over that way." Natalie's hand shook as she pointed into the distance.

Victor turned to look in the direction Natalie pointed.

She eyed Buster and nodded in Victor's direction.

Buster leaped onto Victor's back and knocked him down. Victor dropped the shotgun. It went off and hit a homondie.

"Run, Buster!" Natalie grabbed her shotgun from the ground, slammed Victor in the head with the stock, and darted through the crowd of homondie after the dog.

Seth helped Victor to his feet while the homondie stood around waiting for orders.

"You idiots," Victor yelled. "What are you doing? Get her! Don't let her get away!" Victor wrenched himself from Seth's grasp and stood. He rubbed his head and brushed the dirt from his clothes.

The homondie ran after Natalie and Buster. Natalie looked back and saw them gaining on her, seeming to develop more humanlike forms even as they chased her. "No, it can't be," she cried. "I think their transformation to human forms are almost complete."

"Come, Buster. Come on, keep up . . . Buster?" Natalie peered over her shoulder and saw Buster growling at some homondie. She stopped and yelled, "Buster, no, come back here!"

The homondie surrounded Buster and attacked. They clawed at him and pinned him down. Natalie raised her gun and shot at the closest one just as it bit Buster. Buster yelped and went limp. She feared the worst.

Natalie ran to Buster and shot each of the homondie. She knelt next to him and examined a deep puncture wound in his thigh. “Oh, Buster, this doesn't look good,” she said, holding back her tears. She pressed her hands to his wound to try to stop the bleeding, but it only trickled through her fingers.

She cradled Buster as he lay on the ground and whimpered. “The homondie are coming,” she whispered, giving him a slight nudge. “We've got to get going.” He stood, but his legs gave way, and he dropped to the ground. She tried desperately to pick him up, but he was too heavy. Teary-eyed, she muttered, “Come on, Buster, no time to play, get up. We have to leave now.” She didn't know what to do. Her voice rose loud and firm. “Buster, come on, get up, let's go!” But he made no motion to move.

Natalie evaluated the crowd of homondie fast approaching. Not wanting to leave Buster's side, she readied herself for battle. She reloaded with the last of her ammo. “Well, Buster, this is it. I hope I can hold them back long enough to give you the time you need.”

Just as the homondie closed in, Buster pulled himself unsteadily to his feet.

“Good boy,” Natalie said. “Now run as fast as you can!” She ran backward and shot at the homondie while Buster limped away, but it wasn't fast enough. She grabbed his collar and tried to pull him along, but it didn't help. Blood seeped out from his wound, leaving a trail on the ground. Buster was slowing down, and the homondie were gaining speed.

“Buster, keep going. We need to find the others so they can help us.” Natalie tugged on the dog's collar.

They swayed between the trees and ran until Buster collapsed. “Get up, Buster! They're almost here!” Natalie yanked on his collar once more, but he didn't move. The homondies' moans grew louder as they lurched though the woods in pursuit. Natalie stood ready with her shotgun raised, watching the homondie approach. “Don't worry, Buster, I'm not leaving your side.”

A flock of homondie began to surround them. Natalie's heart raced. She wondered how they were going to make it out alive. She shot one homondie at a time, but it wasn't enough. There were too many of them.

As she spun around to aim at an oncoming homondie, she heard the buzz of a stray bullet whizzing past her ear. The homondie began to fall at her feet as Jameson and Walter ran toward her. Natalie grinned in relief.

"Natalie, come on," Jameson said.

"I can't, Buster's hurt."

Jameson ran to Buster and picked him up. "This way," he shouted.

Victor hollered as he came into view, "There's no place to hide, Natalie! No matter where you go in Homondiem, my homondie will find you!"

As the group ran, Jameson panted and staggered. Natalie could see that carrying Buster was taking a toll on him.

"Do you want me to carry him?" Walter asked, although he could barely keep up.

"No, I got it."

"Jameson, wait." Natalie stopped.

"They'll be here any moment," Jameson said. "Can't you hear them?" He looked around frantically. "I don't know if we can protect Buster, but I can't have anything happen to him. What would we do without him?"

Natalie closed her eyes. "This way," she said, opening them and pointing in a different direction. "We'll be safe for a few minutes over there."

"How can we be safe when they can smell our lives?" Walter said.

"They have to be in range first. Trust me, it'll be safe there."

The men followed Natalie, moving through the woods in every direction. Once out of sight of the homondie, Natalie stopped. "Get down in the underbrush."

Jameson placed Buster on the ground while Natalie removed some gauze from her backpack and held it to Buster's wound. Buster's body shook then went limp. His eyes closed, and he lay motionless.

"Where's the antiserum?" Natalie cried.

"You don't have to worry about him becoming a half-life," Jameson said. "Animals can't be infected by a homondie bite." Jameson lifted the gauze and checked Buster's wound. "This is bad."

Natalie's stomach churned, and she felt a bit woozy.

"He lost a lot of blood. It's up to you, Natalie. Only you can save him now."

"I can? What can I do?"

"Use the chip," Jameson said, gesturing at Natalie's scalp. "Your healing powers through that chip should allow you to heal others as well as yourself."

Natalie stared at Buster. "I'm not sure what to do." She placed the gauze back over his wound, held it tight, and closed her eyes.

"Do something," Walter yelled.

Natalie opened her eyes. "Stop shouting at me and let me concentrate!"

"Think. You'll know what to do," Walter said, his voice having dropped to a soothing tone.

Natalie thought of the wound on her own leg and how it had healed. She placed her hands over Buster's blood-soaked bandages, closed her eyes, and concentrated. She opened her eyes, removed her hands, and lifted the bandage.

Buster opened his eyes, stood, wagged his tail, and licked Natalie's face. All that remained was dried blood and a small scar. "Good thing you didn't die. I don't know how I'd get through this world without you," she said, hugging the dog. "It's hard to believe he's alive because of the chip."

"It's growing and evolving inside you as we speak," Walter said. "The chip has activated a part of your brain that gives you these powers. That's why you healed on your own earlier, and that's why Buster's alive today. Now that you're one with the chip, you have the ability to give life to anyone you choose or to take it away."

"Give *or* take?" Natalie questioned.

Jameson scowled at Walter. "The homondie are coming. Let's get back to the camp. They're waiting for us."

"A camp, with people? Are you saying you saw other people alive in here?" Natalie asked, hopeful. "We haven't seen anyone since we saw that man through the shack portal."

"He's there and so are a few more," Walter told her, "and they're waiting for us to take them home. We can't leave them here to die. We need to get them to the portal and close it so we can all get back together."

"You don't have to worry about that anymore," Natalie said flatly.

"What do you mean?" Walter asked.

"I was at the portal, but I couldn't close it."

"Couldn't close it?" Walter's voice rose as he looked at Jameson.

"Jameson, what did you do to the device?" Natalie asked.

"I didn't do anything." Jameson folded his arms across his chest.

"Then why did it get worse when I tried to use it?" she asked.

"I don't know. Maybe you pressed the wrong buttons."

"I know I did it right," she said. "It must have to do with the portal itself." Natalie thought for a moment. "There has to be a way to close it. In the meantime, we'll get the others and take them to the portal with us. We can figure it out from there."

"Sounds like a plan," Walter said.

Natalie glanced at Jameson, and they heard Victor shouting in the distance, "I've had enough of this! Seth, go out with these idiots, kill all the outsiders, and bring the staff and Natalie's head back to me. Don't fail me this time!"

"I think it's time to get a move on," Walter said. "We have to get back there before the homondie find us and we're all dead. Come on, they're counting on us." Walter got up and took off in the direction of the camp.

Natalie paused, stumbled, held onto a tree, and closed her eyes. So many things rushed through her mind at once that she felt the need to sit and absorb every last detail. The chip was trying to tell her something. Her gaze went right through Jameson. "I don't feel so well. What's wrong with me?"

"Natalie, are you all right?" he asked.

Her head spun as her legs gave out. She fell into his arms, unconscious.

CHAPTER 21

JAMESON GUIDED NATALIE carefully to the ground. "Walter," Jameson called him back. "This is worse than I thought. That chip seems like it's taking full control over Natalie."

"Will we be able to separate it from her?" Walter asked.

"I don't know. It may retaliate if we do."

"What do you mean?"

"It may think we're a threat, but we're still going to have to try. No time like the present." Jameson pulled out his knife. "Get that staff ready." He touched Natalie's scalp with the knife. Her eyes popped open.

Jameson dropped the knife on the ground. "Oh, thank God you're all right. We were so worried!"

Natalie sat up.

"Are you okay to walk?" Jameson asked.

Natalie rubbed her head. "Yes, I'm fine. Let's head out to that camp."

Jameson discreetly picked up his knife and guided Natalie to her feet.

"Let's go, Buster," Natalie said. The dog followed.

They walked briskly with Jameson leading the pack. Jameson stopped and glanced around the woods. "Something's not right."

"You're right," Natalie said.

Another chill filled the air, and their breath caught and lingered. It hovered motionless before their eyes.

"Huh?" Jameson watched as his cold breath hung in the air. He opened his mouth to yell "Run" but while his lips moved, there was no sound.

A surreal silence filled the air as the group sprinted through the woods. Not even their feet running across the dry land made a sound. After a moment, an enormous burst of light cast over the horizon followed by a deafening boom. Jameson's ears felt like they'd been punctured.

The terrain rumbled beneath their feet and heaved up, knocking them over. They landed on their hands and knees, cutting themselves on twigs and jagged rocks.

As soon as the light dissipated and the ground stabilized, the darkened haze brought forth a night sky, and the silence broke. A woman's voice echoed throughout the woods. "Where are they? I want to go home," she screamed.

"That came from over there." Natalie grabbed a flashlight out of her backpack and ran toward the voice.

"Natalie, wait for us," Jameson yelled, ears still ringing. He caught up, not wanting to lose her again. Walter was still on the ground. "Walter, come on!"

"Natalie, slow down," Walter shouted.

The blackened haze slowly dissipated as the light began to peek through the sky once again. A stream of light flowed through the trees revealing Caroline in the distance, crying in panic. She knelt on the ground and covered her ears.

Natalie ran straight to the sobbing woman. She placed her hand on Caroline's shoulder. "It's okay. It stopped. Don't worry, you're safe with us." She helped her stand.

The woman brushed herself off and regained her composure. "Thank you so much," she said.

Jameson and Walter caught up to Natalie. "Natalie, don't run off like that again. We need to stick together," Jameson said.

"Natalie?" Caroline asked.

"Yes?"

"Oh," Caroline said, looking confused. "You're not the Natalie Thompson I know."

"How did you know my name?"

"They told us they had to go out and find you and I thought you were someone I knew."

"Maybe you knew Jameson's girlfriend?" Natalie said. "She had the same name as me."

"It's strange that you two have the same name."

"Yes, it is."

Jameson crossed his arms. "There are probably thousands of people with the same name around the world. It's not that strange."

"But in one place?" Caroline asked.

"It doesn't matter," Jameson said, dismissing the line of inquiry with a wave of his hand. "After that last blast, I don't think there's much of our world left."

"Will we still be able to go back home?" Caroline asked as she guided them into the camp.

"I don't know anymore," Jameson said.

Caroline's face fell as her lips sagged. You could see the hope she'd felt nearly extinguished.

"We may have a problem," Walter said as they walked into the campsite.

"What problem?" Zack stood and asked. "Are you telling us we can't go home now? You said we could when you came back."

"See? I told you they were lying." Wade snickered. "They can't take you home!" He forced his way through the group.

"I didn't say we could," Jameson said. "I said we would try our best. After that blast, I'm not sure."

"What he means is we can't go home—yet," Natalie said. "I'm sure we can figure out a way."

"Who are you to give them false promises?" Wade, with fury in his eyes, gleamed at Natalie, but Jameson stepped between them.

"Calm down." Jameson tensed, ready for an attack.

"Don't tell me to calm down! You gave these people false hope. They waited here, expecting to go home, and now you say they can't? We could have been out searching for a way back by ourselves!" Infuriated, Wade shoved Jameson. "You wasted our time!"

Jameson, ready to strike, found himself held back by Walter. "Look, fighting isn't going to solve our problem. If you give us a moment, we'll explain," Walter said.

"Get out of my way, old man, before you get hurt," Wade said.

"Stop it, stop it now," Caroline screamed. "I can't take it anymore. Wade, just listen to them for a minute, please. We'd all like to hear what they have to say."

The others grabbed Wade and pulled him away to calm him down. Wade flung his hands up, as if giving up, and stormed away.

"I'm not sure what's wrong," Jameson said. "Earlier we tried to close a portal, but the portals seemed to have expanded and formed into one."

"It may have been too strong to close with one device," Natalie interjected, "but that doesn't mean we can never go home. I think we can combine our devices, and using them together, we might be able to close it. Once the closure begins, everything will reverse, and we'll be forced back into our world. But don't worry, no matter what, Jameson is a top-notch scientist and will find us a way back."

"Oh, now all of sudden, we find out he's a scientist and it's all up to him?" Wade had stormed back. "It seems strange that he overlooked telling us that bit of information." He peered at Natalie. "How do you know he even wants to go home?"

"That's absurd! Of course, he wants to go home," Natalie said. "Why would anyone want to live in a place like this?"

"I don't know, but there's something about those two I don't trust." Wade stared through the group, looking directly at Jameson and Walter.

"I don't think we'll ever get back home after that last explosion. I think we're doomed," Zack said, holding his sister in his arms.

"You have to keep your faith." Natalie patted Zack on the shoulder. "We'll be back home in no time."

"Didn't you feel what just happened?" he cried.

"I think our world is in trouble, and I don't see us living past the hour," Zoey whimpered in his arms.

"We may never return home," Caroline said, shaking her head with her hands over her face.

While the group discussed their fate, Jameson waited for the right moment. He stepped back and nudged Natalie and Walter, keeping a watchful eye on Wade. "He's right, you know. It's too late. I believe this dimension has taken over our world."

"If that happened, it's over for all of us," Walter said. "Now I don't know if there ever was a fourth dimension that could repair this situation."

"That's one more reason to keep going," Natalie said, her voice rising in volume. "You dragged me into this, and you're not giving up now. I don't believe our world is gone, and we're going to find a way back home, whether you like it or not, because we're not staying here. Now start thinking, damn it!"

Jameson looked toward the group and shushed Natalie as Caroline approached them. "Is something wrong?" she asked.

"No," Natalie said, staring at the ground. "Everything's fine. We were just discussing the best way to get all of you home."

"What are we supposed to do, wait here for your return again?" Zack asked.

"Not this time. You're coming with us," Natalie said. "Once we get the portal closure started, we're going to use it to get back home. Besides, it's safer to stick together. We could use the help battling the homondie. I'm sure they're out hunting for us as we speak, and they're definitely going to be guarding the portal."

"Rest up and prepare yourselves for battle. We'll leave shortly," Jameson said. He wasn't happy with Natalie's decision but had no choice but to agree with her for the moment.

"I don't know who gave you the right to tell these people what to do, but I'm telling you they're not going anywhere," Wade said. "Most of them don't even know how to fight, and I'm not going to let you get them killed."

Jameson stepped in front of Wade, his face inches away. "Why don't you leave it up to them if they want to stay or leave? I'm getting awfully tired of you."

"They don't know what they want," Wade said. "I tell them what to do around here. I know what they need to survive because

I've been keeping them alive." Wade and Jameson stood chest to chest.

Walter said angrily, "Sitting in a camp waiting to starve doesn't sound like a good plan to me."

"Think what you want," Wade said as he walked toward Walter. "I've gotten us through this mess so far." He waved his hand in a gesture of shooing him away. "Why don't you go back to wherever you came from and leave us alone?"

"Who are you to tell us to leave?" Natalie said.

"I'm the one in charge."

"Says who?" Natalie glared fearlessly at Wade.

"You don't need to worry about it. You just need to walk away from here and leave this to me," Wade said.

"That's not going to happen," Natalie said, stepping closer to Wade and looking him dead in the eye. "We need to make things right, so no matter what, we'll stop this from happening and get these people home safely, with or without your cooperation."

"We'll help however we can." Caroline tried to hide her fear, but her voice shook, giving her away.

"We'll see about that!" Wade sneered and walked away.

Jameson pulled Natalie to the side and whispered, "I don't trust that guy. We just met these people, and we don't know who they really are. We can never be too cautious."

"I don't trust him either," Natalie said, "but it's better to be safe by keeping him where we can see him. Besides, this homondie world has grown, and there are too many of them for us to fight off by ourselves. Every man counts. Without them, we're sitting ducks. The more of us there are, the better."

"All right," Jameson said reluctantly. "I'll go with you on this one, but I'll keep an eye on him, and if he does anything stupid, we're cutting him loose."

Walter stepped up. "I hope you know what you're doing."

"I hope so too," Natalie mumbled.

Jameson was worried. Wade was a threat, but to keep his real plan quiet, he had to agree. "Don't get your hopes up. I don't know if we can even close the portal anymore. This might all be for nothing."

"It doesn't matter," Natalie said. "These people still need something to hope for. I need something to hope for."

Jameson directed the group, "Everyone, check your weapons and make sure you have enough ammo. Walter will pass out what we have if you're low."

Natalie opened her backpack and handed Caroline water bottles and granola bars. "Please pass these out and make sure everyone gets some." She zipped her bag back up and flung the straps over her shoulders. She thought it was odd to still have no hunger or thirst, yet she felt full and vibrant.

CHAPTER 22

JAMESON, NATALIE, AND Walter were talking among themselves when Jameson saw Caroline coming up behind them. "Shh," he said.

Caroline stopped in front of Natalie. "Sorry to interrupt."

"What is it?" Natalie asked.

"I'm ready to go, but I'm having a hard time thinking I might need to battle the homondie. I don't think I can do it." Caroline's lips quivered.

Natalie drew closer and put her hands on the woman's shoulders to force her to meet her gaze. "Caroline, listen to me. I may have only known you for a short time, but you're stronger than you think."

Caroline's eyes misted over as Natalie placed an arm around her. "It's okay to be scared, but we're all here, together, to help each other. You just need to stick with the group, and you'll be fine. We'll all keep an eye out for you, but please do me one favor, would you?"

Caroline wiped her sleeve across her face. "What is it?"

"Hold on to this for me." Natalie pulled a gun from her holster and held it out for Caroline. "Keep it close and don't let it go. It's for your safety, I need you to take it."

"Natalie, no, no, I can't—" Caroline shook her head and backed up. "I can't take that."

"You have to," Natalie insisted. "For the survival of our group, you have to be able to help in this battle. This is a battle for our lives. I can't have you running around without a weapon. It's for your safety as well as ours."

"It's all right. I'll just stay close to someone who has a weapon. I'll be fine."

"We won't be able to protect you if we get ambushed. Believe me, there's no other way around it. You need a gun."

"But Natalie—" Caroline started to cry. "My dad was in the military, and he died in the line of fire. He used to teach me that guns are good as long as you know how to handle and respect them, but I hate them. I swore when my dad died I would never touch a gun ever again." She whimpered. "It doesn't matter. Nothing matters anymore."

"You know that's not true," Natalie said. "Our survival matters."

Caroline turned away to hide her tears and wiped her face.

"Come on, take it," Natalie said. "I think your father would want it this way. I doubt he would want to see his daughter give up so easily." She held out the gun, but Caroline still wouldn't take it.

Caroline frowned and sniffled. She looked at the group. All of them were staring back at her, waiting for her decision. "Okay," Caroline muttered. She took the gun with shaky hands and stared at it.

"The show's over. Get your things together and we'll call you when we're ready to go." Jameson lead Natalie and Walter away from the rest of the group. Caroline followed. She stuck close to Natalie, sensing she was a port in the storm. Jameson worried their connection might pose a threat to his plans for Natalie. He had to find a way to stop it.

They moved to the end of the campsite. Caroline sat next to Natalie. She placed the gun on her lap while Walter and Jameson leaned against trees on the opposite side. Walter pulled out a handful of dog food from his pocket and fed it to Buster while he took a few bites of his granola bar. He drank some water and gave the rest to the dog.

When he was done, Buster went over to Natalie. He sprawled on the ground and laid his head on her leg. She placed her hand between his ears and slid it down to his back, repeating the action over and over.

Jameson took note of the conversation between the two women. He glanced at them now and then, and he heard every word, even though he pretended he wasn't listening.

"I wanted to thank you for helping all of us," Caroline murmured.

"It doesn't seem like they're too thankful," Natalie replied.

"They're scared, that's all." Caroline bit back a sob.

"Caroline, don't cry. We'll find a way back home."

"That's the problem," she said, letting her tears fall freely. "We don't have a home anymore. My town was wiped out, and probably the rest of the world by now."

"We're not sure everything is gone," Natalie said.

"Yes it is, and seeing my hometown destroyed was a terrible thing to watch. I saw people die," Caroline cried. "The people, buildings, homes, everything is gone."

"I know. I was out in it myself," Natalie said.

"So you saw what happened. It didn't just happen to anyone. It happened to me, you, and to the people we knew and loved. After all that, you know what?"

"What's that?"

"We're the only ones who survived." Caroline wiped her eyes.

"There could be others we haven't found yet."

"I don't think so. It was awful. When I woke up, I was lying among the dead. People I'd known my whole life, family and friends."

"I'm so sorry you had to go through that." Natalie gave her shoulder a comforting pat.

Staring down at the gun in her hands, Caroline continued, "When I woke up, I was lying on my back, pinned, and it was dark. I thought, 'What happened?' My head was full of images I couldn't make sense of. When I finally got out and sat up, I felt wet, and I thought, 'What's going on? Am I covered in sweat?' I panicked and tried to figure out where I was, but I had to wait for my eyes to adjust to the darkness. I thought it was a dream." Caroline took a deep breath and exhaled slowly through her pursed lips. She continued, "I moved along the ground and squinted. I couldn't see where I was or where I was going, but I started to remember. My heart began to race when I realized something wasn't right. I could feel my heart pound through my chest and into my throat. I was almost hyperventilating but I managed to calm myself down. I called out, but no one answered. I stood when I saw a light in the distance. The light came at me fast, and I could see where I was. I screamed, but no one heard me because everyone was dead. I stood there, drenched in blood and dirt, looking at the familiar faces from my town. I covered my eyes. That's when I remembered a dark hole growing bigger and bigger until it swallowed our whole town. People were running and screaming, but they had no place to go, and then these creatures . . ."

Caroline started to sob uncontrollably as Natalie squeezed her shoulder.

"You're here with us now," Natalie said.

Caroline sniveled a few more times until she regained her composure. She sat quietly for a moment, then said, "My hands." She held them out and turned them over. "I remember skimming them across my clothing and raising them up to my face. I looked at them, covered in blood. I backed up and fell over several bodies. I didn't know where to go. I was in shock. I tried to scream, but nothing came out. I struggled to move, to find answers, but nothing made sense."

Caroline paused again, emitting short, panicked breaths. "I'm so sorry, Natalie," she said as she tried to control the waver in her voice.

"It's okay," Natalie said.

"I stared at the dead bodies. I thought it was a nightmare," she said, "until I heard that sound, the sound of shuffling feet and moaning came straight for me. I remember I tried to bury myself in the pile of the dead. I thought maybe I could hide from whatever was coming, but it didn't work. I heard something else. It sounded like something sniffing, and that's when it happened."

"What happened, Caroline? It's okay, get it all out." Natalie rubbed her shoulder, trying to keep her calm.

"It attacked. I kicked it and screamed. It tried to grab me. I kicked it back, and it fell down." She sniffled. "That's all I needed, right? Just a second? I got up the courage to move, and I ran. I ran as fast as I could to get out of there, and I didn't want to look back. I didn't have to because I knew, I knew from the sounds behind me that it was chasing me. I was sweating, and my whole body shook, but I couldn't stop running. I kept running until the others found me and killed it." She lifted the gun. "If only I had this on me. Funny how things work out, don't you think?" Caroline chuckled bitterly, pulling herself upright, and drying her eyes with the back of her hand.

Jameson interrupted the women, "Natalie, it's time to leave."

"All right, we're ready."

"Thank you, Natalie." Caroline smiled.

"For what?"

"For listening. I know you're in the same situation, but it's good to get it out so I can clear my head."

"That's all right." Natalie smiled at her. "Do you think you're up for this?"

"I am," Caroline said. "I realize I need to fight for what we lost, for the things they took away, all those things we can never get back." She stood. "Let's do this."

Caroline followed Jameson and Natalie back to the others. "Natalie," Jameson whispered, "I need to speak to you for a minute." He grabbed her arm and glanced over her shoulder. "Alone," he told Caroline.

"Of course," she said. "I'll get my things."

Keeping a firm grip on Natalie's arm, Jameson led her away from the others. He made sure Caroline was out of earshot before he asked, "Is that wise to give her a gun? She seems awfully unstable."

"Yes," Natalie said. "Her nerves may be shot, but she lost more than her nerves, she lost everything."

"We don't know how well these people can handle the homondie, never mind weapons." Jameson glared over his shoulder at Caroline.

"I know she's a bit stressed, but aren't we all?" Natalie said. "Just give her a chance. She could get through this without any problems."

"I'm not sure your word on this is enough," Jameson said.

"We don't have time to sit here and talk about it," Natalie said. "We need everyone to have a weapon. If it makes you feel any better, I'll keep an eye on her. You have your own problems to deal with."

"You better hope she keeps it together," Jameson said. "I'll take that raving maniac and you deal with her." Jameson smirked at Wade, watching as he loaded his rifle. "You know he's going to have it out with us sooner or later. He thinks we're taking his people away from him. He's trouble."

"I know, but we can't leave anyone alone out here. Besides, we don't have time to deal with him. We have to leave."

Jameson agreed with a nod.

Natalie approached Caroline, and Walter stepped up to Jameson. "Do you know what you're doing?" Walter asked. "We can't be responsible for them, not at a time like this. We have a mission to complete, and they'll just slow us down."

"Do I need to remind you again that we need to be careful? It would be suspicious if we told Natalie that Caroline and the others can't go. Don't worry, I have a plan," Jameson whispered. "I'll tell you later."

Jameson and Walter marched over to the group who stood, awaiting orders. "This is it," Jameson directed the group. "Follow us to the portal and keep tight. Once we get there for the final closure, everyone must be armed and ready for anything. We don't know what other surprises may be waiting for us." Jameson looked at Caroline. "Do you have enough rounds?"

"I'm fine."

"Here, put these in your pocket," he said, handing her a few more. "Just in case." He smiled.

"Thank you." She smiled back.

Jameson checked his device. It was working again. He held it up and scanned the area. "The portal isn't far from here. We need to head a bit southwest, over this way." He headed off in the direction he'd indicated, and the group followed.

Natalie walked next to Jameson. "It's depressing thinking about how these people want to go home so badly and knowing this may all be in vain. However it ends, we have to stay strong and believe we can win this. Joining forces with these people may have made our odds even greater."

Jameson ignored Natalie, staring down the path as they walked. He had other more important things on his mind, plans that needed to be worked out. He didn't care about the frivolous things she was talking about.

"What are we going to do about the portal when we get there?" she asked. "Did you figure it out yet?"

"There could be something wrong with your device," Jameson said. "Let me see it."

Natalie handed him the device, and Jameson opened the back of the monitor. He pulled and pushed the wires around. "Oh, here's the culprit," he said. "You had a loose wire, that's all." Jameson fiddled with the inside components. "Here you go. All set." He faked a smile as he handed it back to her. "Ready to close the portal?"

"You said the portal couldn't be closed anymore."

"I could be wrong. Anyway, like you said, we have to try, right?"

Buster growled, and Jameson fell silent. He stopped and ducked behind a tree, pulling Natalie down with him as the rest followed.

"I remember this area. The portal was straight ahead," Natalie whispered and pointed. A glow brightened the forest, revealing its location, and drawing everyone's gaze. "Look how much it's grown since the last time."

When Natalie's eyes met Jameson's, he knew the chip was taking control. *Natalie must be able to feel it by now.* He could see the light run across her irises. It stretched from one end to the other, until it burst, and faded into a flicker while it processed her thoughts. He knew what he had to do, and quickly, before the others noticed.

The homondie came into view. Jameson watched them lift their noses and smell the air, then charged like ravenous wolves. He nodded at Natalie and she nodded back, then stood. "Keep the homondie at bay so Natalie can get to the portal," he instructed the group. "Prepare to fire when the homondie are in range."

Slow and steady, Natalie walked straight to the portal as if being drawn to it. Homondie walked past her and toward the others as if she didn't exist. Jameson watched every movement, amazed.

Weapons ready, the group aimed and fired at the advancing homondie. Jameson could see Natalie getting closer and closer to the portal. She was totally calm. Buster, evidently sensing no threat, kept by Jameson's side.

One of the homondie broke from the pack, and Buster barked. Jameson lifted his rifle, aimed, and fired, killing it.

Natalie began to pick up speed, and then suddenly, she zoomed toward the portal as the homondie closed in.

"Clear the area to get her to the portal," Jameson hollered as he fired shot after shot.

The others followed suit, but the homondie were surrounding them.

"There are too many to fight off, and we're running out of ammunition," Zack yelled to Jameson.

"Save your ammo and start using your knives!" Jameson took his attention off the homondie momentarily.

"Watch out," Caroline yelled.

Jameson turned around and glowered at Caroline, who pointed her gun straight at him. Shot after shot, she fired. Jameson spun and ducked as her shots whizzed by his ears. The homondie lay dead at his feet. He glanced at Caroline, winked, then moved on to another homondie fast approaching. He was grateful, but he wasn't going to show it.

CHAPTER 23

THE OTHERS STAYED behind while Natalie moved steadily toward the portal. Gunshots, grunting, and shouting rang out all around her, but she paid it no mind. She needed to stay focused as she walked through the crowd of homondie, not a hesitation in her step.

The ground began to rumble, and the portal expanded slowly.

"Look out, Natalie," Jameson yelled.

She stood before the massive portal, but before she could use the device, Caroline screamed, "Walter!" Natalie's concentration broke. She flinched and turned to Walter.

A pack of homondie were heading straight for him. As the homondie approached, he aimed and pulled the trigger, but the gun merely clicked in his hand. He ran in the opposite direction, leaving the homondie between him and help.

"Jameson, do something," Natalie screamed.

Walter didn't get far. He was surrounded while trying to reload. He kicked and pushed the homondie back, dropping his ammunition in the process. Lifting the rifle in defense, he brought it down violently until it went through the homondie's head. He swung the rifle wildly at the others and felt around his belt for his knife.

Jameson raised his gun and aimed at the homondie surrounding Walter. "I can't get a clear shot through the trees. Have Wade take it, he's closer."

"You there," Natalie yelled at Wade. "Get those homondie away from Walter."

Walter pulled the knife out and slashed at the closest homondie, killing it. Another attacked from behind. It grabbed Walter and tried to take a bite out of his neck. He spun out of its grasp and the homondie lost its balance, then fell.

Wade spun around, making eye contact with Natalie, then sliced the throat of the homondie next to him. He raised his gun and fired, hitting Walter instead of the homondie.

"You shot Walter!" Natalie clenched her jaw and ran to the old man.

The knife slid from Walter's fingers onto the ground. He dropped to his knees and pressed his hand to his side. Blood soaked through his shirt.

The homondie prepared to attack Walter but paused when Natalie arrived. She stared into the eyes of the homondie before her as she spoke to Walter, "Don't worry, you're safe with me." The homondie seemed to understand and retreated. The others followed, leaving Natalie to tend to Walter.

Wade fired a second time, this time killing the homondie as it turned to leave. It dropped to the ground on top of Walter as Natalie knelt beside him.

Natalie rolled the homondie off Walter and held out a firm hand. He allowed her to pull him to his feet. She grabbed him as he limped along, unable to put pressure on his injured side.

Jameson marched toward Wade, who put his fists up to defend himself, ready for the attack, but Jameson gave him a backhand to the face. Wade's hands dropped, and he fell to the ground.

"Jameson, leave him alone," Natalie said. "Take Walter somewhere safe. There are more homondie approaching."

Walter grunted as Jameson grabbed him. "What are you doing? Aren't you coming?"

"I'll be right behind you to make sure the homondie don't pass." Natalie stared at the group. She felt her eyes twitch as her voice dropped to a calm monotone. She couldn't control it. "Leave now, all of you. Get Walter out of here. I'll hold them off."

Walter's blood trickled through his hand and puddled onto the ground. "I don't feel so well." He swayed as he started to fade in and out, nearly falling over before Jameson caught him.

The portal fluctuated and forced out a gust of air. It pushed them back and knocked them over, but there was no effect on the homondie in its path. Natalie felt nothing either. Strange. A tremor followed and shook the ground, expanding as it passed. It rocked the trees; a few fell.

Jameson threw Walter's arm over his shoulder. "Hang on the best you can," he told the old man. "We're going to make a run for it."

The pair ran, and Natalie watched as she backed up, gun raised, ready to provide cover.

"Something's coming," Jameson whispered.

Heavy footsteps grew nearer.

They stopped and hid amid a cluster of trees.

Natalie helped Jameson place Walter on the ground and leaned him against a tree. They readied their weapons.

Wade pushed through the dense wooded area toward the group.

"You scared us." Caroline put her hand over her heart and lowered her gun.

Natalie looked around as she spoke. "There are no more homondie in the vicinity. We're in no imminent danger."

Wade leaned against a tree, rifle held in his arms.

"Hang in there, Walter. I'm here to help you." Natalie squatted beside Walter and shifted into paramedic mode. "You're breathing well, and your heart rate seems fine." She lifted his shirt to examine the injury. "It looks like the bullet only grazed you, so that's a relief. Let's get some dressings on that wound."

Walter rummaged through his backpack, pulled out some gauze, and handed it to Natalie. She held the gauze in her hands and applied pressure to the wound. He grunted in pain, and she smiled. "You'll be fine."

"I'll be right back." Jameson got up, visibly angry, and headed toward Wade, grabbing his rifle out of his hands. "What were you doing out there? You could have killed him."

"It was an accident," Wade said. "I was aiming for the homondie." He pulled away from Jameson, who put his finger on the trigger. "It's not my fault he twitched. I think he stepped in front of the bullet on purpose."

"Some accident," Jameson said. "Maybe you just don't know how to shoot a gun." They both had their hands on the rifle, tugging it between them.

"I was trying to save his life," Wade growled. They struggled over the rifle, with Wade trying to pull the trigger.

"It didn't look that way to me." Jameson let go of the rifle, raised his handgun, and trained it on Wade.

"What are you saying? That I tried to kill him on purpose?" Wade said.

"Yes, you did it intentionally."

Wade pushed Jameson, and Jameson pushed back.

"If I were to shoot anyone on purpose, it would be you, and it would be more than a scratch," Wade yelled.

"Jameson, no." Natalie grabbed Walter's hand and placed it over the gauze. "Press here," she said.

"That's enough!" Natalie got between them. "Both of you lower your weapons and calm down. You can't go around attacking each other." Natalie placed her hands on the barrels of their guns and guided them downward. "You want to shoot each other, you'll have to go through me first."

Jameson lowered his gun. "I told you not to bring him," he said to Natalie and stormed off.

"So you wanted to leave me out there to fend for myself?" Wade asked.

Jameson whirled back around. "That's exactly what I wanted to do!" He got back in Wade's face.

"Stop it!" Natalie wedged herself between them again.

"Wade shot Walter! He could have killed him!" Jameson clenched his fists.

"Maybe, maybe not, but we can't stand here worrying about it. It already happened, and there's nothing we can do to change that." Natalie pulled Jameson aside to not arouse the group. "We have to think of Walter right now. He needs some rest before the homondie attack again because I don't know if I can control them every time and we can't stay here."

Jameson and Natalie turned to look at Walter, who was slumped over on the ground.

"Walter, are you all right?" Natalie asked.

"Wha—huh? Oh, I'm fine. Just a little tired is all," Walter said. He sat up with a jerk and leaned back against the tree with Natalie's help. "I'll be better in no time." He smiled, then grunted as he adjusted his body.

"Thankfully, your wound isn't life-threatening," Natalie said. She took the blood-saturated gauze from Walter and released the pressure to expose the dried blood and a slight scar that remained. Natalie leaned in and whispered into the old man's ear, "I've healed it to the best of my ability. Let me make sure you have no other injuries."

"What? I can't believe it," Caroline said as she glowered at Walter. "How could he heal so fast?" She turned to Natalie. "First the homondie leave you alone, now this?" The others moved closer to look.

"The wound wasn't as bad as I thought, and the homondie probably didn't see me," Natalie said as she grabbed Walter's shirt and moved it up a little higher.

Walter had begun to sweat. Tiny droplets formed on his brow, and he fidgeted when she lifted his shirt.

Her eyes widened and her mouth was agape when she saw a deep gouge in his side. "What happened to you? Is that a . . . bite?" Natalie back away and stared at Jameson.

Jameson looked like he was going to say something but dropped his head and stared at the ground instead. Natalie had no doubt that he knew what had happened but wouldn't say a word.

Walter tugged his shirt back into place, covering the bite mark.

Natalie glared at Jameson again. He made no motion to answer.

Natalie turned back to Walter.

"Well, I—" Walter cleared his throat. "I had an incident. Let's just say it was an experiment gone wrong, but hey, I survived. Now don't you worry about me, I'm feeling better now. We can get moving if you'd like." He looked at Natalie, his eyebrows raised.

"Are you sure you're okay to walk?"

Walter glanced at Jameson then back at Natalie. "Yes, I'll just use the staff as a crutch. I'll be all right."

"There's something awfully weird going on here." Wade sneered.

"All right, let's get you up on your feet and we'll get going," Jameson said to Walter, ignoring Wade.

Walter stood, sweat streaming down his face. His face had turned pale, and his skin was clammy. He swayed and almost fell over. Jameson caught him and Natalie stepped up to take his other side.

"We're going to have to settle down here for a few more minutes so he can recover a little more fully before we make the trip back to the portal. I'm certain the homondie are going to be waiting there for us, and we'll need him to be functional." Jameson lowered Walter back down.

"You're going to what?" Wade asked.

"This doesn't concern you." Natalie stood in front of Wade, warding him off.

"I think it does. You're jeopardizing the safety of this group. I'm making the call, and I say we're not stopping anywhere. We're going right back to that portal, and you're going to take us home," Wade yelled.

"You don't get an opinion here," Jameson said. "Walter needs to rest a bit, and that's what we're going to do."

"We're sitting ducks," Wade shouted.

"If you don't like it, you can leave. No one's stopping you," Jameson hollered back.

"Why don't you leave him here?" Wade said. "We can go back to the portal and get the reversal started, then you can come back to get him. That way, we don't get ambushed and he won't slow us down."

"What? We should have left you behind like I wanted to." Jameson's face was red. "Next time, you can save yourselves."

Natalie watched Jameson storm off as she shouted, "We're not going to leave anyone out here alone!"

"Yeah, run away, you pansy," Wade yelled.

CHAPTER 24

JAMESON WAS LIVID when he heard Wade's comment, and it lit a fire of rage inside him. He spun around and walked back, his glare so intense it would strip the paint off a car.

Wade took a swing at him. Jameson ducked, then came back full force, punching Wade square in the face. Wade's nose cracked, his eyes watered, and his knees buckled. Jameson stared at his opponent on the ground. "Had enough?"

Natalie stood between them. "Both of you, calm down! I'm tired of this macho crap. Just stop it! Fighting won't help us get out of here."

Wade stood and touched his face delicately. "You've got a mean punch," he mumbled. Blood trickled out of his nose as he cupped his jaw and worked it back and forth, testing it.

"You're both out of control," Natalie screamed. "What's wrong with you? Dealing with the homondie are bad enough, and I'm not going to take you two fighting anymore." She glowered at Wade. "If you want to do that, you're on your own!"

"He came after me," Wade said, barely above a whine.

"I don't want to hear it!" Natalie raised her revolver and pointed it at Wade, her finger on the trigger. "Do you really want to go down this path? I didn't want to take it this far, but you've given me no choice. You're trying my patience!"

"Whoa there," Wade said, holding up his hands. "You don't need to get excited. It's just us guys having a little fun, that's all."

"The fun is over," Natalie said. "We aren't safe with the two of you acting like this. I'm cutting you loose."

"Why me?" Wade said, his eyes gone wide. "He's the one who started it." Wade pointed to Jameson.

Natalie tucked her gun back into its holster. "We don't have much time left, and we can't spend it here arguing." She turned and walked past the two men.

Wade laughed and slowly began to reach for his gun. Jameson saw him and pulled out his own gun, training it on Wade. "I wouldn't do that if I were you," Jameson said.

Wade's fingers touched the handle of his gun, but seeing Jameson's revolver trained on him, he lifted his hands and held them up in front of him.

Without turning around, Natalie said, "Wade, don't think you're a quicker draw than me. You're not." She signaled that they should keep moving. Walter hobbled behind Jameson and Natalie.

Natalie turned around, grabbed the old man around the waist, and tucked her shoulder under his arm. "We'll get you somewhere safe for a while," she said.

Wade followed them at a distance.

"Where do you think you're going?" Jameson stopped, held up his gun, and pointed it at Wade.

"I'm going with you." Wade stood firm. "I have to keep an eye on you. I don't trust you, and I don't need you doing something to hurt these innocent people."

"You're not going anywhere with us. You're dangerous." Jameson turned and continue walking, catching up to Natalie.

"*I'm* dangerous?" Wade yelled. "Seems like you're the dangerous one." He followed them a few feet more and hollered, "Natalie, I understand it's you who is truly in charge, and I'm pleading with you, you can't leave me out here alone!"

Jameson turned and shoved Wade back, who drew his weapon.

"Touch me again!" Wade warned, his gun aimed at Jameson.

"If you want to keep your gun, you better lower it now or I'm going to take it from you."

"You're not going to intimidate me and control this situation while I stand here quietly."

Jameson lunged forward and grabbed Wade's gun, snatching it away from him, then pointed it back at him. "If you calm down, I'll give you your gun back, and you can possibly have a fighting chance out there alone. If you keep shooting off your mouth, you won't have your gun. It's up to you."

Natalie stopped, sighed, spun around, and drew her gun, aiming it at Wade. In a calm voice, she said, "I'm sorry, but you're too unstable for this group, and you can't be trusted."

"I can't be trusted?" Wade yelled, incredulous. "You should be saying that to those two!" He pointed at Jameson and Walter.

Caroline tried to walk past Wade, but he blocked her path. She maneuvered around him, but he grabbed her arm. "Caroline, tell them how I saved you all," he pleaded. "Tell them how I saved you from being stranded in the woods. You owe me!"

"If I have to choose between you or them, I'm choosing them," Caroline said, pulling her arm free of his grasp. "I'm sorry, but you've changed, and I don't think you can be trusted anymore."

"How can you be so ungrateful?" Wade yelled as Caroline joined Natalie and Walter.

"She's with us now," Jameson said.

Natalie motioned to the group with a wave of her hand.

Wade briefly dipped his head in acknowledgment and moved to the side to allow the rest of the group to pass. They turned their backs toward him, walked away, and left Wade behind all by himself. After the group passed, Natalie looked at Jameson and nodded before she, too, turned away.

Wade swore under his breath and waved farewell. "You'll see who you can trust around here soon enough when those two show their true colors," he shouted at the group.

Jameson glanced at Wade again, wanting to be sure he was behaving.

Wade's eyes widened with belated understanding. They really were going to abandon him. He ran after Natalie and grabbed her arm. "Wait, please, you don't understand what they're up to. I can't see you getting hurt. They're manipulating you. You don't know what you're doing."

"Stop it, Wade! You did this all yourself. There's nothing I can do now." Natalie yanked free.

"Don't leave me out here alone! You'll be sorry I'm not around when they turn on you! They'll be the cause of everyone's death," Wade shouted.

"I don't know what you're talking about." Natalie kept walking.

"Don't pay him any mind, Natalie." Jameson gave Wade one last lingering stare, then threw his gun on the ground. "Don't make a move until we're clear out of sight."

Wade picked up his weapon, stepped back, and slipped away, disappearing into the woods.

Jameson caught up to Natalie. "I think he's doing this on purpose to get me all fired up. What is it that he's expecting me to do, shoot him?"

"For a moment I thought this wasn't going to end well," Walter said.

Caroline gave one last glance behind her, still dawdling as they stomped through the undergrowth in the forest. "It's for his own good as well as ours. Best to be safe."

"Wade was too self-assured. He was more in tune with his own pride than working together," Natalie said.

Wade yelled from somewhere in the woods. "You'll be sorry I won't be there to save you. Just wait until Jameson turns on you. Then what are you going to do?"

"You know, he keeps saying we all shouldn't trust you." Caroline stared oddly at Jameson for a moment then said, "Obviously, he isn't all there."

"I didn't want any trouble, but on the other hand, he can rot out there by himself for all I care," Jameson griped. Wade's words left him unnerved. Did Wade actually know what he was up to?

"I guess that's what this place does to some people," Natalie said.

"You did the right thing. He was off his rocker," Walter said. "He cornered you. You had no other choice but to leave him behind, for the safety of everyone else." Walter smiled and patted Jameson's shoulder. "You're always making friends, buddy." He chuckled.

"That's not funny. He has a serious problem, and I don't want to worry about him tracking us down and killing one of us," Natalie said.

"Don't worry. If it ends up that way, let it be. I'll be waiting for him." Jameson had no concern for Wade anymore. He wasn't going to let him get under his skin again. He took a few more steps and analyzed the area. "We can have Walter rest over there." Jameson pointed to a cluster of large trees that were surrounded by heavy undergrowth.

Walter grunted as he walked. "I'll be all right. Just give me a minute or two and I'll be good to go."

"Natalie, why don't you stand guard?" Jameson said, helping Walter to sit with his back against a tree. "Let me know the minute you see anything. I'll stay here with Walter."

Natalie nodded and stood on the other side of the group which gave Jameson the chance to speak to Walter alone. Walter twirled the staff in his hands. He stared at the orb as if mesmerized by its beauty.

"Walter," Jameson muttered as he plopped down next to him.

Walter peered around the tree then whispered, "Good job getting rid of Wade. He was becoming too nosy, and I didn't think you could make Natalie leave him behind."

"You were the one who had to take a bullet for it. Thanks for stepping in front of that."

"You owe me for that one. That stung, and it could have been worse. The things you talk me into." Walter rubbed his wound.

"I knew Natalie would heal you," Jameson said dismissively. "Now that Wade's gone, it's time." Jameson pointed at the staff. "She's held on to the chip long enough. We need to take it before Victor gets another chance."

"Is it safe though?" Walter asked. "She's not looking much like Natalie lately. It's happening more often than not." His voice cracked and rose. "If the chip knows what we're planning, it'll convince Natalie to kill us."

"That's why it's imperative that we convince her to give it to us first."

"How are you planning on doing that? Wade can't save her, and I'm not too worried about the others, but Caroline's still here."

"You let me take care of Caroline." Jameson pulled out his device and held it up. The monitor displayed the portal, pulsating and expanding. "The portal is unstable, and we can use it to our advantage. I'll lure her toward it and set it off so she gets caught up in the explosion."

"Don't you think someone will notice?" Walter asked.

"I'll make it look like an accident," Jameson said, "but there's a problem."

"What's that?"

"It could explode anytime," Jameson said. "Are you rested enough to walk?"

"Oh, I've been fine from the beginning." Walter chuckled.

"You're getting as good at pretending as me." Jameson smiled.

"I learned from the best."

"Keep the others busy and follow my lead. You'll know when it's time." Jameson stood, attached the device to his belt, and grabbed hold of Walter's arm, helping him to his feet. "Walter's rested and ready to go," he called to Natalie. "We'd best be on our way." Jameson walked in the opposite direction of the portal.

"Jameson, where are you going? The portal is that way." Natalie pointed behind her.

"We're going to head around the back side to try and avoid the homondie."

Natalie nodded and the group followed Jameson.

Natalie and Caroline walked on either side of Walter. Jameson grabbed Caroline's arm, tugging her away from Natalie. "Caroline," he said. "I never got the chance to thank you for saving my life earlier."

"It was nothing," Caroline said, staring at Jameson's hand gripping her arm. "It got me to fire the damn thing, so I'm grateful I had the courage to do it. I've been afraid for too long."

Jameson looked behind him. Walter and the others were far enough behind. He pulled Caroline and forced her to walk faster as he thought, *This is a good place.* He reached down at his device. The ground shook violently then exploded. The dirt gave way under Caroline's feet. Caroline screamed as a dusty mist flew into the air, hanging over both her and Jameson. The ground quaked and started to sink, creating a cliff.

Caroline looked over her shoulder, down at the ravine, and back at Jameson. "What are you waiting for? Pull me out," she said as she scrambled to find a solid piece to plant her feet. Jameson grinned devilishly as he lessened his grip on her arm. Caroline's eyes widened in terror as he released more pressure, her life teetered on the cliff's edge.

Natalie ran into the dust cloud and grabbed Caroline's arm from Jameson. She pulled with such force that Caroline was flung upward and straight into Jameson's arms. Natalie nearly threw herself over the cliff in the process.

Jameson held Caroline tightly and whispered, "You tell Natalie about this and I'll kill her."

"Let go of me!" Caroline pulled herself free of Jameson's grasp and ran toward Natalie.

As the ridge was about to swallow her whole, Walter extended the staff toward Natalie. She grabbed it just in time.

Jameson stepped in and grabbed Natalie's arm. "Hang on, we'll pull you in."

The ground continued to give away. The tips of Natalie's toes teetered on the last patch of dirt beneath her.

"Don't let go, please." Natalie looked over her shoulder and down the rocky ledge. The ground began to pull farther away from her. Her palms were sweaty, and she started to lose her grip on the staff.

With one last hard pull, Walter and Jameson yanked her up, propelling her toward them. Walter fell backward and landed on the ground, Natalie on top of him.

Caroline helped her up. "Are you all right?"

"I'm okay," Natalie said, wiping dirt from her clothes. "Are you okay?"

Caroline sniffled and wiped her eyes. "I'm fine," she said, glaring at Jameson.

"Sorry about that, Caroline," Jameson said. "You almost slipped through my fingers. Lucky Natalie was there to save you."

"Yes, I guess it was lucky, huh?" Caroline said, coldly.

Jameson ignored her and walked away. He knew she wouldn't say a word for Natalie's sake. He approached Walter and whispered, "We don't have any more time. We don't need to worry about the others, but keep Caroline away from Natalie."

CHAPTER 25

"NATALIE, I NEED to have a word with you, in private." Jameson and Natalie stepped aside as he kept an eye on everyone else. He whispered, "I don't want to shock anyone, but after that last encounter, I think we may have run out of time. I believe this world consumed ours faster than we could close the portal. If we try to go through it now, there may be nothing left to go to and we could be stuck in a void."

"Are you saying that last explosion might have been the destruction of our world?"

"Yes."

"We can't give up now, not after all we've been through." Natalie rubbed her forehead as if trying to activate the chip. "There's got to be a way to bring life back to our world."

"There could be a way," Jameson said. "If there's even a sliver of our world left, we may be able to bring it back."

"Tell me, whatever it is, we'll make it work."

"I think we need to place the chip in the Staff of Life."

"What are you saying?" Natalie stepped back guardedly while she placed her hand over the chip.

"The chip is part of this world. It knows all about it and has learned from it. There may be a way to use it to secure our world back to normal."

"I thought you said I could control it?"

"Take a look around," Jameson said, spreading his arms to indicate the destruction. "There must be more to it than you can understand, because it obviously isn't working. Our only option is to put that chip into the staff."

"You didn't give me a chance to try," Natalie said.

"We're out of time."

"I could die if you take it out, right?" Natalie asked.

Jameson locked eyes with Natalie. "Either you give up the chip or we'll all die here in Homondiem."

Jameson held out his hand to Walter. "Give me the staff."

Walter limped over and handed Jameson the staff and a knife. Jameson nudged Walter with the end of the staff and pointed to Caroline. The old man nodded. Jameson watched Walter put his arm around Caroline, leaned on her shoulder, and hobbled away with her help.

"We'll have to remove the chip now," Jameson said.

Natalie sighed. "I guess I have to trust your judgment. If I'm not strong enough to control it, I can't save our world. If you think you can control the dimensions and set things right with the chip in the staff, I have to do it. It's our only choice." Her eyes grew teary. "I'll do whatever it takes to bring our world back, even if I won't be there to see it."

Natalie sat on the ground and Jameson placed the staff next to her. He opened the top flap and readied it for the chip. Jameson guided Natalie down. She lay flat on her back. He pulled a handkerchief from his pocket. "Bite on this," he said. "It's all we have."

"What are you doing to her?" Caroline had extricated herself from Walter and ran to Natalie. She stared at the knife in Jameson's hand, and her eyes grew wide. "What do you think you're doing? I won't let you!"

Caroline grabbed for the knife, but Jameson held it out of her reach. "She has something in her head that may help us to get out of here," Jameson explained. "I need to take it out."

"What are you talking about?"

"You don't have to worry about it," Walter said, taking a firm hold of Caroline's arm as he pulled her away from Jameson.

Caroline tried to pry out of his grasp, but he grabbed her hand and squeezed tight.

"What if you kill her?" Caroline asked.

"That's a risk she's willing to take," Jameson said. "If it means you'll all be free."

Zack, with Zoey by his side, approached and said, "Maybe there's another way."

"This is none of your business." Walter released Caroline and aimed his gun at Zack. "Step back before I have to use force."

Zack stepped in front of Caroline and Zoey, shielding them with his body.

"Go ahead, Natalie," Jameson said as he leered at Caroline. "Tell her."

"It's okay." Natalie smiled with considerable effort. "I have to."

Caroline said nothing but looked at Natalie, desperation in her eyes.

Jameson gazed down at Natalie. "I won't lie to you. This is going to hurt."

"Do it quickly, and if I'm dying, please don't let me suffer," Natalie said, her voice stoic. "Make it fast."

Walter moved in and knelt next to Natalie, pinning down her legs and holding her arms. Natalie clenched her fists into the dirt and readied herself for the pain as Jameson made a small incision across her scalp.

Her eyes welled up with tears, and she let out a muted scream. A brief, ragged sound escaped her throat, muffled by the cloth, followed by short puffs of air as she tried to catch her breath.

Blood trickled down the side of her face. "There it is." Jameson could feel the chip with the tip of the knife.

Natalie's eyes twitched, and a ray of light flashed within then expanded across both irises. The chip was aware of imminent danger, and Jameson knew he had to hurry. He pressed down a bit harder, and a burst of electrical current flowed through the metal blade. The zap caused him to drop the knife. Cursing, he cradled his injured hand and tried to control his pain, but his grunts drew the attention of nearby homondie.

Jameson picked up the knife and was about to pull the chip out when a homondie groaned behind him. He turned around and noted the homondie staring at Natalie being pinned to the ground. It cocked its head to the side and advanced. It ignored the others and moved only toward Jameson and Walter.

"Buster, why didn't you warn us?" Walter shouted at the dog, noting the approaching homondie. "You must have known it was coming!"

Buster ignored Walter and allowed the homondie to close in on them. He lay next to Natalie and placed his head on her chest with a whine.

Jameson pulled out his gun and shot the homondie. "It's probably because they're too much like humans now," he said. "Buster can't identify them anymore."

A group of homondie came into view.

Walter released Natalie, picked up the knife and staff, and stuck them back through his belt. The two men aimed their guns and fired into the crowd of homondie.

Once freed, Natalie sat up, spit out the cloth, and wiped the blood off her forehead with the back of her hand. The incision had already closed.

Caroline ran to her, and the others scrambled to hide from the homondie. She helped Natalie up. "Your head, it's healed?" she said, clearly confused.

"Caroline, get back!" Natalie pushed her toward the others, then hollered, "Stop shooting!" She stood in front of Jameson's and Walter's weapons. Her eyes were black as night with rings of fire encircling them.

Caroline yelled, "Natalie, what's happening to you?"

"Natalie, get out of the way," Jameson shouted.

"Stay where you are," Natalie said. Her red-rimmed eyes glowed as she stared at an advancing homondie, its hands and face still bloodied from its last meal. She held up her hand and unconsciously spoke to it in a language no one could understand. The homondie replied and left. It headed back to its group.

Walter's eyes widened. "What did she say? She sounded like Victor with his incantations."

"I don't know," Jameson said. "I don't know the language."

"What did you do to her?" Walter asked, panic rising in his voice.

"I might have accidentally activated the remaining portion of the chip and released its full power into Natalie."

"You did what?"

"I think the chip's energy is now flowing through her veins and flooding her soul. It has full control of Natalie, and she has full control of the homondie and their world."

Caroline ran to Jameson, who was staring at Natalie in amazement. "Whatever you did to her, you need to undo it!" Caroline cocked her gun. "She better be all right!"

Walter came up behind Caroline and pointed his gun at her head. "Lower it," he said with a calm voice.

"Calm down, Caroline, everything will be fine," Jameson said soothingly. "When I touched the chip with the knife, it activated it just like it would have in the Staff of Life. Now she's communicating with them. We're safe as long as she controls them."

"I hope you're right for our sake," Walter murmured, "because if Natalie ends up on their side, we're doomed."

Natalie stood there as if she was waiting for something.

Caroline backed up. "What are we going to do?"

"Absolutely nothing." Jameson said, arms crossed.

Zack approached. "We can't leave her like that. Look at her."

"She's in no pain, and there's no immediate danger," Jameson said, not taking his eyes off Natalie. "She's in limbo between evolution and regression."

"How can that be?" Caroline asked.

"Electronically, she's evolved because the circuits connected to the chip which is used to transmit data signals have become part of her, integrating throughout her mind. On the other hand, the homondie world held within the chip has regressed and is connected to her life capacity. You see, the chip, comprising the processing and memory of units, is working the same in her as it would inside the staff. The semiconductor material of her body, embedded within the integrated circuitry of the chip, created a sort of transmitter through her. It combined the pair into one, causing her to become more powerful than any being in existence." Jameson gazed upon the group as they regarded him with incomprehension. "In other words, she's still human-based, but with a fraction of mechanical qualities."

"I don't understand. Should we fear her?" Zack asked. "Did the circuitry take over or will her human side maintain control?"

"Look." Jameson pointed at Buster, standing calmly next to Natalie. "Buster's by her side, and he's not afraid. If she wasn't the Natalie we all know, Buster would attack her."

Another homondie lumbered toward Natalie, and Natalie headed straight for the homondie. Walter grabbed her and tried to hold her back. "Natalie, snap out of it. We need you."

She paused for a moment and turned to Walter. With her eyes engulfed in flames, she replied, "Let me go."

Walter raised his hands, and Natalie turned to the group. Her eyes slowly returned to normal. "Everyone stay here."

Buster followed her and Jameson yanked Walter forward. "Come on! We can't afford to lose her now. We need to stay close."

A creature staggered and swayed toward Natalie. Its eyes were glazed over, and its body was covered in dried blood. Jameson didn't dare rush to her aid, but Natalie had to be protected somehow, especially when he was so close to getting the chip back.

"There has to be a way we can still get that chip," he said to Walter. Jameson readied his gun in case the creature attacked.

As it neared her, he studied its posture and noticed how human it was. Upright and full of life, he was baffled. It has some noticeable similarities, but he didn't recognize that particular homondie. There was something different about it.

They stood only two feet away from one another. It could easily destroy any one of them, but it didn't. Even with Natalie's quick regression, there seemed to be no behavioral, physical processing, or communicative interaction that would cause this connection between them. So how was it they both seemed to understand each other fluently? Jameson's train of thought was interrupted as Natalie spoke to it.

"Can you understand our language? We only want to go home," Natalie said.

Everything went silent as the group waited to see if the creature would answer.

CHAPTER 26

THE CREATURE STOOD motionless. It glared at Natalie through half-open eyes. It should have been incapable of understanding, but they were communicating nonetheless.

She waited patiently as its lips chattered open and closed. Whispers shaped into words and formed speech. The creature grunted as if speaking pained it.

"Yes, I understand you, but I prefer to use your language," it replied in the humans' native tongue.

"What do you mean my language?" Natalie said. She was baffled. She wondered how a homondie had the capability to speak, but to speak to a human?

"You do not remember?" It began in a different dialect.

Natalie found herself at a loss for words. Her mind sorted through the sounds, and she found that she could understand. "This can't be happening," she whispered. Somehow, she and the creature understood each other.

The creature turned to the others in her group. "Ask those outsiders."

With every sentence, the homondie's language became clearer. "I don't understand?" The new language freely passed her lips as she had begun to speak the homondie's language. It seemed to flow effortlessly, and it felt good to speak this tongue. There was a connection, but she didn't want to accept it. Her gaze lingered on the creature before her. "Who are you speaking of?"

"Those two." The creature pointed at Jameson and Walter. "Those outsiders, who gave them authority over this world?" it asked. "They are treacherous and deceitful. Do not trust them."

"I do trust them, with my life," Natalie said.

"They do not care about you," the creature told her. "They only want the chip."

"The chip? Why?" Natalie asked.

"I will only warn you once. Do not give them the chip or we will all perish."

"What are you afraid of?"

"They want this world for themselves, and I will not allow them to have control over us. If anyone is going to take over, it is I who will be leader."

"Why do you think they're here to take control of Homondiem?" Natalie asked.

"Because they took the Staff of Life and they are planning on placing the chip into it," it explained.

"How do you know this?"

"I know because I was one of them. I am a half-life."

Natalie searched its facial features, where she found a hint of humanity. Like a lightning bolt, she realized who he was. "Seth, is that you?"

"I am not that human anymore. I only have a small memory of his life left. The more I become a half-life, the less I remember my past."

"Who did this to you?"

"Victor," Seth explained. "He had his homondie attack me for allowing you to escape. If I was not strong-willed, I would be dead. I was one of the lucky ones to survive, but now I have been sentenced to a life of misery. We half-lives do not have the same appetite as the homondie. We cannot extract life to use as our own, but eventually the homondie will finish us off once there are no more living."

He paused and licked his dried, cracked lips then spoke again. "Once my brain process began to regress from my human form, it is slowly disregarding my human memory. Soon enough I will not remember what Victor did to me." Seth held out his arms. "Look at me," he shouted in the homondie language and howled as he spoke. He paused and inhaled deeply, then said, "There is some good to it. This homondie world has something extraordinary that the outsiders do not have."

"What's that?" Natalie stepped closer, cautiously.

"They do not kill their own kind, except for you. You are the exception because the chip gives you the choice between giving life or death to those around you."

"I don't understand. What are you saying?"

"Once the human race is exterminated, the homondie can never die."

"Exterminated? Why?"

"They are a threat. They all must die."

"Not all are bad," she said. "Some just need guidance."

"Humans do not learn from their mistakes," Seth said. "They never have and they never will."

"You don't know that for sure."

"I know from experience, but I can be compassionate, the homondie behind me cannot," Seth said. "I can give you a chance to save them."

"How?" Natalie asked.

"You must force them to leave Homondiem and give me the chip. I do not want to live like this. I want to use the chip to bring back my human form."

"We can't," Natalie said. "Jameson said we're all stuck here and there's no way back unless I give up the chip, but the chip can't be taken out anymore. It's attached to me as I am to it."

"You could have left Homondiem anytime you wished."

"Jameson said the portals wouldn't close."

"That is what he wanted you to believe. He always knew how to close the portals. You could have left at any time."

"He's known how to fix this all along? Why did he force us to go through this?" Natalie asked.

"Once inside Homondiem, he never planned to leave, and he could not allow you to go without getting that chip first."

"Why did he do this to us?"

"His deception runs deep. He wants the same thing we wanted, to control this world, and being here with that chip is the only way he can do it."

"How do I know you aren't deceiving me as well?" Natalie asked. "What if I force them to leave and there's nothing to go back to? Won't they all die?"

"That is the chance you will have to take. I would think you would rather risk sending them home, because if they do not leave, the homondie will have no choice but to kill them all."

"What about the chip, how can I give it to you? Jameson already tried and failed."

"I do not know. That is something you will need to figure out. But once I have that chip, I will close off their world from ours so they can no longer return to Homondiem. Then I will search for a cure for us half-lives."

Natalie, torn, didn't know who to believe. "Stay here." She walked away, surprised that Seth obeyed her.

As she headed back to the group, Seth called to her, "Hurry. I do not know how much longer I can hold back my transformation. Once I fully transform, I will not remember who I am or that we made this bargain."

With each step, she felt the chip inside her, taunting her, and erasing her memory. She fought to maintain control but was losing the battle. The chip was taking over, manipulating her, making her cold and unfeeling. She could feel her emotions fading fast. She was succumbing to the circuitry and leaving her human qualities behind. She paused and thought, *Why am I here?* She gazed at the group, all eyes on her. She stared at Caroline, slowly remembering. She'd almost forgotten about the promise she'd made to bring them home. Will she be able to control the chip before it takes over completely? She stared back at Jameson and continued walking.

CHAPTER 27

"HERE SHE COMES." Walter said, backing up slowly. "I don't know whether to stand here or run."

Everyone stepped back with Walter.

Natalie's eyes never left Jameson as she walked briskly toward him. When she spoke, her voice was calm and her words patient. "I have a renewed energy," she said. "I believe you've given me an eternal connection to the homondie with the chip you activated. Now that I understand, there's no longer a need to remove the chip, for *I am* the Staff of Life. I must ask all of you outsiders to leave this homondie world before you die."

"Are you going to kill us?" Caroline asked, putting her trembling hands over her mouth.

"No," Natalie said, "but they will." She gestured behind her to the pack of waiting homondie.

Lines of light shot across her irises. They stretched and burst then faded to a flicker. The chip was now one with her and could never be removed—the chip wouldn't allow it. She was becoming more robot than human. Her compassion was ebbing as her emotions faded away.

"Are you coming with us?" Caroline asked Natalie.

"No, I must stay here."

Jameson listened to her speak, but he wouldn't fear his creation. He stepped up to her, grabbed her shoulders, and stared deep into the bottomless pits of her eyes.

Caroline pushed Jameson aside. She grabbed Natalie's hand and held it tightly. "Natalie, I won't fear you, and I definitely won't leave you. I'll stand by your side, no matter what happens."

"I can't allow that."

"Yes, you can."

"They'll kill you."

"I know you won't let them," Caroline said. "Just tell me how to help you."

Natalie pulled her hand from Caroline's grasp and looked down at the dog. "We're ready, Buster. Let's go." Buster trotted to the front of the group.

"Ready for what?" Jameson asked as the group followed Natalie and Buster straight into the crowd of homondie. Natalie gave no reply.

"Look at them staring," Walter said to Jameson. "We're not going to make it out alive."

"Just keep going until I figure out what Natalie's up to," Jameson mumbled.

Natalie came to a halt. Everyone stopped behind her. She stood directly in front of the group of homondie, the humans cowering behind her.

She stood before them and said, "Seth, I can't let them leave. We must all live here in peace."

"Seth?" Jameson whispered to Walter. "That's why it looked familiar."

"I will not allow it," Seth yelled for all to hear.

Jameson knew the homondie wouldn't allow the outsiders to exist among them. The battle had to be fought. Who would control life and this world, the outsiders or the half-lives?

Before Jameson could speak, Buster barked. Victor stepped out of the woods.

"There's my staff," Victor yelled. "Get him, get Walter, and retrieve my Staff of Life!"

The homondie charged the group and advanced from all directions.

"We've almost won," Victor shouted at his minions. "Take back the staff, and I'll get Natalie."

Natalie didn't flinch as Victor approached. Jameson and Walter stood next to her and pointed their weapons at Victor and the oncoming homondie.

"I guess this is it," Walter said, resigned.

Natalie stared at Victor. The approaching homondie suddenly stopped.

Victor looked at his homondie. "What are you doing? Get that staff! Move! She's not your leader, I am!"

Jameson's eyes widened as Victor and Natalie stood face-to-face. Jameson turned to the group. "Be ready to charge. We don't know how this will end."

"Well, why aren't you attacking?" Victor asked Natalie.

"There's no need for you to take the chip because it's now one with me," Natalie told Victor.

"Jameson, what have you done," Victor growled.

"He activated the chip and it can no longer be removed," Natalie said, showing no emotion.

Victor pulled a knife from his waist and pointed it at Natalie. "I'm taking that chip and you can't stop me." He lunged toward her, and without hesitation, two homondie blocked Victor and pushed him back. "Homondie, get out of my way.

"You'll never get the chip, it won't allow it," Natalie said as more homondie surrounded her. She turned to Jameson. "I can no longer wage war against the homondie. You're on your own." She moved aside and Buster followed her.

"Jameson, you'll pay for what you did." Victor shouted, "Homondie, attack!"

Seth growled and marched toward Victor. "I remember who you are and what you did to me."

Victor raised his hand and halted his troops. "Seth? You should be dead."

"Thanks to you I am now stuck living as a half-life."

"I never thought to hear human words come out of such a disfigured creature. What are the odds? No matter. Get back in line with the others and attack these outsiders," Victor demanded.

"I will no longer take orders from you." Seth's teeth chattered. "Now it is time for you to sacrifice *your* human life."

"You may think you're intelligent enough to make commands," Victor said mockingly, "but I don't have to obey them."

Seth stared at Victor, rage in his black eyes. He lunged. Victor stepped behind another homondie while Seth advanced.

"I see your intelligence is highly developed. We could work together," Victor said, backing away.

"I will not work with you," Seth said. "It is time for you to die so I can become leader of Homondiem."

"Now, now," Victor said as Seth closed in on him, the homondie following close behind. "Maybe I was a bit harsh. We could work this out. My understanding of this world combined with your half-life capabilities, we'd be unstoppable."

"This is *my* world now," Seth said. "You do not belong here. You are one of them."

"One of them?"

"An outsider," Seth said. "There is no place for you here."

"How dare you?" Victor bellowed. "I created this world. It's mine to rule!"

"Not anymore," Seth said. "You will be feasted upon as I was, but you will not survive." He turned to the others. "I am a part of your world now and he is an outsider with life. Do what you must. He is yours."

"No, wait!" Victor stepped back, tripping on the uneven ground.

"No human is allowed to live. They all must die. You said it yourself," Seth said.

"No, don't do it," Victor pleaded. "Forgive me!"

"Forgive you? We have worked together for years. You were like a brother to me, and you condemned me to death. You deserve everything that is coming to you."

Victor fought his way through the crowd of homondie.

"Do not let him escape! Kill him," Seth said.

The homondie surrounded Victor. They attacked, ripping at his skin and ravaging his body. They shoveled his torn flesh into their mouths.

Natalie's group backed away as the homondie feasted.

Caroline averted her eyes and hugged Zack and Zoey while Jameson watched, taking no small pleasure in Victor's demise.

The faces of the homondie were smeared with blood as Victor's last breath exited his body with a gasp. Seth shrieked, moaned, and snarled at his victory. He stepped up to Victor's body and boldly addressed his peers. "You have done well. Victor was an outsider and we have no room here for outsiders. They will try to take over our land, but we will not let them. We will kill them all to make our world safe." He let out a final victorious screech.

Walter whimpered. "We're the outsiders. Better run."

"I think you're right," Jameson muttered. They ran off together.

"They're leaving us behind!" Caroline signaled the group to follow Jameson and Walter.

Jameson grabbed Natalie's arm as he passed. Dragging her along, he said, "Natalie, look what this has come to! You want us to end up like Victor?"

"We must all live in peace." Natalie walked beside him, forcing him to slow down.

"But they're after us, not you," Walter said.

"Natalie, you know we can't coexist." Jameson stared at her. "You need to help us."

"Get them! Kill the outsiders," Seth shouted.

"Natalie, come back, we need you!" Jameson shook her. "Don't let it get the best of you. You're stronger than that."

Natalie smiled. "I can understand the homondie and this world is growing within me as the chip grows. I won't harm them."

"I need you to use your homondie connection against Seth to save us," Jameson pleaded.

"I'm sorry, there's nothing I can do."

Natalie pulled free from Jameson's grasp and turned away as the homondie sniffed their prey. They licked their lips and gazed at the meal set before them. Hunger filled their eyes.

Jameson knew he was in trouble. The portal was looking better every minute. Maybe trying to take control of this world hadn't been such a good idea. He pulled out his device and checked for a portal. The screen was blank. He slapped the side, and a faint signal came through. It would have to do.

Jameson grabbed Natalie's arm and forced her to run with him. Buster barked at him, following Natalie's every move.

"Let me go," Natalie yelled.

"You're coming with me to the portal. Now hurry."

"I thought you said we couldn't access the portal." Natalie tried to pull away.

"There isn't time for a discussion. We're going to the portal, and I'm getting out of here," Jameson hollered.

Jameson caught sight of the group fast approaching with the homondie right behind them. "Perfect timing. They'll keep the homondie busy and we can slip right through." Jameson led Natalie deeper into the woods.

"I'm not leaving," Natalie shouted.

"I don't need you to leave. I just need you to get me out of here." Jameson hurried toward the portal while the homondie continued to follow the straggling group.

The weakened portal came into view, barely pulsating off in the distance.

Jameson aimed the device at the portal. "We have to hurry, Walter, it's going to close for good."

The group faded in the distance, but that wasn't going to stop Natalie. She shouted, "Caroline, follow us. You need to get everyone to the portal!"

Caroline redirected the group, following Natalie's lead.

Jameson wrapped his arm around Natalie's waist and placed his hand over her mouth, pulling her close. "I said you're getting me out of here. I didn't say anything about the others."

Buster barked at Jameson. Natalie bit his hand as hard as she could.

Jameson moaned in pain and released her. He reached into his backpack and pulled out a syringe only to find the needle broken. He threw it on the ground in disgust.

Natalie ran toward Caroline and the others. The mass of homondie followed close behind with Seth in the lead. "Keep going. I'll meet you there," she said to Caroline. Natalie changed course and ran toward Seth. "Stop! You're not going to kill these outsiders."

The homondie halted, looked around, then paused as they focused on Natalie.

"What is wrong with you? Get them now before they reach the portal," Seth roared, but they made no motion to move.

Natalie approached Seth. "I don't want any trouble for these outsiders. Let them go home, and I'll do whatever you ask."

"How dare you help the outsiders," Seth growled. "You know they cannot be trusted. They want us all dead."

"Not all of them," Natalie said. "There are good people here."

"They will eventually turn on us. If my homondie will not kill them, I will do it myself. They all must die." Seth charged the group.

"Seth, no!" Natalie ran after him. Buster and the homondie followed.

Natalie ran past Seth to the awaiting group at the portal. She stood before it and was about to retrieve her device when Seth caught up, grabbed Zoey, and held a knife to her throat. "Your time here has ended," he said.

"Let her go," Natalie shouted.

"No outsider is going to leave here alive." Seth addressed the group. "You all must die!"

"You told me I could save them, and I will," Natalie said to Seth.

"Your time to save them has ended." Seth touched the blade to Zoey's neck.

CHAPTER 28

AS HUMAN LIFE hung in the balance, there was a huge eruption at the portal, stronger than any before. The ground rocked and cracked open. It seemed the worlds collided with a force powerful enough to set a new dimension into place. The homondie paused and watched Natalie's every movement. Everyone lost their balance and Seth released Zoey.

Natalie grabbed the knife from Seth and the homondie stood guard to prevent Seth from advancing. She stared at the portal. It flickered, then faded. She knew something wasn't right. She turned to Jameson and Walter as they stepped out from the woods and into the clearing. "Jameson, how do I stop it from closing?"

Jameson didn't say a word.

"Jameson, the portal is fluctuating. It's shutting down," Natalie shouted. "If that portal disappears, there'll be nothing left to connect to, and our world will be truly gone."

Jameson crossed his arms and smiled.

The portal flickered, followed by a flash of light and a burst. A bang echoed shortly after, and the portal faded away. The last portal had disappeared, leaving no trace.

"Was that the end of our world?" Natalie looked at the group, hope fading from their eyes. Buster sat by her side as she struggled to figure out how to save them now that the portal was gone.

If the dimensions had combined into one, that meant Homondiem was their new home. Could the world she once knew be the passage to death? Who knows what happened to the remaining people who had been there? Could they have survived? As the worlds merged, the last parts of their world combined into this one. The remaining hills, trees, mountains, and streams formed around them, leaving no trace that Homondiem had ever existed.

Buster barked uncontrollably at Natalie, snapping her out of her daze. He must have sensed how she felt. She realized the battle hadn't been lost and she still had to guide them to victory so they could all live in peace.

All eyes were on Natalie. She wouldn't admit defeat, but was their world really gone? No one knew. Who was she to dash their hopes? There could still be a way to get everyone back home, if home still existed. Her mind was set. She strode toward Seth, Buster following. It was time to end this frivolous battle here and now.

"Jameson, look who it is." Walter pointed to another batch of homondie in the distance.

Natalie stopped and turned around. Victor was coming toward them, dragging a leg and one of his arms was twisted and chewed.

"I hope he likes being a half-life." Jameson smirked. "At least he got what he deserved." He shouted at Victor, "I've been waiting for this day to come!" He raised his knife and marched toward Victor, leaving Walter behind.

"Victor?" Seth turned his attention away from Natalie. "He is mine!" He forced his way through the homondie toward Victor. The homondie followed. He picked up speed and charged at him.

Victor changed course and headed straight for Walter.

"Walter, watch out! Victor's after the staff," Jameson hollered as Victor gained speed. He fired shot after shot, but Victor didn't go down.

"I . . . must . . . have . . . staff," Victor mumbled, his first words as a half-life. "I . . . will . . . take . . . Staff . . . of . . . Life . . . back."

Natalie watched Victor approach Walter. He barreled straight at the old man, his arms outstretched, and knocked Walter down. Walter wasn't quick enough to evade the blow, nor was he prepared for the sheer force that slammed him to the ground. It knocked the wind out of him. He gasped for air as Victor hovered over him. Victor lashed out and held him down, trying to grab the staff.

During the struggle, Walter relinquished his hold on the staff. Victor raised it in victory. An enraged howl echoed across the battlefield and grew louder as Seth approached.

"I will not let you have that staff, Victor," Seth bellowed. He reached Victor just as he stood. Walter got up and ran away as Jameson fired a final shot straight into Victor's head. He dropped the staff and fell to his knees. Seth picked up the staff and raised it in victory.

"I have it. The Staff of Life is mine! I will rule all!" Seth shrieked with joy, Victor's blood was splattered across his face. He held it high. Nothing happened. He shook it. "What is wrong with the staff?" he asked, looking at it quizzically.

Jameson stood face-to-face with Seth. "Did you forget? The staff is useless without the chip." He chuckled.

Seth howled and fled toward the group.

Buster chased Seth, warding him off with his bark.

Natalie yelled, "You want the chip? I still have it!" She drew his attention to her and moved Seth away from the group. She was determined to stop him at any cost, but he wasn't fooled.

Seth grabbed Caroline, nabbed the gun from her hand, and placed it to her head. "Give me the chip or I will kill her," he roared.

Caroline screamed, and Buster leaped at Seth. He let go of Caroline and tumbled backward. Seth got up and lunged at Caroline. Buster jumped up and pushed Seth back.

Seth aimed the gun at Caroline. "This is the moment I have been waiting for. No one will stop me from becoming leader. Now you will all die."

He squeezed the trigger. A gunshot rang out. Caroline covered her head and ducked. Seth fell to the ground, Natalie's gun aimed at him.

The Staff of Life flew into the air. It landed hard and shattered the orb, which created a blast that broke the staff into pieces. An abrupt sound followed by a flash of bright light came from the staff, and each splinter emitted flickers of light. The fragments flew in every direction as its light gradually grew dim.

"Not the staff!" Jameson crawled across the ground, collecting the pieces. "I can still get it to work."

With the battle nearing its end and their leader gone, the homondie were confused. They stopped their attack and whimpered at Natalie. They watched the outsiders as they joined together and approached Victor and Seth, eyes drawn to the two bodies lying side by side. Jameson shot each one a final time in the head. "You bastards," he said.

Natalie spoke to the homondie in their native tongue. "Victor and Seth are gone. You don't have to fight. The battle is over."

The homondie walked away. Exhausted, they had lost the urge for life, yet their hunger was not fulfilled.

Walter nudged Victor and Seth with his foot.

"It's a pity they fought so hard for something with no power, and it cost them so much," Natalie said. "If only we could have worked together, they would have enjoyed this new world."

Natalie wanted desperately to make everything right. She walked to where the last portal had been and stared at the emptiness before her. She closed her eyes and searched her mind, but nothing happened. Could their world be beyond saving?

The reversal might not have been a success, but it wasn't too late for them to survive in the new world. Somewhere, someday, they could figure out a way to bring their world back, but for now, she had to think of the outsiders.

The outsiders grouped together, Jameson standing behind them. He rubbed his hand where Natalie had bitten him.

"What do we do now?" Caroline asked. "We do have to live somewhere, even if it's here."

"You're right," Natalie said. "We're going to have to make the best of it until we figure out if our world still exists." Natalie paused for a moment to think, then continued, "We have to find a place to settle until we figure out how to get back home. I think our best bet is to go to Victor's town. At least we'll have shelter there."

"It would be nice to finally get a good night's rest," Zoey said.

"I heard Jameson say that there was food and water there too," Caroline said.

"Really?" Natalie shot Jameson a malicious glare. "I guess he forgot to tell me." Natalie decided the priority was getting the people to safety. She'd deal with Jameson later. She started down the path, the others following behind. Somehow she knew exactly where to go.

"Be careful, there may be some lingering homondie." Caroline's gaze darted along the path.

"I'll take care of them," Natalie said. "They won't stop us from living there."

They headed to the town Victor had created, returning to the exact spot where it all began. Natalie was wary of what might be lying in wait for them, but she pressed on regardless.

They set off to try to recreate the civilization they had once known, in hopes that one day they could merge their lives with the world of the homondie. Natalie thought they might have a chance. They could begin a new life in Homondiem, now that the rivers and lakes were filling with fresh water. A whole new ecosystem was forming around them.

They moved quietly while Natalie kept her distance from Jameson. She had to guide these people in the right direction. Her mind wandered as she took in the scenery changing before her eyes. The last of the dead trees had grown full of life. Leaves sprouted from their branches, and flowers bloomed. The warmth of the landscape grew. The birds chirped a happy tune as a rabbit hopped by. A few deer drank from a newly formed lake.

Natalie paused and picked a flower. She brought it to her nose and smelled its sweet aroma. A cool breeze passed, and the air no longer carried the stench of rot. Instead, it bore the scent of a new beginning, even better than what she remembered from back home. She couldn't remember a time when she'd felt so peaceful.

There were harsher conditions coming their way, and the homondie would eventually continue their feast unless she could figure out a way to stop them. They had to be ready for the homondie, but she was determined to persevere.

They continued down a new path, leaving their past behind. They have a chance to make a new beginning, but doing it right would be a challenge.

At last, they arrived in Victor's old town; the only place they could call home. Exhausted from the day's events, they found themselves standing there facing their fears. They gazed upon it as if waiting for a sign that they weren't alone. They had survived, but it wasn't over.

Natalie looked at the center of the town where the three trees had once stood. They were connected, having merged back into a single tree. "That must be the sign that our dimension has completed its transformation," she said, slightly above a whisper.

"We're stuck here, aren't we?" Caroline asked.

Natalie stood in silence, not wanting to believe their world was gone. She remained hopeful they would see more of their kind one day, but for now, in this new world, humans no longer existed, only outsiders.

CHAPTER 29

NATALIE STOOD, ALL eyes on her, frightened by the emotions playing through her mind. She stepped in front of the others. She knew they were exhausted from the unending days of the struggle to stay alive and needed some well-deserved rest. She smiled at them, barely remembering how. She gazed at their saddened faces. They couldn't respond with anything more than a half-hearted attempt at cheer, but it was good enough for her.

Natalie didn't want to cause them more stress. This might be the last chance they had to hang on to something positive before tomorrow arrived, but they had to know the truth.

Natalie had more to contend with than just the homondie. Silent for a moment, she examined the group carefully. She knew deep in her heart that she couldn't give them the hope they needed. Everyone had been struck hard by this ordeal, but she still summoned the nerve to speak. Turning to her peers, she lifted her head proudly.

"The events we've all lived through may have been inevitable," she said, "but this isn't the end. We must face facts. We can't go back. We can only go forward. Today, we have a new life before us, the start of a new adventure. Here we have new memories to look forward to. Every day will be a new beginning with new obstacles to face, but it won't get us down. Here, today, we start a new chapter in our lives."

Natalie gazed at Buster, who wagged his tail reassuringly. She prepared the group to move on. She put herself before the others to show them she wasn't afraid. "Let's go into that town. We'll find a place to sleep for tonight and figure out the rest tomorrow."

Natalie was relieved that the path into town was deserted. As they reached the center, Natalie caught sight of a dwelling in the distance away from the others. It was the largest structure for all of them to fit. She pointed and said, "We'll head to the building at the end of the path. We'll all stay together tonight for our safety and figure out what to do for a long-term tomorrow."

They approached cautiously, and Natalie opened the door. "This will be good enough." She stepped in, and the others followed.

Boxes of food and water, enough to last months, were piled nearly ceiling high in the corner of the room. The group tore into the boxes.

"Get your fill, but remember we must make everything last until we can grow crops and find clean water," Natalie said as she lit candles around the room.

"Don't you want any, Natalie?" Caroline asked, holding out some crackers.

"No," Natalie said. "I'm not hungry." She picked up a long piece of wood and laid it across the metal brackets on either side of the door, latching it closed. "Sleep with your weapons," she told everyone.

Jameson threw something at Natalie and walked away. She caught it. It was Natalie Thompson's license.

"Here you go," Zoey said, holding out a blanket. "I found some for everyone."

"Thank you," Natalie said, taking it. "Now get some rest."

"I'll try." Zoey hugged Natalie and joined her brother, who was preparing a makeshift bed on the floor.

Natalie tucked the license in her pocket as Walter followed Jameson to the corner of the room, near the door. Jameson sat with his back against the wall and cradled his wounded hand. He glared at Natalie silently.

Walter opened a water, drank some, then sliced the bottle in half with his knife and Buster finished the rest. He reached in his pocket and pulled out a handful of dog food, placing it in a pile on the floor.

Exhausted, she watched everyone settle in, then she chose a place to rest in the opposite corner of the room, as far away from

Jameson as possible. She placed the blanket on the floor, lay down on top of it, and folded it over her, tucking it under her chin.

She lay there terror-stricken, her brain running through all the possibilities for the days to come. She stared at the ceiling without blinking. *If only we could go back to before this started.* She desperately wanted to wake up in her own bed the next morning.

Buster finished his food and water then came to lie next to her. With the dog nuzzling at her side, Natalie gave him a reassuring pat. "It would be nice to start over, wouldn't it, Buster? Like none of this ever happened." Natalie stroked the dog repeatedly.

Finally, she relaxed enough to succumb to her fatigue. As worried as she was, exhaustion got the best of her, and she dropped into a deep sleep.

Sweat beaded on Natalie's brow. Her sheets were warm from the morning sun, shining between the curtains that refused to stay closed. Turning to the window, she saw daylight.

Mind fuzzy, she opened her eyes and squinted. She rubbed them hard and blinked. Her sheets soaked and heart pounding.

Natalie focused and found herself lying in her own bed. Her eyes fluttered up and down, then closed again. She couldn't keep them open. She pulled the blanket over her head and hid there until she heard, "Sweetie, you're going to be late." The voice was faint but familiar calling to her.

"Mom?" Natalie's eyes were still closed. She lay still, puzzled and frozen in time. Her eyes shot open. She gazed at the window. "It's morning already? I can't be late again!"

Natalie looked at the alarm clock and realized she'd forgotten to set it. Drained and confused, she jumped out of bed. *Was it all a dream? It seemed so real.*

She dressed hurriedly, hopping about with one leg in her pants until she could get the other one to follow suit. She grabbed her backpack and headed downstairs.

"Honey, I have breakfast for you."

"I don't have time, Mom." Natalie knew her mom was always worried about her eating habits. Her dad sat at the table chomping on a piece of toast.

"Natalie, your hair," her mom shouted as she passed. "That girl is always running late."

Natalie flew out the door. "Good thing it's only down the street," she murmured. She ran to her car, but paused—something caught her eye. She looked up at the sky and saw a blackening haze beginning to waft over the town. *There's not supposed to be a storm today.* She hopped into her car and drove off. It seemed like the darkness followed her all the way to school.

She ran up the building's steps and sprinted down the hall toward her class. As she ran, she reached into her backpack for her comb, trying to untangle a head full of morning knots.

She pushed the classroom door open. It swung hard and made a loud thud, drawing the class's attention to her. She stopped short, mouth agape, as her teacher introduced the man beside him.

"Good morning, students," he said. "Before we get into today's class, I'd like to introduce Dr. Jameson Walker. He's a renowned theoretical physicist and holds degrees in both biology and genetics. He has also made several medical research discoveries in the past and is one of the youngest people ever to reach the highest rank in the science field. He'll be hosting a conference tonight regarding the feasibility of interdimensional travel and the effect other worlds would have on ours. His colleague Dr. Walter Beerman will also be present. He specializes not only in genetic engineering but also in neuromorphic and artificial intelligence technology. He'll be there to speak about a breakthrough revolution with an active chip and how it mimics the human brain. This AI even processes its own thoughts as it learns and builds its data. I would strongly advise those of you writing your final thesis or dissertation to attend."

Natalie stood immobile, staring at Jameson. Her head ached. She touched her temple gingerly and felt a small lump. Her eyes twitched uncontrollably as she tried to process what she was seeing.

Jameson stared at Natalie. Their eyes met, and he smiled, sending a chill down her spine.

Natalie thought. How does she know this man? She felt a pinch in her pocket and pulled out a license—Natalie Thompson's license. Was she Natalie, or was she stuck with Natalie Thompson's thoughts? She was a grad student, right? Was this a dream, or was this real? Was she out there fighting the homondie, trying to save the world? Did she figure out how to use the chip implanted within her to find her way back home, or had she never left her bed?

Questions ran though her head as she heard a voice in the distance. "Young lady, you there in the back, close that door and have a seat." Her professor's voice pulled Natalie out of her trance.

Her classmates giggled as she closed the door. She hurried to the first open seat.

"Dr. Walker, it's always a pleasure," her professor said. "Thank you for stopping by."

Shaking hands, Jameson replied, "Thank you, Professor, and I presume I'll see you tonight?"

"I wouldn't miss it for anything."

Jameson headed for the door, staring at Natalie. She stared back, feeling as if his gaze was burning a hole through her. The closer he got, the more afraid she became.

"Now then," her professor said, "open your books to page—"

The professor's voice faded as Natalie's attention was drawn to Jameson. She tried to look away, but still watched him out of the corner of her eye.

Suddenly there was a crackle of lightning, followed by a deafening roar of thunder. It rattled the classroom windows and Natalie's nerves. She peered out the window. The blackened haze grew and swirled around overhead while buildings crumbled in the background. She turned back to her classmates. They faced the teacher, emotionless.

A scratching noise caught Natalie's attention. She peered out the window again and saw a homondie clawing at the window, trying to get in. Natalie gasped as the homondie stared back at her.

The homondie changed and morphed into a human. It took on Natalie's appearance. It was as if she was looking into a mirror.

Palms sweaty, heart thumping through her chest, Natalie forced herself to stop staring and looked back at Jameson. He edged closer and stopped right next to her. She looked up at him. He peered out the window and back at her, then bent down and whispered into her ear.

"We have some unfinished business to tend to after the conference." Jameson straightened up and stepped back. "I'll see you tonight," he said softly. He winked and smiled, then headed for the door.

Tonight? Natalie blinked slowly, but her heart hammered against her chest. She stared at the backpack on her lap and opened it to find the device still inside. She looked for Jameson, but he was gone.

She felt a part of her brain activate as it took control of her thoughts. She stared out the window. The homondie was gone, but the blackened haze grew. A boom echoed outside. She jumped in fright. The sky darkened, and the trees began to die. The dead walked. She gazed around the room and watched her classmates change into homondie.

Natalie zipped her backpack and jumped out of her seat. She ran out of the classroom. The door slammed behind her as she sprinted to the exit. She pushed the door open to reveal Walter waiting for her outside the building in the town in Homondiem. He grabbed her and held on tight.

"What's going on? What are you doing? Leave me alone," Natalie cried, looking around. "I was home, in college. How did I end up back in Homondiem?"

"You never left," Walter said. "Hush now, before I hurt you."

A stream of visions flooded her mind. The chip processed Natalie's thoughts and her mind cleared. It was her illusions that had caused her to run out the exit, but it wasn't the door at her college. It was, in fact, straight out the door of Victor's house and into Walter's grasp.

Jameson rounded the building. "Natalie."

"Jameson . . .," she whispered.

CHAPTER 30

WALTER HAD NATALIE held tightly in his arms, facing Jameson. Memories of her life, Jameson, Homondiem, and the homondie flashed by in a blur and flooded her mind. She shouted for help and squirmed wildly to get out of Walter's grip.

Jameson glowered at her. The gleam in his eyes filled her with fear as she found herself defenseless. "Don't worry about calling out to anyone. They're not here."

"What did you do to them?"

"Nothing bad. While you were sleeping, I told them to take Buster and search the area for more survivors. I told them not to wake you, that you needed your rest. I sent them so far out that no one can hear you. They won't be back for hours. Too bad you won't be able to say your goodbyes."

"They aren't going to let you get away with this! When they get back—"

Jameson cut her off. "They'll be told you went crazy from that chip and ran off."

They led her away from town and into the woods with a firm stride. Walter pulled Natalie along.

Natalie swatted his hand away. "I can walk on my own." No one was around to help her. She had to remain calm as she walked between the two. She didn't want to lose her head. "What are you going to do to me?"

Jameson laughed and held up his device. "Walter, we need to head south and go deeper into the woods, this way."

"Where are we going?"

"You should know. This was once your home."

"What are you talking about? This was never my home," Natalie said. "I've never been here before until the portal sucked me into this world."

"Think about it." Jameson smiled. "Have you eaten at all?"

His smile gave her an eerie feeling inside.

His voice cracked as he said, "You had always been drawn to Homondiem by an irresistible force, haven't you, but you'd never known why?"

"My home is where my family is, if they're still alive."

Jameson glared at her. His eyes turned as black as the night sky. He smirked and laughed.

Natalie watched as his skin paled and his eyes sunk into his face. "What's happening to you? Are you . . . changing?"

Jameson paused and grabbed her arm. He pulled her in close and said, "Yes, I am, because of your bite."

Natalie grunted as she yanked out of his grasp. "I don't understand. How could you turn? I'm not a homondie."

"Remember? This was once your home before you were taken, but now you're back where you belong."

Her eyes twitched as her thoughts processed through the chip. "I was that homondie? The one you captured?" Natalie asked but didn't want the answer. "I don't want to believe it. This has all got to be a dream."

"I'm sorry to tell you it's not," Jameson said. "You're a homondie, and Homondiem is your home."

She could feel her senses heighten. Something clicked. All the pieces of the puzzle began to connect. "Now I remember," she said slowly. "I *am* the one you captured from Homondiem." Natalie stuttered, "I'm, I'm a, homondie. I remember now. I remember when you implanted the chip in my scalp and fed Natalie Thompson to me until I absorbed her life and became human." Natalie shuddered with disgust, remembering ripping the poor woman to shreds. "That's what Seth was trying to tell me," she whispered. "But if I'm a homondie, you should only become a half-life from my bite."

"What do you mean?" Jameson asked, slurring his words. He smiled, revealing his razor-sharp teeth. He leaned in and stood so close to Natalie that their noses almost touched.

Natalie pushed him back. "How can you change yourself into something other than a half-life?"

He pulled a syringe from his pocket.

"I thought the antiserum was to keep you from changing?" Natalie asked.

"This isn't the antiserum, that needle broke. This is different. Since I didn't have the antiserum to inject myself with, I decided to go one step further. I don't want to be an ordinary half-life. I need to be the ultimate one. With this, I'll be unstoppable, and the homondie will have no choice but to be under my control."

"How is that possible?"

"I created a DNA changer." Jameson laughed, coughed, then bent over with a grunt. He stood upright, revealing his thinning lips and decomposed ears.

"What are you talking about?"

"Do you remember Walter's side? He said it was an experiment gone wrong. You were the experiment."

"Victor said the same thing. I didn't put it together until now." Natalie gasped. "Walter's bite mark was from me—I was the one who bit Walter."

They led her farther away from the town.

"Yes, and you would have killed him or at least made him a half-life if it wasn't for the antiserum. I drained the fluid inside of you to create it. I gave it to Buster first. Once he survived, I gave the same dose to Walter before it was too late. That gave him a counter-balance to your homondie genetic makeup, tricking Walter's DNA into thinking he was already a homondie, thus preventing him from turning."

"Then if you already had the antiserum, why did you create another?"

"That antiserum was only intended for Walter and me so we could stay human, but I still needed to find a way to force the humans to accept me as their leader. That's when I came up with a solution," Jameson explained. "I was able to create a serum that let me design the perfect mix of human and homondie. I designed it specifically for all our human guests in Homondiem. I can control the effects of them becoming a half-life, depending on the amount of the injection. The more dose I give them, the less human they'll be and more homondie they'll become. Humans will no longer exist, as I create the perfect species, ones who will obey me."

"You're out of your mind."

"Isn't it uncanny how much this Natalie is like the real Natalie?" Jameson asked Walter. "She seems to have gained her personality. That was the very same thing she said to me right before she died."

"She walks and talks exactly like her too," Walter said. "She even understands the background of our work, just like the Natalie you met in college."

"Ahh, yes, I'll never forget the first day I met Natalie Thompson. She came to my conference that one evening, and we hit it off instantly."

"That lecture was on interdimensional travel," Natalie said.

"You shouldn't know about that. I didn't give you all her memories." Jameson rubbed his chin. "Interesting. I think you absorbed the essence of her being when you extracted her life. It's as if the fabric of her life is a part of you now. That makes sense. I didn't think a homondie could ever have compassion, but you're so much like the real Natalie, wanting to save the human race and all. It's like the real Natalie was showing through you all along. Too bad we couldn't hit it off." Jameson caressed her cheek.

Natalie flinched at his touch. She turned to Walter. "You're both sick!"

Jameson looked down at his device. Natalie pushed Walter aside and started to run, but Jameson reached out and grabbed her arm before she could escape. Walter seized her other arm.

Natalie groaned. She looked into Jameson's eyes, fearless. "How could you be so heartless?"

"There are always casualties in war," he said. "Nothing I can do for them now. Don't you worry, though, you'll be as heartless as me soon enough."

"What do you mean?" she asked, frightened of the answer.

"That chip doesn't allow for compassion. Once it melds with you, you'll never have feelings again and one day you'll need to eat. Too bad you won't be around. I would have loved to see that."

They pulled her along, but Natalie dug her feet into the ground. "Let me go and I'll give you the chip."

"It's too late for that," Jameson said. "I no longer have the Staff of Life to control the chip, so you and the chip both have to go. I have to destroy both it and you and take my chances with the homondie."

"You were the one who tried to kill me," Natalie said, realization dawning.

"Yes, but you did try to kill Walter first. If it wasn't for the chip, you wouldn't be here. Then of course I had to give you some sort of memory to hide who you truly were, so I programmed the chip with some of Natalie's memories."

"Why would you think she deserved that?" Natalie asked.

"She tried to stop me. She stole one of my devices, but before she could get away, I found her in her car and brought her to that basement. That's where Natalie, the homondie, was strapped to the table."

Natalie gasped, remembering the surgical table.

"We let you do the dirty work. When you were done, we sedated you and strapped you back down. She deserved everything she got, and now it's your turn." Jameson looked at the sky. "Walter, we need to get her to the portal right away."

Jameson headed down a narrow path. Walter guided Natalie through, holding her tight to prevent another escape attempt.

"I thought there were no more portals?" Natalie asked. She pushed through the branches and tripped over a few rocks as she tried to keep in step with Walter.

"You're so naive," Jameson said. "We tell you what we want you to think. We always have."

"How could you ruin so many lives?" Natalie struggled, but Walter gripped her arm tighter.

"They're just pawns," Jameson said.

"You're insane."

Walter's face grew slack. "Jameson, you don't look too good."

"We don't have much time before I change completely." Jameson grinned. His razor-sharp teeth chattered.

"Hang in there," Walter said.

Jameson lifted his head, eyes darting about. "My senses are heightened. They're coming for her. We've got to move faster."

Walter shoved Natalie.

"Who's coming for me?" Natalie asked, still struggling against Walter's grip.

"The homondie are coming to rescue their leader," Walter said. "That chip inside of you is calling them."

"Me, their leader, how?"

"Before we trapped you, you were the leader of Homondiem. Didn't you notice that you could control the homondie so easily? Not anyone, not even Victor, could do that." Walter tightened his grip and pulled Natalie in close. "Can't you feel it? You're one of them."

"I can feel it," she said.

Jameson scanned his device. "We're still on track. The portal is this way." He led them farther into a remote area of Homondiem.

"You should be thankful we brought you into our world and gave you life. It's something you didn't have before. We made you who you are today," Walter said.

"I should thank you?" Natalie said. "All you gave me was a false sense of hope. Nothing you told me was true. I'm not even human!"

"That doesn't matter anymore. It's time to end this." Jameson's sardonic tone worried Natalie.

"How?" she asked.

"I have something important planned for you. I can't kill you because the chip will only heal you again. I've already tried. So it's time to move on to bigger and better things."

"Like what?"

"You must be exiled from Homondiem so I'm going to open a dimensional portal and throw you into the nothingness of our old world to ensure you won't make it back. With you gone, I might still be able to control the homondie without the chip, as Victor could, but your presence would mean my death." Jameson leered at Natalie. "Now it's time for the real leader to step up."

"And who is that?" Natalie asked.

"Haven't you figured it out by now?"

"You've been after this world since the beginning, just like Victor and Seth said."

"Yes, indeed." Jameson smiled at her.

Natalie twisted out of Walter's grasp. Walter grabbed her again. Natalie grunted in pain as Jameson grabbed her other arm. The two of them pulled her through the remaining woods.

"You were never going to save our world, were you? You never intended on closing the portals."

"Of course not! We pretended we were going to close them so you wouldn't discover our plans. I couldn't allow you to know what Walter and I had in store for you, the chip, and Homondiem. Besides, the devices only work to open and close them, not to fully repair the dimensions back to normal. Only the chip could do that."

"So I had the means to restore our worlds all along."

"Yes, you were the key. Your homondie connection combined with the aid of the chip, you could have reversed the dimensions at any time, and we'd all be back home by now. That's why I never gave you a chance to close the portals. I couldn't allow the chip to be activated and end up restoring our world."

"All those lives lost because of me," Natalie whispered, disheartened at the thought that she could have saved them.

"As a precaution, in case you did try to close the portals, I sabotaged all the devices to force them to expand to speed up the process before you figured out how to use the chip."

"That's why my device didn't work when I tried to close the portal," Natalie muttered.

Jameson chuckled. "I must say, it was difficult to keep up this charade, but we did a smashing job, didn't we?"

"So Wade was right about you all along!" Natalie stood, slack-jawed. "I didn't see any of this coming."

"You should have listened to him instead of being so determined to let him go off on his own." Jameson chuckled. "Funny thing about Wade. He actually didn't mean to shoot Walter. It was Walter that purposely stood in front of the bullet so that we could get rid of him."

"Walter, you led me on this whole time?" Natalie cried. "I trusted you, and you lied to me." She felt her cheeks flush, and a knot settled in the pit of her stomach. "How dare you trick me and kill all those innocent people!"

"Why should you care about them? This is your home, not theirs." Jameson snickered.

Natalie's face tightened.

Jameson grunted and leaned forward, grabbing his stomach. Natalie watched his human qualities fade away and the homondie's features emerge.

"Take a look around you. I may have risked lives, but see what I've gained. This world changed before me as I stood and watched Victor command the homondie. I could see how they reacted to a human as their leader. And to see Seth stand up to Victor as a half-life. To see the homondie actually learn to build and speak? That was all amazing!" Jameson grinned. "No one before me has ever tried, and no one after me will follow in my footsteps. I'll make sure the homondie remain as helpless creatures obeying my commands."

"I won't allow you to take control of them!"

"Sorry, but you won't be here when it happens," he said. "You won't be around for much longer." Jameson's skin slackened, and his hair fell out, leaving behind only a few thin, straggly strands.

"Why so sad, Natalie? Don't worry," Walter said. "When you're gone, this place will become a magnificent world for Jameson to rule. With him in charge, the outsiders will become a new breed." They emerged from the woods and stepped into a clearing.

"I'll be the one who decides who lives and who dies," Jameson said. "It all depends on who behaves and abides by my rules." He looked up at the sky. "We're running out of time. I must say goodbye."

"Shh, listen," Walter interrupted. "I can hear the homondie coming closer."

"They're coming to save me and kill you," Natalie said.

"Hush," Jameson said to Natalie. He turned to Walter. "Walter, we must hurry before the others arrive. I need to get rid of her." He sneered at Natalie.

Natalie didn't know what to do. No one knew where she was. She felt Jameson's gaze rip a hole through her as goose bumps layered her arms.

"Then I guess it's too late," Caroline said, stepping out of the woods with Buster by her side. She aimed her gun at Jameson's head.

"Caroline," Natalie shouted. "How did you find me?"

"Buster and I arrived back at the town, but he must have known something was wrong. He took off running into the woods and I followed him right to you." Caroline stepped closer to Jameson. "I heard what you said and it's time for us to say our goodbyes to you and Walter."

"You don't have the guts to kill an outsider like yourself," Jameson scoffed and knocked the weapon out of Caroline's hand. Buster barked at Jameson as she bent down and picked it up.

"I wouldn't do that if you want Natalie to live." Walter put his gun to Natalie's head. Jameson plucked Caroline's weapon from her hands, ignoring Buster's aggressive advances.

Jameson grabbed Caroline and chuckled. "You should have killed me when you had the chance."

"Let her go," Caroline screamed.

Natalie saw fear and heartache in Caroline's eyes.

"What do we do with her, Jameson?" Walter asked. "We can't shoot her and leave her behind. The others would eventually find her."

"We'll just have to take her with us and tell them she went after Natalie and they disappeared," Jameson said. "They'll just assume they were attacked by homondie."

Natalie focused her attention on the homondie through the chip. She could feel the connection she had to them. The rustling continued in the woods around them. "Hear that?" she asked Jameson. "They're coming for you. Do you think you have enough homondie in you to keep them from finishing you off?"

Jameson began to sweat. He stared into the woods. "We have to get out of here now, Walter." He hunched over in pain. His mouth twitched, and his eyes sunk deeper into his skull. His words slowed, and his speech slurred. "We have to get them to the portal fast."

Jameson and Walter dragged them across the field. Buster followed their every step, not leaving their side. Natalie jerked and tugged to get out of Walter's grasp, slowing him down.

"This is it." Jameson leered at Natalie. "Natalie, do you remember this place? This was the first place we met when I dragged you out of Homondiem and into my world. I thought it would be ironic by ending your life here at this location." Jameson pressed buttons on the device.

A ghastly blackened haze descended from the sky and formed around them. A loud crack rumbled throughout the woods, followed by a burst of light, and an opening appeared. Lightning shot from the portal, through the device, and up into the sky. The flash was so bright that she was momentarily blinded. Every time she neared the portals, she could feel her blood run cold. Her body tingled, and the hair on her arms stood up. Would this be her last time? There seemed to be no way out.

She peered into the darkened opening and watched the rippling waves float through its center. They expanded across the portal as the pulsating outer layer grew. The darkness before her swirled and crackled.

"Goodbye, Natalie." Jameson smiled.

Natalie struggled to get away.

"Walter, don't do it," Caroline yelled. "How do you know Jameson won't turn on you when he's fully transformed into a homondie? You'll need Natalie if he does!"

Walter stood Natalie before the swirling dark hole. The wind picked up through the entranceway. Natalie's eyes watered. She turned away, not wanting to see her demise.

Buster stood between Natalie and the portal. He growled and barked at Jameson and Walter.

"Buster, come here! What's wrong with you?" Walter hollered.

A gunshot went off in the distance. Jameson's body twitched and fell to the ground, releasing Caroline.

"Walter, release Natalie," a man's voice rang out from behind them. The man stepped out from the woods into the field.

"Wade!" Walter let Natalie go. He stared down the barrel of the rifle aimed straight at him.

"Natalie, help!" Jameson crawled toward her. He reached out for her hand and begged for his life.

Natalie stared at him, emotionless.

Wade approached, ready to pull the trigger again.

"No, wait," Natalie yelled. She stared at Jameson with tears in his eyes. She bent down and touched his once-human face and gazed deep into his eyes. His skin began to wrinkle.

"Natalie, what are you doing to me?" Jameson tried to wriggle away but failed.

Natalie sensed the chip's energy within her as it began to take hold of the entire essence of her being. She was left with no choice. "I remember what Walter said earlier. I'm the giver of life, but I can also take life away. You don't deserve yours."

Jameson cried, "Natalie, listen. We can work this out."

"Don't you remember? This is your doing. You were the one who fed the deceased life and look what it got you—your assassin." She held his face for a few moments, then released him and stood. Jameson let out a short scream as his skin deteriorated and his bones were exposed. He edged closer to her and extended his hand for her to take. Natalie backed away.

His last breath came out as a screech. It burst into a mist that floated in midair until his bones were reduced to a pile of ashes.

Caroline ran to Wade. Buster continued to bark as he backed away from Walter but stayed close to Natalie, ready to attack. Walter dropped his weapon and put his hands up. "Don't let them kill me, Natalie. I didn't have anything to do with this. It was all Jameson. He forced me to get involved."

Natalie moved away from the portal and stood next to Caroline and Wade. "Wade? I thought you'd be dead when we left you behind."

"I'm stronger than you think." Wade smiled. "Besides, it was all an act. I'm part of the Special Forces working with Central

Intelligence on a national security breach. It's a different division of the government than Victor and Seth were in."

"How did you get involved?" Natalie asked.

"I was sent to retrieve the chip that Victor and Seth stole from the government."

"How did you get into the town? Wasn't it cut off? I thought even military personnel couldn't get in."

"I was dropped off by helicopter and ordered to retrieve that chip before all hell broke loose. Evidently, I'm too late."

"How did you know about Jameson and Walter?"

"I was trailing Victor, and I found out those two idiots were involved. Then I figured out what Jameson was planning. I overheard them talking. I knew I couldn't convince you if you didn't hear it straight from them, so I tried to force him into revealing what they were up to. I tried to get under Jameson's skin hoping he'd make a mistake. Since that didn't work, I've been tracking his every step. I had to wait for the right time for them to tell you the truth before I killed him. But I was too late. They'd already destroyed our world before I found out you were the one with the chip."

"I'm sorry for doubting you," Natalie said.

"It wasn't your fault," Wade said. "Everyone thought they knew who he was. You didn't even know you were a homondie. Jameson lied to all of us."

Walter pulled a knife from under his shirt, leaped forward, and grabbed Natalie, raising the blade to her throat. He backed away and pulled her along. "Wade, back off before she dies."

Buster growled at Walter.

"Now, now, don't do anything drastic." Wade lowered his weapon.

Walter backed up, pulled Natalie to the ground, and grabbed Jameson's device. "I'll finish this for Jameson," he said. "He'd be proud."

Buster barked as the homondie came out of the woods, all with human qualities. They encircled them, but made no motion to advance. As Walter focused on the homondie, Buster leaped up and pushed him, forcing him to drop the knife.

Walter stumbled but hung on to Buster as his body was sucked into the darkness, swallowing both him and the dog.

"Buster, no," Natalie yelled as he disappeared. She flung herself headfirst into the darkness.

"Natalie," Caroline screamed.

Wade grabbed her legs as she was halfway into the portal. "Hang on, Natalie."

Natalie could feel her body stretching as Wade was being pulled in behind her.

"Caroline, help me pull her out," Wade yelled; half his body was lost in the darkness.

Caroline grabbed Wade's waist and pulled.

"Come on, Caroline, pull harder!" Wade grunted.

Natalie could feel them slipping in farther, but there was nothing she could do.

Caroline and Wade gave one final yank and flew backward onto the ground.

Natalie sat up hugging Buster. "Don't you ever scare me like that again!" Natalie scolded the dog then covered him with a flurry of kisses.

In a flash, the sky appeared to bend, and they all glanced upward. The light curved as it was sucked into the portal then disappeared. It collapsed just as Walter had predicted.

They had reached the edge of space-time itself.

As the portal disappeared, silence descended. Only Natalie and the other homondie could move. Natalie felt as if she was floating in a higher dimensional space. She watched the humans, frozen where they stood.

She went to Caroline first, then Wade, shaking each of them. "Wake up, damn it!" She dropped to her knees and wrapped her arms around Buster's neck. "Please," she moaned, holding back her tears as she buried her face in his furry neck. When she lifted her head, she focused on Wade. She noticed his watch had stopped.

The homondie stood around, staring at Natalie.

She didn't know what to do. She put her face in her hands until she heard a faint bark. She raised her head. "Buster?" He twitched, then moved, followed by Wade and Caroline. As they slowly came back to life, they moved tentatively, leaving a trail of their distorted self behind like an afterimage.

As their mobility increased, Natalie noticed something odd. Several identical images of each of them moved in a different fashion, carrying their different versions of reality, as if Natalie was looking through multiple parallel universes—a multiverse. Time sped up, and they merged back into one self, then in a flash, it was over as if nothing had happened.

Natalie jumped up and hugged each of them. "I thought you all left me."

"What happened?" Caroline asked.

"I think we just witnessed the destruction of our world, for good," Wade said.

"Wade, let me see your watch," Natalie said. The hands on his watch were moving normally. "I think you're right. Time has officially reset itself. I wonder what happened to Walter?"

"Maybe he went into an alternate universe?" Caroline said.

"We'll never know." Natalie gazed at the group of homondie surrounding them. She'd never forget their once-straggly hair, decomposed ears, and sunken eyes with that crazed, rabid stare of hunger; their thin lips, and their razor-sharp teeth chattering for a bite. Now all their homondie features were gone. Once pale and lifeless, they stood before her fleshed out and almost entirely human. To think she was one of them. "What do you think they want?" she asked Wade while staring at the homondie.

"It looks like they're waiting for a command from their leader." Wade winked at Natalie. "I think that's you."

Natalie turned to the homondie.

Caroline smiled. "They need your guidance."

"I don't know what to do."

"They may look like us now, but they're still homondie. You can help them so we can all live in this world in peace." Wade backed away to give Natalie room to pass. "Look at them. They're waiting for your command."

"Will it be enough to hold them at bay?" Natalie was concerned for the well-being of the outsiders.

"I don't know, but with you in charge, they shouldn't try to eat us anymore, right?" Caroline asked.

Natalie knew the outsiders wondered about her connection to these homondie, but she was their only option. Maybe it was a good thing, being able to communicate with them—a godsend, possibly.

Natalie turned away from Caroline and Wade and walked toward the homondie, Buster at her side. She cocked her head and closed her eyes, not wanting to watch as the homondie approached. *Am I brave enough to take on this task of keeping the outsiders safe?* She opened her eyes and stood still as she tried to regain her composure.

As she stared, she saw the torture in the homondie's once-wild eyes. She hoped over time all the homondie would become more human, able to live in peace, but that was a long time in the future. Perhaps it was only a pipe dream, but she could hope. It was time to deal with the here and now.

With their transformation complete, Natalie believed the homondie would no longer continue with their hunting instincts, but only time would tell. For now, the homondie might be the majority, with the human outsiders as the minority, but who knows where the new world would take them? Maybe everyone would become so similar that no one could tell who was human and who was homondie anymore—just ask Buster.

In the meantime, the outsiders would need to develop their own survival skills. They would have to not only survive in this new world with the homondie but also maintain sources of food and water. Everything they once knew was gone, stores, transportation, even their homes, and they had to come to terms with that, no longer living in fear of the unknown.

With the reversal of the dimensions unsuccessful, they had to begin a new life with the others who had survived their entrance to Homondiem. They were on their own to recreate their old world in this new, unfamiliar place. Natalie hoped to bring about peace between their kinds and keep peace among themselves.

She nodded at the homondie, who gazed back at her, as if they knew what she was thinking. They turned around and wandered back into the woods from where they came.

Natalie stared at the retreating homondie while Caroline and Wade stepped next to her.

"What do we do now?" Caroline asked.

"I guess we find the others and call this place home," Wade said.

ABOUT THE AUTHOR

ORIGINALLY FROM MASSACHUSETTS, P. F. Donato, uprooted and braved the unknown with her three children. Ending up in Pennsylvania, her family grew by two—Yorkshire Terriers that is. As a young adult, she loved to write poetry and songs, and now she has found that writing novels are her passion. Her inspiration for writing this book came from a dream, and she continues to write with her two Yorkies by her side. In her spare time, she loves riding her Harley and traveling with her pups as they go on exciting adventures together. Welcome, readers!

CPSIA information can be obtained
at www.ICGtesting.com
Printed in the USA
BVHW032127141220
595752BV00002B/3